Innocent Eyes

Doyle Suit

To Kelly,
Enjoy the tale.
Doyle

Innocent Eyes

Doyle Suit

Mockingbird Lane Press

Innocent Eyes

This is a work of fiction. While some names, characters, places, and incidents are the product of the author's imagination, some are accurate, but are used to further the story. The publisher does not have any control over and does not assume any responsibility for author or third-party websites or their content.

Mockingbird Lane Press—Maynard, Arkansas

ISBN: 978-1-64316-872-4

Library of Congress Control Number: In Publication Data

0 9 8 7 6 5 4 3 2 1

www.mockingbirdlanepress.com

Cover graphics: Jamie Johnson

My mother provided for and rode herd on five unruly boys. She inspired all of us to get an education and accomplish something with our lives. In her seventies, she took up writing, oil painting, and sculpture. Hopefully I inherited some small part of her talent.

My wife grew up in the French and German border country in Alsace during World War II. She helped me to understand the culture and hardships endured by French people forced to live as Germans during that terrible war.

Numerous friends and colleagues helped me complete this book. Members of Saturday Writers, Coffee and Critique, and Scribes Tribe groups reviewed and critiqued the manuscript as the book took shape. The book is fiction based on a true story.

I'm grateful for my editor, Regina Williams, and the folks at Mockingbird Lane Press for helping me prepare this manuscript for publication.

Special thanks to my wife, Irene, for her wise counsel and for allowing me time away from chores to hide in my office and write this story.

To Irene

August 20, 1959

The flight attendant smiled as she accepted our boarding passes. “Welcome to Air France Flight 1140 to New York.”

With my carry-on bag in one hand and the other arm cradling my infant son, I entered the airliner that would carry me from Paris to a new life in America. My husband, Dale, had traveled on a military flight. He’d be released from the army and meet us at the New York airport. We spent the last of our savings to buy tickets for me and our baby boy.

The airliner’s four big engines roared to a screaming pitch, and the big plane lurched forward on the long Orly Field runway. I reached out to touch the two-month-old child beside me and reassure him his mother was here. The gesture proved to be for naught because he was already asleep. The airplane gained speed and gathered itself to leap into the gray Paris sky. Our journey to our new home in Kansas was underway.

My mind drifted back to that September afternoon in 1939 when the approaching war shattered my peaceful young life. I’d been five years old when we evacuated the village to escape the Nazi invasion. My baby brother had been only two months older than my infant son. Life under German rule had been about to begin. I checked my purse again for the notes I’d written about my experiences during those troubled times.

Relieved we were safely on our way, I consulted my notes. Reviewing the events I’d recorded brought back memories that shaped who I’d become during those turbulent years in the war. Perhaps I’d write about it someday.

Chapter 1

I sat on the ground under an apple tree, enjoying the early fall weather and watching over my four-month-old brother, Roger. We lived in the French village of Kaschel near the German border. It was Monday, September 4, 1939, and all the adults were talking about a war that was sure to come.

The canopy on Roger's baby carriage protected him from the cool breeze. I had just changed my doll, Brigette's, red dress and held her up to admire. Mama was gathering laundry from the clothesline when a loud clanging on the street corner interrupted the quiet afternoon.

I jumped to my feet. "Mama, the town crier is ringing his bell."

She picked up her basket and hurried to put it inside the house. Then she ran to take Roger from his little buggy and called out to Papa. "Ádolph, come quickly. The crier has news."

Papa slammed the gate to the chicken run and hurried toward the corner. "Come, Mina. Bring the children."

Confused, I followed Mama as she rushed past the Schmidt's big house across the street and on to the corner. A crowd had gathered, and everyone talked at once. I sensed something bad was about to happen.

The crier spoke. "The government has information. The Germans are preparing an attack through the Maginot Line and Alsace. The French Army will occupy Kaschel to block the Nazis. All civilians must evacuate the village."

I tugged at Mama's skirt. "What is evacuate?"

My mother shushed me with a motion. "It means we have to leave our home."

Chapter 2

A neighbor shouted over the noise of the startled crowd. "The Germans can't reach us here. We're protected by the Maginot Line."

Waving his arms for silence, the crier continued. "The Nazis have tanks and armored vehicles that might break through the fortifications. French troops will occupy the village to block any advance by invaders who might penetrate our line of guns at the border."

A shrill outcry rang out from the back of the gathering. "Where can we go?"

"Any place you can find shelter. Everyone must be out of the village by five o'clock. You have two hours. The army needs all civilians gone so they can fortify the road crossings."

Questions continued while I stood frozen in fear. I didn't understand why we had to leave. Where could my family go? What would happen to our cows and rabbits and chickens and pigs? Could I bring my toys? Would the Nazis come with tanks and find us? My baby brother was too little to travel. It would soon be dark, and we would have no place to sleep. I held tight to Mama's hand and clutched Brigette to my breast.

Finding no answers for my fear, I bit my lip and wiped away a tear. The fresh wind penetrated my warm sweater, and I shivered.

Panic spread through the crowd as the crier moved on to deliver his warning. Most people lingered on the corner, trying to understand what they must do next. Some stood with blank stares. Others cursed the Nazis.

Our neighbor, Mrs. Rolf, stood without moving, tears streaming down her cheeks. I wanted to offer her sympathy, but I didn't know what to say.

Papa recovered from the shock first and started to shout orders. "Mina, pack our clothes and bedding. Bring the dishes. I'll hitch the cows to the wagon and load the food we've stored for winter."

He turned to me. "Irene, go tell Opa and Oma they will ride with us. Tell them to pack only what they must have. Then hurry home."

I ran three long blocks to my grandparents' house as fast as I could make my short legs move. My breath came in gasps as I barged into my grandmother's kitchen. "Oma, the Nazis are coming. Papa said we have to leave. You can ride in our wagon."

"I know, child. We're packing." She wiped her brow with the sleeve of her dress. "Go home now and help your mother. We'll be ready soon."

At home, Mama raced frantically back and forth selecting things we would need most and stacking them on the kitchen floor. She looked up as I entered. "Roger is starting to fret. Feed him his bottle and stay with him. Hurry."

With a trembling hand, I prepared the bottle and ran outside to pop it into the baby's mouth. That quieted him immediately. Fighting back tears, I watched him devour the warm milk and brushed away a fly that tried to share his meal. Why did we have to leave?

Papa brought the wagon around to the kitchen door, and our two milk cows plodded to a stop and waited patiently. My parents loaded sacks of potatoes, beets, carrots, dried fruit, and flour near the front, and a few heavy farm tools spread across the floor. Then came our kitchenware, clothing, and bedding.

Mama brought our winter coats and laid them on top. When the load reached higher than the wagon's cargo box, Papa attached higher side boards. He stored fragile items under the driver's seat.

I fought to contain my fear as I listened to Papa and Mama argue about what items were needed most and whether or not the wagon carried too heavy a load for the cows to pull.

"Can I bring my doll?" I asked.

Papa shook his head. "No room for toys. Only necessary things."

My chin dropped as I watched from the shade of turning leaves on the big tree. We were being forced to go. I might never see my house again. Frightened, I gazed at the solid old stone building. Papa said it was almost three hundred years old. A century old grape vine covered the end of the house next to the narrow street. Tears came into my eyes as I realized we were really leaving.

Some things I wouldn't miss, like the pigs' pen next to the cows. It stank, and I held my nose when I walked by. The greedy porkers ate scraps from the family table and weeds I pulled from the garden. Papa fed them a small amount of grain, and they made a muddy mess on the ground. The rabbit hutch rested against the back wall of the building near our small garden plot. The rich soil provided fresh vegetables during warm weather. Some of the plants had turned brown since the nights had cooled. A shed alongside the house sheltered our winter firewood. A stone outhouse faced the neatly stacked rows of wood. The outhouse smelled almost as bad as the bin containing cow manure beside it.

I decided I would even miss the stink from the pigs. I still didn't understand why the Nazis threatened us. I puzzled over what we might have done to make them angry, and a sudden thought frightened me. “Papa, who will feed the animals while we're gone?”

He lifted his hands toward the sky. “I've given them food and water to last a few days. My job on the railroad should allow me to stop and check on them from time to time. If I can't come, the soldiers will surely care for them while we're away.”

His answer didn't reassure me. The soldiers might not feed them, and the poor animals would be left to starve.

Mama interrupted with a thought. “We should go to Wolfskirchen. My family knows people in the village.”

Papa paused for a moment to consider the idea, then he nodded his head and grunted. “Yes. It's not too far away, and the train stops there.”

After the top-heavy vehicle was loaded, Papa closed the kitchen door and snapped the reins to start the cows moving. The Schmidts across the street had brought a wagon and two horses from their cement business and were busy loading what they would take with them as we passed.

I turned my head to take a final look at our house and walked beside the baby carriage as Mama pushed it behind our wagon. Roger made happy sounds as his little cart bounced along the rough pavement during the short ride to my grandparents' house.

Chapter 3

My grandparents waited out front as Papa stopped the cows and wagon close to their door. They stood defiantly beside several suitcases and two large bags of food and bedding. They wore their winter coats as Papa loaded the possessions they'd brought.

"Where is Uncle George," I asked. "Is he going with us?"

Opa shook his head. "He just started his job at Solway, and he doesn't want to lose it. He plans to stay with a friend in Sarralbe until the fighting stops."

Their belongings filled the wagon to a mound heaped above the top of its side boards when it was loaded. Papa tied the bulky cargo down with lengths of clothesline to prevent it from shifting. My grandparents climbed aboard to take their place beside him on the bench seat.

Mama gave me a quick hug and waved at Papa. "Irene can ride on top behind Oma and Opa."

I shook my head. "I'll walk with you."

"It's a long way to Wolfskirchen. It will soon be dark," my mother said. "You'll be a tired little girl before we get there."

Oma beckoned from her perch on the bench seat. "Come ride with me. I might get lonesome up here."

"I'll walk with Mama and Roger."

My mother smiled. "All right. Tell me when you get tired."

When Papa snapped the reins, the cattle leaned into their traces. The heavy vehicle began to move toward the highway. Refugees crowded the street. People pushed two-wheeled handcarts or wheelbarrows. Several wagons preceded them as everyone rushed to seek safety away from the village. One man passed us riding a bicycle pulling a small cart. Everyone hurried like they were afraid of something.

After we reached the edge of the village and turned south onto the Route De Phalsbourg, we overtook Mr. and Mrs. Mueller, elderly neighbors who lived a block east of our house. The pair appeared to be tired already as they struggled with large bags filled with more than they would be able to carry for any distance. They made their way south with uncertain steps.

Papa reined the cows to a stop beside the couple. “Climb on top. You’ll never hold out to reach safety with all that luggage.”

Mr. Mueller lifted his eyes to the mound of goods we carried. “You are already overloaded. There is no room for us.”

Papa jumped down from the high seat and took the heavy sack from Mrs. Mueller’s hand. “You will have to sit on top of the load, but it’s better than walking.”

He helped the old couple climb onto the pile of belongings they had carried.

I tried to entertain my baby brother as he became impatient that his carriage had stopped moving. The Muellers found places to sit atop the pile, and the cows plodded onward. The gentle animals moved slowly, so my short steps had no trouble keeping up with their pace.

Mama tugged at my arm and moved the baby carriage to the edge of the pavement as an automobile overtook the wagon. Bags filled the interior of the vehicle, and more had been strapped on top. I waved as it chugged ahead. Only a few cars crept past us on the road filled with wagons, bicycles, and people walking, struggling to carry as much as they could.

The odor of exhaust lingered after the automobile was gone.

An airplane approached from the north, and Mama cried out in fear. Papa stopped the wagon beneath the branches of a large oak tree to hide it from above.

My body shook as I looked up at Mama. “Will the airplane drop bombs?”

Mama watched the craft’s swift passage for a long moment, and then she shook her head with a tentative smile. “No. He’s only going on a trip.”

After the airplane continued on without changing course, Papa snapped the reins, and the cows resumed their slow journey south and away from the Maginot Line.

I worried the Nazis might come before we could escape.

The sun sank beneath the horizon, and a brisk chill descended on our little group. The placid cows maintained their steady pace along the paved road, and the people riding on the wagon sought covers against the cold. I marched alongside Mama. The exercise and my wool sweater kept me warm. Roger slept, and another blanket made him comfortable in his cozy nest.

A few bicycles, usually heavily laden with precious belongings, went by and weaved through the struggling line of refugees to disappear in the distance. An occasional automobile passed us and would quickly be blocked by the hordes of people. Pedestrians struggled to carry heavy loads and frequently faltered. They sat at the side of the road resting as we passed by.

One elderly man, sitting on a large suitcase waved a hand at us when we reached him. “Could you give me a ride?”

I heard sadness in Papa’s voice when he answered. “I’m sorry. We’re already too heavily loaded. Our cows might not be able to pull the extra weight.”

A small truck carrying a half dozen soldiers approached from the opposite direction. The driver blew the horn constantly to force a path through the oncoming crowd.

We passed an orchard by the side of the road, and the smell of rotting fruit littering the ground reminded me of the plums I'd gathered to help Papa make a recent batch of schnapps. There had been no room to bring the fiery brew with us.

Bedtime approached as we reached the town of Sarre Union. Businesses had all closed, and the dark streets were quiet. Most residents stayed inside as we made our way through town and turned onto the Route De Fenetrange toward Wolfskirchen.

We'd left home in haste and didn't take time to eat our evening meal. Hunger gnawed at me, but I ignored my growling stomach and continued to walk.

Mr. Mueller broke his silence. "I have a niece in Sarrewerden. She will take us in until we find someplace to stay."

Papa nodded. "It's only another two kilometers. We'll take you there."

Refugees had scattered in different directions from Sarre Union. The line of travelers thinned, and only an occasional bicycle passed us. We soon found ourselves alone on the dark road. The cows kept their deliberate pace as they encountered a number of low hills in their path. Sarrewerden was on our route, so we wouldn't have to go out of our way to leave the Muellers with their relatives.

The niece lived only two hundred meters off the paved road, and she agreed to take the old couple in. Papa unloaded their belongings and acknowledged their expressions of gratitude. He asked to water the cows, and the niece filled a tub for them. They drank it all.

While we were stopped, Mama passed out cold ham and bread. I ate like my next meal might not be in the near future. When the food was gone, we said goodbye and resumed our trek.

Mama put her hand on my shoulder. “There’s more room on the wagon now. Wouldn’t you like to ride?”

My head snapped up to stare at her. “I will walk with you and Roger.”

Thick clouds turned the night to black. We encountered larger hills, and Papa stopped occasionally to rest the cows. Mama changed the baby’s diaper at one of the stops. Potholes in the road were hidden by the darkness, making walking more treacherous. Another bicycle carrying two people passed us. The lady sitting on the luggage carrier waved as they went by.

I tripped on the uneven pavement and fell. When I stood, pain from the scrape on my knee stung me. Bending down to touch it, I didn’t find any blood. “I’m all right.”

Mama leaned over to examine my wounded knee. “It’s only scratched. I’ll put some salve on it when we get there.”

Our journey followed the Sarre River as it meandered through the fields and passed by several small villages. No lights shone to guide our way. A fitful breeze chilled the night air, but my sweater kept me warm. Iron wagon wheels grated on the pavement, and the cow’s rhythmic footfalls provided a cadence. I kept pace beside the little baby carriage.

Mama didn’t say anything, but I saw her trip occasionally. Her stride faltered from time to time.

My sturdy shoes felt heavier with every step, and my legs began to tire as we tramped up and down the rolling hills. Mama pushed Roger’s carriage and kept up with the wagon without complaining. I gritted my teeth and refused to admit I was tired.

As we passed by a farmhouse, a large hog, startled awake by our passage, snorted and scrambled away from the noisy wagon. Hearing what sounded like an angry wild animal made me cringe in fright, but I relaxed when I recognized the stink of the hog lot.

I didn't know where we were going, but I stayed determined not to give in and climb on the wagon. I'd promised to walk with my mother beside Roger's carriage. Insects chirped and night birds called from the forest. Dogs barked at our passing, and I continued to put one foot in front of the other.

Roger started to fret, and Mama took a milk bottle from the small bag containing his needs. "Irene, you can feed the baby while we walk. I have to push the carriage, and we can't stop here."

Walking close beside the carriage, I almost tripped again trying to avoid the closely spaced wheels while holding the bottle to the baby's mouth.

Roger expressed his wrath when I bobbled, and he lost the nipple.

I walked sideways and held the side rail to steady myself. "The carriage won't hold still."

Even with the interruptions, the bottle was soon empty. Roger gave a loud burp and drifted off to sleep again.

"I don't like those dark clouds," Mama said. "It smells like rain."

I didn't respond. Fatigue made my legs feel clumsy, and I tripped frequently on the uneven surface. Tucking my head, I continued to keep pace with the wagon. Rain failed to appear as we followed the plodding cattle. Faint streaks of gray had softened the eastern horizon when we finally reached the turnoff at Wolfskirchen.

Papa allowed the cows a rest stop at the narrow lane leading uphill to the village. The pavement ended. After a moment, the cows leaned into their harness to pull the heavy wagon up a rutted dirt street that climbed the steep hillside toward the cluster of buildings.

"Only about another half kilometer," he announced.

My feet slipped and stumbled on the graveled path until they reached level ground, where the village perched on top of a large hill. My strength had waned, but stubborn pride kept me walking beside my mother and baby brother.

After the steep climb, Papa pulled the tired cows to a stop in front of the Lutheran Church near the center of town.

The pastor was up and fully dressed as he came out to greet us. He spoke the same dialect as our local patois at home. It was similar to German, even if we were loyal to France. "It appears we have more refugees. Welcome to Wolfskirchen."

"We're from Kaschel." Papa dropped down from the wagon and approached the pastor. "We've traveled all night, Reverend. We need a place to rest."

The pastor nodded. "The church is already filled, but you can stay in the schoolhouse around the corner."

A few minutes later, we had settled into a classroom that already contained another family. Mama brought bedding from the wagon, and Papa found water for the cows and fed them the bag of hay he'd brought from home. I collapsed onto a folded blanket laid on the classroom floor and fell into a deep sleep.

Chapter 4

The noontime sun rode a clear sky when Mama shook me awake. “Time to get up, sleepyhead. Pastor Zimmer brought us lunch.”

My empty stomach growled as I rose from my pallet on the floor and dressed. The room we shared with another family included three noisy children who complained about not having their bed. The fresh bread, butter, and warm porridge tasted wonderful, and my fatigue had faded while I slept. We were all in better spirits after the meal. I even remembered to thank Pastor Zimmer for bringing food. A half hour later, Mama washed our dishes and took them back to the parsonage.

When she returned, she and Papa discussed our situation and decided Mama should find her family’s acquaintances as soon as possible. They might be able to help us locate a place to stay while we couldn’t go home.

Feeling better after I’d eaten the good food, I joined my mother to visit the family she hoped might help us. Along the way, I noticed the closely spaced houses we passed. Most of them were built of stone and very old. Ivy that Mama said took decades to grow covered several of the walls. A short walk across the village took us past a butcher shop and a bakery. A block farther, and we arrived at a weathered stone house.

An elderly lady met us at the door. Her eyebrows lifted as she spoke, “Yes?”

Mama’s voice sounded thin at first but quickly strengthened. “Good afternoon, Mrs. Bauer. I’m Mina Reeb, daughter of Emile and Caterine Lang of Schopperton. We’ve been forced to evacuate our home in Kaschel because the government expects the Nazis to invade."

The lady smiled at us. "Come in. We think of your parents often. Are they well? Do they still have the tavern?"

I followed Mama as she stepped inside and nodded. "Yes, they are well, and they keep the bar open even if it doesn't make much money. I still remember being fifteen years old and staying up to serve beer until the last customer wobbled out the door in search of his house."

Mrs. Bauer hesitated. "I'm sorry you were driven from your home. How can we help?"

"The pastor arranged for us to sleep in the schoolhouse for now, but the students will need the space. I was hoping you might be able to help us find a place to stay."

Mrs. Bauer pursed her lips. "War is sure to come. You may be here for a while. How many in your family?"

"We have two children. My husband's parents are also with us, and we have two cows."

Mrs. Bauer's brow wrinkled for a moment. "If you allow us time to empty our storage room, I'll make a place for you and your children. It's small, but you can stay there until you find something. You can cook on the fire pit in the backyard. Tether your cows behind the house. The grass is tall, and it should last for a few days. I'm sure one of the neighbors can find a place for your husband's parents."

* * *

We spent another night in the school, and then the four of us moved into the Bauer's storeroom. My grandparents moved into vacated space in the church so the school could reopen. The Bauer's tiny room had a wood floor and a single window. A round table and one chair were the only furniture. The place needed to be aired out, but it sheltered us from the rain. Roger slept in his carriage, and Papa brought in a mattress for himself and Mama. There wasn't space for another, so I laid my pallet on the bare floor. Papa tied the cows to a nearby tree, and the rest of our belongings were left in the wagon behind the Bauer's house.

When I woke the next morning, my father was gone. "Where's Papa?"

"He's at work," Mama said. "You slept too long. I've already milked the cows."

She set a bowl of cold porridge and a glass of milk on the table. "He caught the train to Kaschel. He has to go to his job at the station."

A pang of fear stabbed me, and I pinched my eyebrows closer. "But the Nazis are coming. We had to leave the village."

Mama's face softened, and she took my hands. "The trains have to run, and someone must keep the signal lights lit. The last train will bring him back tonight."

Why Papa had to stay in the village and work still confused me. Everyone else had to leave. The Nazis might hurt him. I turned to the carriage to play with my baby brother, but Roger was sound asleep. With nothing else to claim my attention, I sat on the steps, holding my head and pouting for a time, wishing I could have brought my doll.

Later that morning, I tagged along to mind Roger's carriage while Mama approached Mr. Bauer with a question. "We may be here until it's safe to return home. Do you know of a place we might rent?"

He scratched his head before answering. "We have several refugees looking for housing in the village, but Charles Merkle has an old house he uses to store equipment and hay for his cattle. He might clear everything out if you paid rent."

Mama responded quickly. "I'd like to see the house if he would agree to rent it."

"I'll come along and introduce you," Mr. Bauer said. "Perhaps I'll be able to help."

Mama and I followed him as he walked south toward the edge of town. The homes were more spacious and well maintained on this street. Several large oak trees provided shade, and most of the yards were weed-free and neatly trimmed.

Mr. Bauer led us to a large stone farmhouse and knocked.

An elderly lady with her gray hair tied in a bun answered the door. "Good morning, Paul. Who did you bring with you?"

"This is Mrs. Mina Reeb and her daughter, Irene. They were evacuated from Kaschel and need a place to stay. I thought you might be willing to vacate the old house Charles uses to store farm equipment and hay."

The lady smiled and opened the door. "Come in for a glass of tea, Mina. I'm Liliane. I'll have to speak to my husband. He might be willing."

"I'd also like to rent a plot of land near the house for my cows, and I will plant vegetables next spring if we're here that long," Mama said.

A half hour later, Mr. Merkle agreed on a price to rent the old building if Mama liked it. "I'll have to move my farm equipment. "The house is small and needs to be cleaned, but the roof doesn't leak. There is a good well behind it."

He led us to a dilapidated structure that stood in the middle of cultivated fields, separated from a cluster of homes by about a hundred meters. The yard was filled with weeds, and the condition of the building offered proof it hadn't been inhabited for years. When we entered, the pleasant smell of drying hay overpowered the stink of dust and rotting vegetation.

The downstairs consisted of a large open room, much longer than it was wide, and a small kitchen containing a wood-burning cookstove. A fireplace in the main room would provide heat during cold weather. The stone walls were solid, and Mr. Merkle promised the roof was weather tight. Four windows provided light. The front door was in good repair, but the back door needed its hinges reset and a new latch. A few windowpanes had been broken. The floor was rough-finished concrete, and it held an assortment of farm implements that would need to be moved out. A rickety ladder led to a pair of upstairs rooms filled with hay. Layers of dust and trash covered the floors. The house needed a lot of work before we could live there.

Mr. Merkle pointed to a long shed adjacent to the building. "It goes with the house. You can keep your cows there, and I'll leave you the hay upstairs, so it will be close to the animals."

The house didn't look nearly as nice as our home in Kaschel, and my chin dropped at the thought we would be forced to live here. The hay-filled rooms upstairs were creepy, and we would all stay in the single big room. I'd miss having a bedroom for myself.

The next day, Mr. Merkle emptied the ground floor of the house. Then Mama grabbed a broom to sweep the mess while she heated a tub of water. The building had been infested with mice, birds, and other wildlife, so it needed a lot of cleaning before it would be fit to inhabit.

"Can I help you?" I asked.

Mama pointed to the baby carriage. "Watch your brother while I clean this place."

I soon tired of taking care of Roger. He spent most of the time sleeping and only wanted to eat when he was awake. Dust from Mama's vigorous cleaning got in my hair and eyes and made me sneeze. The boring day seemed to drag on forever. Playing outside would have been much more fun. My mother killed spiders and used the broom to wipe cobwebs from the ceiling. Then she scrubbed the walls and floors until they were spotless.

During the afternoon, Mr. Merkle brought several panes of glass to repair the broken windows. He nodded to Mama. "The place looks better already."

Mama wiped her hands on her apron. "Do you have a wire brush I might borrow? The cookstove is rusted and scrubbing doesn't get it clean."

Mr. Merkle walked home and returned with a stiff wire brush. "This should do the job. I brought my tools, and I might as well reset that back door while I'm here."

Mama attacked the old stove with the brush, and scales of rust flew. Then she washed the kitchen floor to remove the flakes and cleaned the newly repaired windows.

After Mr. Merkle leveled the door, and it opened and closed freely, he told Mama, "I'll have to find a new latch, but you can use it now."

I could see that the long room would be too small for all of us to be comfortable, but at least we'd have a place to stay. Mama kept me busy for the rest of the afternoon, helping clean our new home and watching my baby brother. Cleaning was hard work, and I welcomed the opportunity to care for Roger.

My boredom was interrupted when a small mouse crept out from the kitchen to race across the floor and scamper up the ladder to the hay-filled rooms above.

"A mouse!" I screamed.

The sight of the creature made my skin crawl, and I spent the rest of the afternoon looking over my shoulder for another of these fearsome rodents to appear.

Thoughts of mice would keep me awake at night, fearing one of those dirty things might crawl under the covers with me.

I began to feel better at sundown when Mama stopped working to lead me back to our cramped little room in the Bauer's house.

At least it didn't have mice.

Chapter 5

Papa came home from work at nine o'clock that night carrying a wooden box filled with his homemade schnapps. "The French army barricaded the intersections and requisitioned all the houses to quarter troops."

"I hope they don't damage our belongings," Mama said.

His angry voice roared. "I had to prove who I am to get in my own home. It's a mess. They act like they own it. Our soldiers are helping themselves to the wine and food."

Mama's eyes rolled upward as she exhaled. "Can't their leaders control them?"

"The sergeant in charge is using my coffee cup. I can't stop them, but I'll bring what I can carry on the train each night."

Mama's face looked drawn. "They're acting like animals."

"There's more," Papa said. "Great Britain and France declared war on Germany. There's no way fighting can be avoided now."

Mama nodded and changed the subject. "Did you take care of the livestock?"

"The soldiers watered them, so I fed them. They've already eaten a couple of chickens."

Mama lifted her chin in a gesture of defiance. "We'll have to bring the animals here."

Papa nodded. "We need a place with enough space to keep them."

"I rented a house today."

"Here? In the village? What kind of house?"

"It's small, but we can make do with it for now. It has one large room and a kitchen. Hay is stored upstairs."

Papa ran his fingers through his thick dark hair. "We need room for the cows."

"We have a hectare of land and a shed for them. There is a well behind the house with plenty of water, and the shed has lots of room for storage."

I ran to stand in front of my father. "We have a mouse."

Papa laughed. "I'm not surprised with the hay stored upstairs. I'll find some mousetraps when I stop at home tomorrow."

My parents discussed the rented house, and I watched the baby when they left to see it. They soon returned, and I fell asleep while they talked about what must be done.

* * *

I slept late the next morning and had just begun to eat my buttered bread and milk when my grandparents came to visit. They shook their heads when they saw the tiny room we had been crammed into.

Oma recoiled at the sight. "You can't stay here."

Mama smiled. "It's better than living in a school room with a dozen other people. We have already rented an old house. I'll start moving our belongings tomorrow."

Opa pulled his pipe from a bib pocket on his overalls and stuffed the bowl with tobacco. "We'll look at it later. A man from the government talked to us yesterday evening. They expect it will be a long time before we're able to return home. He recommends that refugees move to the south of France to avoid the fighting that's sure to come."

I breathed in the familiar smell of his pipe tobacco. Opa often smoked it when he talked to people.

"But you'll have to leave your home and all your friends," Mama protested.

"We already left home. Everyone knows I don't like the Germans, and the Nazis may not treat us kindly if they take control of Alsace."

"Are you sure you'll be safe there?"

Opa rubbed his whisker-stubbled chin. "Nothing is sure. A lot of Jews live in Sarralbe, and the Nazis are sure to persecute them. The government requested that all of them move to the South of France."

Mama threw back her head to stare at the ceiling. "The world is going mad. The Nazis are persecuting anyone who doesn't worship the Fuehrer."

"Oma and I have decided to leave. I don't want her to be caught in the fighting. The Nazis are sure to invade. They claim Alsace and the Moselle as part of Germany. They'll overturn our lives."

"Adolf has a job with the railroad," Mama said. "We'd hate to lose that. We don't think there will be any fighting here, and we plan to move back home when everything is settled."

After expressing doubt, Oma and Opa left to make their way back to the church.

That evening, Papa gave a big sigh when he returned. His chin dropped as Mama told him of his parents' decision. "No one can know what is best. There will surely be fighting, and people will be killed. We could go, but we need my job, and I don't want to lose our home."

Papa and Mama spent the evening discussing the decision they must make. They were still talking when I fell asleep.

* * *

By the time I rose from my bed on the floor, Papa was gone. Mama brought me another bowl of porridge and started repacking the wagon. Mr. Bauer helped her load the mattresses and a few boxes of linens, clothing, and dishes. By noon, she had harnessed the cows and brought our belongings to our rented house.

After unloading everything she could lift, she tried to arrange the room and soon realized she would run short of space. Some of our things would have to be stored in the shed. Papa would need to build shelves for storage and make sure it was weather tight. She left the farm implements in the wagon for him to unload and staked the cows out to graze on their tiny plot of land. Later, she brought the gentle animals into the shed for milking before closing them in their stall for the night.

I spent the day caring for my baby brother and pouting about losing my good life in Kaschel. Roger slept in his carriage and complained loudly whenever he needed to be fed or changed. I missed my friends and my toys. Mama checked on the baby frequently, so I had no opportunity to shirk my duty.

Inside, Mama stacked boxes for a makeshift cabinet to hold silverware, dishes, and cooking utensils. Mr. Merkle loaned us a table and three chairs so we could eat dinner like civilized people. Mama spread our mattresses on the floor and added the bedding we brought from home. As evening approached, she gathered sticks from the field and prepared dinner on the stove. Only a small amount of smoke escaped into the room while she cooked.

"It's dark in here," I said.

"You're right. There's not enough light," Mama said. "Only one socket on the ceiling and it has a fifteen watt bulb in it. I can't see to cook. The living room is just as bad."

Papa arrived later carrying two heavily loaded metal buckets with towels covering their contents. When he lifted the first towel, I saw the bucket was filled with bottles of wine.

"The soldiers are drinking it fast," he said. "There wouldn't be any left if I didn't take it away quickly."

When he lifted the second towel, my doll, Brigette, clad in her red dress, rested on top of the bottles. Unable to speak, I pressed her to my breast and wiped away sudden tears that filled my eyes. After a moment, I ran to Papa with a big hug. I failed to find my voice to say anything.

When Mama put food on the table, the pleasant smells of potatoes and sausage filled the room. The kitchen felt more like home as we sat down to eat. I still clutched the doll as if I feared it would escape. Papa continued his report on what was happening to our house.

"The soldiers ate another one of the chickens and one of the young rabbits. At the rate they are going, we will soon lose them all."

Mama brushed back her hair with open fingers. "I'll take the wagon home tomorrow and bring back whatever I can haul. We need to save our chickens, and we can use the eggs here."

"Don't bring a lot of furniture," Papa said. "We don't have room."

It was pitch black outside when Papa harnessed the cows. "I'll be in Kaschel, so I can take off work and help you load the wagon. We'll start back during the afternoon and drive the cows to Wolfkirschen at night."

An hour before daybreak, Mama started her journey. I barely managed to say goodbye before going back to sleep.

Oma stayed with Roger and me. She made breakfast and fed the baby. Then I watched him while she cleared space in the shed for things Mama would bring from home. Cloud cover and a light breeze put a chill in the air. Oma wore her sweater while she worked outside.

The day dragged on as I took care of the baby and fed him his bottle. I had to call Oma to help me with his diaper. He wouldn't stop wiggling. I played with the doll and daydreamed while Roger slept. I even pushed his carriage outside and took him for a short stroll up and down the path to the village. During the afternoon, Oma enlisted my help to cobble together some makeshift shelves to keep our belongings off the dirt floor in the shed.

"You can hold the boards while I drive nails," she said.

After dinner, I slept while Oma cleaned the room and spent the night with us. Skittering sounds from above woke me, and I shuddered at the thought a mouse might invade my bed.

The sound of wagon wheels on the rocky path woke me before daybreak. Mama and Papa were back, and I heard a pig grunt. They had tied it behind the wagon and brought it from home. It was almost time to butcher it. The animal could stay with the cows for now. They left a dozen chickens in their crate until Papa could arrange space for them. Then he and Mama slept for the hour of darkness that remained.

Later, Oma walked back to her room at the church, and I helped my mother unload the wagon. She had brought our kitchen cabinet to hold dishes and food. A table and chairs replaced those Mr. Merkle had loaned us. Two sturdy chests held our clothes. Mama assembled the beds and I danced a jig when my small cot fit in a corner. Maybe mice couldn't reach me there. Familiar furnishings made the house feel more like home.

Mama opened a small paper bag and beckoned to me. "Look what I have here."

"Mousetraps! Now we'll catch those varmints." This was something we really needed. I'd sleep better tonight.

She smiled at me. "I'll set traps in the kitchen and at the top of the ladder."

I sat on the side of her bed feeling safer. "I hope we catch them."

That evening, Papa brought home a large box containing bottles of schnapps. "That's the last of it. Soldiers drank at least a dozen bottles before I rescued it. They can't get to it here."

Mama glanced at the ceiling and then at Papa. "I need your help to change light bulbs. These are too dim to see what I'm doing. I brought some from home."

When he'd finished Mama pulled the strings to flood the rooms with light. "That's much better. Twenty-five watt bulbs make a big difference."

On his day off work, Papa drove scrap lumber into the ground at the end of the shed to serve as posts and lashed straight tree branches across them to make a roost for the chickens. At sundown, the big birds flapped their wings and jumped on top of the rough frame. High off the ground, they'd feel safe from predators during the night.

The following day, Papa brought back a half dozen rabbits in their cage. "This is the last of our animals. The soldiers butchered the other pig and the whole company had a party that lasted all night."

"That's stealing." I looked up to stare at him.

"That's not all," Papa said. "A fire got out of hand, and the Krieger's house down the street burned. The soldiers all claimed they don't know how it happened. Looks like nobody will be held accountable."

Mama's hands covered her face, and then she leaned against the back of a chair. "Poor Anna. Is there nothing we can do?"

Papa shook his head. "The army is preparing for a battle. The whole village is at risk. We're fortunate. Our house is a mess, but it's still standing."

Mama sniffed as she put a large bowl of sauerkraut and pork on the table. "I knew our home might be damaged in the war, but I didn't think French soldiers would do it."

Papa made a face. "I went to my parents' house. It's in better shape than ours, but the soldiers have looted it too. I'll try to bring what is left of their things here."

Everything that happened was just too much for me to accept. I put my hands on my hips in protest. "I want to go home."

Mama wrapped an arm around me and pulled me close. "We can't go now. The Nazis will come, and it won't be safe there."

I sat down for the meal, but my appetite had disappeared.

While we ate, Papa told us the news he'd heard during the day. "Nazis have captured the western part of Poland. The Russians attacked from the east."

Mama looked up with a hopeful expression. "Hitler has already taken Austria and Czechoslovokia. Maybe he will be satisfied he has enough *lebensraum* now."

Papa grimaced. "Not likely. The Fuehrer wants all of Europe. France will be next."

* * *

Later that evening, my grandparents came to visit. Opa fished out his pipe and lit it. "The train to the south leaves tomorrow morning. We'll be resettled in the Haute Vienne Province. It is a mountainous area with no large cities. Beautiful country. The government man says the fighting won't reach us there."

Papa grunted. I hope you're making the right decision."

Opa shrugged. "We will be limited to 30 kilos baggage on the train. We'll need to store a few things in your shed.

"We have the room," Papa said. "I hope you find a safe haven in the south."

Mama's gaze traveled back and forth between my grandparents. "You must do what you think is best. We'll miss you."

Opa held his pipe in both hands. "At least a dozen people from here will be on the train tomorrow. The government expects to transport tens of thousands to the safety of the interior."

Papa's forehead wrinkled as he nodded. "The soldiers have looted a lot of valuables in your house, but I'll try to bring some of your belongings here."

Oma reached out to touch Papa's arm. "Only *things* are left there. We will be safe in the south of France. This war can't last forever."

Papa met her eyes. "I'll save what I can."

Chapter 6

Emptiness lay like a weight on my chest as my grandparents climbed aboard the train the next morning. Several of the people, mostly elderly or disabled, were given priority to board. Opa and Oma were in the next group, and they pushed their way into the crowded railcar. It looked like most of the seats had already been taken. Oma waved at us from the window.

My chin trembled, and I cried when the engine chugged to life. It began to move, and the clanking string of cars disappeared around the curve. My mind wrestled with the thought I might never see them again. I missed home. I missed my friends. Now my grandparents were leaving, too. No longer would I be able to go to Oma's house for a piece of apple cake or a bite of chocolate. The Nazis had ruined everything.

Papa managed to rescue more of our belongings during the day, and he stacked things that wouldn't fit in our room inside the shed. He purchased a roll of net wire and made an outdoor pen for the chickens. A few scraps of wood lifted the rabbit cages off the ground.

One Sunday when he didn't have to work, Papa helped a neighbor cut a storm-felled oak tree into lengths for firewood. At the end of the day, he brought home a half filled wagon. "It's a blessing I can work for this instead of buying it," he said to Mama. "Prices are high and money is scarce."

He built a small fire in the fireplace.

I found a seat close to the flames. "I don't need to wear my coat in the house now."

* * *

October arrived with brisk winds and cooler temperatures. Dry foliage flew in the stiff breeze, and the days grew shorter. The smell of turning leaves and the crisp, cold air announced that winter was coming soon. Roger's carriage was usually parked in the kitchen, and Mama made sure I stayed busy watching my baby brother while she worked elsewhere. Roger delighted in throwing his toys, and it was my job to keep them picked up.

"The mice might nibble on them if you leave toys on the floor," Mama told me.

While Roger slept, I picked up his playthings and spent a lot of time feeling sorry for myself. I daydreamed about being in my roomy house in Kaschel and playing with friends I'd known since I could walk.

Lots of things had changed. Things we used disappeared from the stores. Chocolate and sugar couldn't be found. Mama said we would use what we had.

I soon met several of the other kids in the neighborhood, and Mama allowed me to go play with them. They jumped rope and threw a ball against a wall. The challenge was to catch it on a return bounce. Making new friends brightened my days. But these friends were not quick to accept a new girl. I persisted, but I still wanted to go home.

* * *

November arrived, and the weather turned colder with rain and a dusting of snow. I was delighted when Papa brought me a pair of rubber boots and helped me try them on.

He gave the boots a critical look. "They fit. Your feet will stay nice and dry."

I immediately ran to show the boots to my new friends. On the way, a shallow canal carried water from springs on the hillside as it passed through the village. I waded in to find out if they were truly waterproof. One of the bigger boys urged me to venture into deeper water. His challenge sounded too big to ignore.

"Oops." Icy water surged over the top of a boot and drenched my foot. I waded out and shivered as I emptied the inch-deep liquid from my boot.

"I thought you said they were waterproof," the boy taunted.

Afraid Papa would punish me, I ran home to hide in the kitchen and change into my other shoes. It would surely be safer not to tell my parents the boots leaked if the water came over the top. Mama caught me changing, but I breathed a long sigh of relief when she promised not to tell Papa. This experience led me to be more careful, and the boots worked like they should if I stayed out of deep water.

* * *

One morning, Mama noticed a red rash on Roger's chest. It got steadily worse for the next few days. Angry red splotches covered most of his body. She looked down at the miserable little guy and tried to soothe him by dusting his body with baby powder.

"I'm sorry, little one. Maybe this will make you feel better."

The rash didn't improve, and Roger became more quarrelsome. His crying made me nervous. I wanted to comfort him but didn't know how.

"Can't you make him stop crying, Mama?"

She picked him up and held him often. His cries would subside for a few minutes, but he continued to squirm and paw at the irritation.

I talked to him and tried to interest him in his toys, but he didn't appear to notice. The toys lay untouched.

Ominous black clouds appeared, and a blustery wind blew cold rain against our windows. Gray skies and the gloomy, damp chill only made our situation worse.

After talking to Mrs. Bauer, Mama spread olive oil over his body. The treatment seemed to fight the itching for a time, but Roger made things worse by scratching the red bumps. The spots got bigger and angrier looking.

She made him a pair of linen mittens to protect his skin from tiny fingernails, but Roger became frustrated by being unable to scratch. His protests grew louder and upset the household for days before he accepted the mittens. The rash persisted, and it dragged on for several weeks before it finally faded.

* * *

I felt left out when my friends went to school while I had to stay home to watch my baby brother. Life wasn't fair. They were learning to read while I did chores at home and took care of the little guy. It didn't take me long to come up with a plan to remedy this situation.

The next morning, I took action. Standing outside when the neighbor kids started their short walk to school, I announced "I'm going with you."

One of the boys laughed. "You're too little to go to school."

I crossed my arms and flashed him a determined look. "I'm going to school."

The boy shrugged, and I followed the small group of children to the schoolhouse. After entering the classroom, I slid into an empty seat in the back row and waited for the lessons to begin. I started to feel uneasy about being there and watched with eyes wide as the teacher brought the class to order and called roll.

She didn't call my name.

The elderly lady wore a long gray dress under her sweater even though the room was warm. Her fading hair was pulled into a tight bun. She didn't smile when she speared me with an inquisitive stare. "What is your name, little girl?"

I returned her stare. "Irene Reeb."

"Did your parents enroll you in school?"

A feeling of uncertainty crept over me. I couldn't think of a good way to answer the question. "I don't know."

The teacher nodded. "How old are you?"

Several seconds passed while I hesitated. I could feel all the other students' eyes on me. "I'm five."

"Do your parents know you're here?"

I fidgeted in my seat. This talk wasn't going the way I wanted. "Papa's not at home."

The teacher smiled as she walked down the row of desks to rest a hand on my head. "Five years old is too young to go to school. Run home now, and tell your mother we will welcome you to the first grade next year."

Defeated, I trudged back to our house with a heavy heart. All my new friends were allowed to go to school, and I couldn't go.

Later that day, Mama brought home a letter from the post office. It was from the government and addressed to Papa. Even to me, the letter looked ominous. Her face stiffened as she held the official-looking envelope with her fingertips and placed it on a shelf to await Papa's return from work.

I sensed my mother's concern and asked, "Who sent the letter, Mama? Why don't you open it?"

She glanced down at me with drawn lips and the skin around her eyes pulled tight with worry. "The government."

"What does it say?"

"Your father will open it when he gets home."

For the rest of the day, I noticed Mama didn't always respond when Roger cried for attention. She forgot to tell me to bring in the eggs, and she was late in preparing our dinner. When Papa came home, she handed him the letter before he had a chance to take off his coat.

His face turned pale, and he frowned as he looked at the envelope. His movements were slow as he sat on a chair and stared at the letter.

Finally, he used his pocket knife to open it and removed a single sheet of folded paper. A moment later, his jaw clenched. His body slumped and he seemed to wilt as he studied what was written on the page.

Mama's hand rested on his shoulder. "Do you have to go in the army?"

He was slow to answer, and his body looked smaller when he spoke, "I'm to report at Soissons for induction in four weeks."

Chapter 7

Worry about my father being drafted and going away to the army kept me awake. My eyes popped open every few minutes during the night to hear crickets chirping and our cows moving in their stall. Papa and Mama spent most of the evening discussing what this bad news could mean for the family. With him away, life would be difficult for those of us left at home. They also agreed there wasn't much they could do about it.

From my bed in the corner, I watched and listened to their conversation. Why did Papa have to go? Who would look after our house in Kaschel? What if he got hurt in the army?

"You could be killed," Mama said. "France and Germany have declared war. The fighting could start any time."

Papa lifted his hands in frustration. "We could all be killed at home. A bomb doesn't care where it falls."

A vision of bombs dropping from the sky struck terror in my heart. We hadn't done anything to the Nazis. What made them so mean?

"How will we live?" Mama wrung her hands. "The army will pay you almost nothing."

"You will need to be thrifty, but we have some savings. Maybe I can find a way to earn a little extra money while I'm in the service."

"Will Uncle George have to go to the army, too?" I asked.

"No," Papa said. "He's only sixteen. The army needs grown men."

Mama clutched the back of a chair. "They need you at the station. Can't your boss do anything to keep you?"

Papa rubbed a hand over the top of his head. “I doubt it, but I’ll ask him tomorrow.”

With Papa gone, who would do the work at home? All during the night, I fretted and woke frequently from an uneasy sleep.

Sunlight streamed through my window when I climbed out of bed and dressed. Papa had already left for work. Mama looked smaller when she prepared our breakfast. Her hands fumbled with the dishes, and tears glistened in her eyes. We ate our oatmeal and bread without talking. The only sound was the clinking of silverware on our plates.

The day passed slowly. My normally active mother spent a lot of time sitting at the table holding her head in her hands. She appeared to be distracted by bigger concerns while she cleaned the kitchen and the single large room we lived in. Roger demanded frequent attention, and Mama was slow to care for him. I tried to play with my little brother, but he seemed to sense our downcast mood, squirming and fussing for no obvious reason.

The room felt stuffy and sad. “May I go play outside?”

She nodded without looking at me.

Intending to bounce my soccer ball off my head and knees to keep it in the air as long as possible, I sat on an overturned box staring at the empty sky instead. Nothing happened to dispel my gloom. Our family faced some bad problems if Papa had to go to the army.

During the afternoon, Mama asked me to care for Roger while she did chores. “Make sure he stays warm and doesn’t start crying.”

Wanting to allow Roger a chance to enjoy the sunshine, I pushed his carriage outside. For a time, he waved his arms and made gurgling noises. A half hour later, he started to fret, so I made faces at him and tickled his chin. He responded with a big smile and reached for me. When the sun passed behind a cloud, a chill wind penetrated my sweater. The sleeves had become too short, and it barely reached to my waist. The fit didn't matter since it was the only sweater I owned. I pulled the covers tighter around Roger, and he soon fell asleep.

Playing with the ball and listening for Roger kept me close to the carriage. Sunlight warmed me despite the wind. Bare trees looked lonely as they stood in stark contrast against a clear sky. Dry leaves fluttered in the breeze. Winter couldn't be far away.

Mama cleaned the chicken run and brought a half dozen eggs into the kitchen. After that, she cleaned the small pig pen.

Creeping closer to watch, I wrinkled my nose and complained. "It stinks."

Mama's laugh sounded odd, not her usual happy sound. "It stinks worse where I'm standing."

When she finished taking care of the animals, she used the axe to split a few round blocks for firewood. Then she carried them into the house to fuel our fireplace.

The flames soon gave off a warm glow, and she came back outside to take care of the baby. "Our wood won't last all winter. I hope your father can find more before he has to leave."

My teeth clamped onto my lower lip. "Why does Papa have to go to the army?" My fingers fumbled with the hem of my skirt. "He doesn't want to fight."

"The Nazis are bad people who intend to take our country from us. The army needs more soldiers to keep Germans from coming here." Mama smoothed her apron with a shaking hand. "We can only pray he doesn't have to go."

My chin dropped to my chest. "It's not fair. We need Papa here."

After all the chores were finished, Mama appeared to be more relaxed and gave me a hug. Then she checked on Roger again. "He needs his diaper changed."

She rolled the carriage inside, and I sat on the step to fret about our problems. After a few minutes, I gathered myself to trudge up the hill to the Koeppel's house. They were refugees from Kaschel like us. Mr. Koeppel had worked in the cement plant on the other side of the village, and they lived on a street close by. I didn't know them well. They had been fortunate to rent a small house uphill from the old building where we lived.

The weathered stone walls looked ancient. The roof had been repaired, and some of the newer tiles weren't faded like the older ones. The downstairs had a kitchen and living room. The upstairs had two bedrooms. Two small shrubs were separated by the front door. The house looked like a friendly place.

Their daughter, Maria, was younger than me. Older kids were my first choice for playmates, but they were all in school. Maybe Maria and I could play with her dolls.

I knocked on the door and waited.

When Mrs. Koeppel answered, I asked, "Can Maria come outside to play?"

She shook her head with a smile. "*Bonjour*, Irene. Maria is taking a nap. You can come back later when she's awake."

Turning away disappointed and staring at my feet, I made my way home with reluctant footsteps. Having nobody to play with, I sat on the step, idly tugging at strands of my hair. I missed my playmates at home. My mood perked up when Mama came outside carrying something in her hand.

The trap she showed me held a mouse. "We caught him in the kitchen. We're sure to catch another one when I reset it."

I shrank away from the dead mouse. My stomach felt queasy, but I was glad the creature wouldn't sneak up on me during the night. There had to be a lot more of the nasty little critters lurking in the hayloft. Maybe Mama would catch all of them.

After dark, Papa came home from work with another box and set it gently on the table. "I brought some of Oma's set of good china. Part of it is missing. Several pieces were broken. I'll save what I can."

Mama's whole body tensed. She didn't even bother to look at the dishes. "Did you ask your boss if he could do anything about your draft notice?"

Papa's face broke into a wide grin. "He said a lot of people are being drafted, but he needs me to stay on the job. The trains can't run if nobody is there to tend the signals that control their movement."

"Will he do anything to help you?"

Papa shrugged and chuckled. "He can't guarantee results, but he promised to write a letter declaring that my work is essential to the war effort. He'll explain the need for rail service when the fighting starts. Nothing is sure, but I'm not gone yet."

Dinner was turnips and potatoes with milk, fresh baked bread, and butter. It tasted wonderful. After Mama tucked me in bed, I slept soundly all night long.

Chapter 8

On Sundays, Papa liked to visit Mr. Bauer. The men always listened to news broadcasts on his radio. When Papa got home, he would bring us an account of what happened in the war.

"France has positioned troops to reinforce the Maginot Line and guard against Nazi aggression," he said. "That's why we had to evacuate Kaschel."

The news sounded more sinister the next week. "German submarines sunk a British battleship, and the Luftwaffe dropped bombs on one of their naval bases."

"The British are the only allies we have left." Mama continued to stir the dough to make dumplings for our dinner.

I cringed. What would happen if the Luftwaffe dropped bombs on us?

A few weeks later, Papa came home, shaking his head. "Germany and Russia agreed to split Poland between the two countries. Hitler will rule the west and Stalin will rule the east."

Mama wiped a hand over her eyes. "Mr. Merkle told me the Nazis are rounding up all the Jews and sending them to concentration camps."

Papa nodded. "They appear to be taking anyone who opposed them, like reporters, intellectuals, and people who work for the government. I wouldn't want to be a Jew living any place the Nazis control."

On another Sunday, Papa brought home more unpleasant news. "Hitler has started to kill sick and disabled people in Germany and in the countries he conquered. He rounds people up by the dozens, and they disappear."

"He's determined to rid the world of what he calls non-productive people." Mama dried her hands on her apron and sighed.

I stayed scared from listening to daily conversations about the status of the war and the certainty that Nazis would invade. The French army claimed they could stop the Germans at the Maginot Line or in the Ardennes if they attacked through Belgium. I didn't understand what the war was about or where all these places were, but I wondered when the soldiers would come to us. People I heard talking in Wolfskirshen weren't sure we could stop the German Army. At night, I woke frequently from bad dreams about what the Nazis might do to us.

The next morning, I questioned my mother. "Why do the Nazis kill sick people?"

Mama stared at the ceiling before looking directly at me. "Nazis are evil. People who are old or helpless need care. Those who need help to stay alive are not able to contribute to winning Hitler's war."

My shoulders curled over my chest when I heard these terrible things. My skin crawled from thinking about Nazis coming here to decide who lives and dies.

One afternoon, Mrs. Koeppel stopped by to visit. "Mrs. Bauer told me a German airplane circled over Sarre Union for ten minutes."

Mama frowned. "How did she know it was German?"

Mrs. Koeppel explained. "It had a big cross painted on the bottom of the wings. It's easy to see. They call it the iron cross. All their airplanes have it."

I felt a catch in my throat. An iron cross sounded scary.

* * *

The weather grew colder, and I woke on an icy December morning to find snow covering the ground. I remembered Papa pulling me down the street on our sled. Looking at the snow outside made me long for the battered little sleigh. It would be leaning against the side of the woodshed in Kaschel if the soldiers hadn't broken it. Not having the sled, I decided to tromp through the snow with my new boots.

It was Papa's day off work. He ate quickly and prepared to leave the house. "I'll help Mr. Merkle repair his broken wagon. In return, he'll give us more firewood."

The snow soon melted in sunlit patches, and I stayed home to take care of my baby brother while Mama sat at the dining table knitting for hours. The sound of other children playing outside made me feel sorry for myself. Fortunately, my doll and the task of looking after my brother kept me occupied.

During the afternoon, Papa came home long enough to harness the cows to the wagon and leave again. An hour later, he returned with a big load of firewood.

He grunted in satisfaction when he lifted the last chunk of wood onto the tall stack in the shed. "This will be enough to get us through the winter."

* * *

On Papa's next day off work, a thin film of ice formed on the livestock's tub of water. Mama woke me early. "Papa slaughtered our pig, so this will be a busy day. Get dressed and eat your breakfast quickly. We need to prepare the meat to last through the winter."

After I'd eaten, I ran outside to see what Papa was doing. The pig's carcass hung from a tree fork. Its belly had been cut open. The insides lay on the ground in a stinky pile.

I covered my nose with the palm of my hand. "Yuck."

Papa laughed as he handed me a pan filled with chopped intestines. "Take this to the chickens. They'll have a feast."

The idea didn't appeal to me. "Will the chickens really eat it?"

Papa grinned. "They'll love it."

I carried the smelly pan to the chicken run and set it inside. The hens surprised me by making a mad dash to compete with each other for the choice morsels. At that moment, I wondered if I'd really want to eat eggs tomorrow.

Papa had already scraped all the hair from the pig's body, so I watched him remove the skin. Next he washed the carcass and cut it into pieces with a big knife. The fat would be reduced to lard. He took care to separate the hams, shoulders, and loins to be salted so they wouldn't spoil during the coming winter. Later, he would hang the hams over a smoky fire. Most of the fatty meat would be made into sausage which the whole family loved. He would clean the large intestine to make a casing for the sausages, and it would keep for a long time. The brain and organ meat were set aside for a special treatment.

Papa handed me another pan of chopped pig guts. "Take this to your mother. She can feed it to the chickens tomorrow."

I took it without answering. Obviously, the chickens liked it, but I couldn't figure out why they should.

We fed almost half the meat through a hand-cranked grinder to make sausage. Mama turned the crank for almost an hour before she raised up to shake her arm. "This is hard work. Think you could turn it for a while?"

The handle felt heavy as I grunted and gave it a mighty pull. It moved halfway around and stopped. I pushed harder, and it turned some more. Determined, I used all my strength to turn it a full circle. Pride kept the crank moving for a couple of minutes before my arms cramped and I stopped to rub them.

Mama took the handle and awarded me a smile. “Thank you for helping. I’m rested now.”

Papa hauled the rest of the pig guts out into the fields and returned to take care of the meat. “The varmints will eat most of the intestines tonight. I can bury anything they leave.”

While Mama and Papa took care of the meat, I spent most of the afternoon watching the baby. It was comforting to know we would have plenty of pork for the coming winter.

The fresh ribs we had for dinner tasted great. It had been a long day, and I was tired. “We have a lot of fresh meat left. Will it spoil before we can eat it all?”

Papa shook his head. “I’ll take some to Pastor Zimmer, to Mr. Bauer, and to Mr. Merkle. They have been kind to us. The meat will be our way of saying thank you.”

Exhausted, I fell into bed early and went to sleep as soon as my head touched the pillow. I didn’t even think about mice nibbling at me.

During the next several days, the weather grew colder as more snow covered the ground. It didn’t melt this time. Ice froze thick on the cow’s tub, and Mama had to break it with an axe. I was happy when Papa brought my sled to haul things he salvaged from home up the steep grade to the village. Pulling it was easier than slogging up the snow-covered hill from the station and carrying the load on his back.

* * *

As Christmas approached, everyone grew more excited. I anticipated the holiday and frequently broke into a dance or a song of joy for no apparent reason. Even Roger seemed to sense something special in the air. He smiled and kicked his chubby legs.

A sudden thought sent me into a momentary panic. “Will Kris Kringle be able to find us in our new home?”

Mama’s face wrinkled as if she was doing some serious thinking. Then she gave me a reassuring look. “Kris Kringle is very smart. I’m sure he knows how to find us here. Don’t you agree, Papa?”

My father nodded immediately. “Don’t worry. Old Kris knows the way.”

A few days later, as darkness approached, Mama finished washing the dishes and then she declared, “It’s Christmas Eve. Let’s all go to church and give thanks to the Christ Child for keeping us safe.”

Papa declined. “I have to do some work at the station, Mina. You can take the children to the service. You’ll have to carry Roger. His carriage would get stuck in the snow.”

She shrugged. “All right. The three of us will go without you.”

The big bell sounded out loud notes as we approached, and we found the church all decorated for Christmas. Bright ribbons and garlands of evergreen branches hung over the front of the church and all the windows. Candles illuminated the podium and pews. I breathed in the fragrance of freshly cut boughs and marveled at the bright lights and decorations. Pastor Zimmer wore his white robe as he preached about blessings the Christ Child brought to humanity. Church members shared their joy with neighbors by greeting those around them.

While I watched the festive service with wide eyes and growing anticipation, Roger slept through most of the excitement.

After the service, Mama took time to speak with other villagers. "I'm so glad to meet you Mrs. Klein. Mrs. Merkle speaks of you often. She tells me you're the best cook in Wolfskirchen."

Later, Mama said her goodbyes and carried Roger as we trudged through the snow back to our house.

Papa was not in sight when we arrived. I opened the door to slip inside first. Suddenly, Papa appeared behind us to follow as we entered. A cheerful fire warmed the room, and we started to remove our coats. Then I turned toward what had been a dark empty corner which now held bright pinpoints of light on a beautiful fir tree. Lighted candles were firmly attached to its branches, and the flames gave off a cheerful glow. Warmth from the candles filled the room with the spicy smell of the evergreen boughs. Several newspaper-wrapped packages lay on the floor beneath the tree.

I screamed with delight. "Kris Kringle found us."

When we opened the packages, we discovered presents for everyone. Papa pulled off the wrapping to find a new wool shirt. Mama gave him a long hug when her package held a bright scarf and gloves. Roger had several noisemakers and soft rings to chew on. He'd enjoy them when he started teething. My package held a knitted wool sweater that was big enough to fit me and a beautiful little blue dress for my doll.

We reveled in warmth and safety as we enjoyed our Christmas. Excitement kept me bouncing around the room until Mama finally chased me off to bed. I'd already tried on my sweater several times and admired the new dress on my doll.

I went to sleep clutching Brigette in her new outfit. Thoughts of armies or invasions or Nazis or mice didn't enter my mind.

Chapter 9

Shortly after the New Year began, Mama picked up a letter from my grandparents at the post office. She waited until Papa came home before opening it. I stood close, watching with interest as they sat down at the table to read it together.

After a moment, Papa leaned back and shook his head. "It sounds like they are fortunate, living in luxury with a countess. They did a lot better than we did."

Mama pointed to a line in the letter. "They don't live in the castle. They live in the garden house behind it. The countess and her husband live in the castle. Oma says the owners are very kind to them."

"It sounds like the owners are providing food and lodging. I don't see anything about any meaningful work that could take care of them long term."

Mama laid the letter on the table. "We don't know how long they'll be there."

Papa rubbed his temple with two fingers. "She says it's all mountains and beautiful country there."

"The best news is they feel safe. We can't say that. The Nazis could invade tomorrow, and we're too close to the border."

I listened without speaking. My grandparents had been fortunate to find a safe place to stay. They must be a long way from Alsace. Mama and Papa made it plain they didn't feel safe here. That scared me.

* * *

Winter set in to stay. Mama took care of Roger, me, and the animals. Papa worked from early till late. Both my parents dealt with the bad weather and constant labor.

Then I developed a cough.

Papa listened as I had several of my hacking spells before he suggested his favorite remedy. "You sound terrible. I'll get you a spoonful of sugar and schnapps. That will cut through the congestion. You'll feel good as new."

Mama didn't agree. "I wish it were just a cold, but several children in the village have whooping cough. I'm afraid that's what she has. It can be serious."

The next morning, my cough was worse, and I felt warm all over like I had a fever. Mama kept me inside. She put hot compresses on my chest and fed me some tasteless tea. Nothing seemed to help. The cough deepened, and the spells happened more frequently.

"It hurts, Mama," I complained in a raspy voice.

"Just lay quiet," Mama said. "Stay warm and rest. I'll try to find something to make you comfortable. Roger is sleeping, and I'll only be gone a few minutes. If he wakes, don't go near him. We don't want him to catch it."

"I'll stay in bed," I promised.

She grabbed her coat and rushed out the door.

Ten minutes later, Mama returned with a different sort of tea. "Mrs. Merkle says most of the children in the village have the whooping cough. She wants you to try this. It seems to help other children feel better."

I tried the bitter tea. It tasted bad enough to be medicine, but the cough stayed with me. Waking up with each new spell of hacking kept me miserable for the entire night. My throat and chest hurt all the time.

Mama gave me more tea and put evil-smelling compresses on my chest. “Just rest and you’ll be better soon.”

After a few days, I felt better and began to play with my doll. Then I became restless to go outside. “I’m fine, Mama. It doesn’t hurt anymore.”

She shook her head. “Not yet.”

I stayed away from my baby brother, but the next day he began to cough. We all hoped it was just a cold.

Roger’s fits of hacking and gagging hit him hard. He cried without stopping until he fell asleep from exhaustion. I felt sorry for him as his pitiful wailing filled the room. It was obvious he felt miserable and was too young to understand what happened. I tried to play with him, but nothing I did seemed to console him. He spit up the tea, and Mama ran out of ideas about how to help him.

His cough got worse and worse. After each spell of violent coughing, he struggled to breathe. His lips and fingernails turned blue. He began to vomit thick mucus, and soon he couldn’t keep his milk down. I helped clean the bed after each spell. His little body got thinner as he lost weight and strength. Days passed and Mama stayed at his bedside without rest. I tried to help when she could stay awake no more.

Papa would normally have taken charge and told everyone what to do. Now, he sat in his chair by the table on his day off work, not speaking, wrinkling his brow, pinching the skin on his throat.

He always had an answer when we had problems. I looked up to him and expected him to tell us what to do. His silence scared me.

Most children in the village recovered, but Roger’s condition got worse. He vomited everything he ate. We feared he wouldn’t recover.

When Papa came home from work with a five kilogram bag of sugar he'd obtained from a rail shipment, Mama rationed it. Not knowing when we might get more, I decided my baby brother should have first call on it.

"I don't need sugar, Mama. Save it for Roger." I hoped it would help him get better, and this bit of self-sacrifice made me feel more grown up.

After Roger had been sick for almost two weeks, Pastor Zimmer appeared at our door, accompanied by Sister Gertrude from the Catholic Church. "With your permission, Sister will try to help you care for the baby."

Sister Gertrude stood tall and straight in her black habit. Wire-rimmed spectacles perched on her nose as she glanced at the family. Her black robe frightened me. I ducked my head and retreated to a corner of the room.

The elderly nun went to Roger's bed and looked down at him. Her wrinkled face looked calm and friendly as she nodded to Mama. She reached to touch the baby with the tips of her fingers. "How have you treated his illness so far?" she asked.

"I used hot compresses and a mustard plaster," Mama said. "We tried to give him some tea from Mrs. Merkle, but he spits it up. He's getting weaker, and nothing seems to work."

"I have medicine that may allow him to rest," Sister Gertrude said. "I believe we can help him fight this disease."

Tears streamed down Mama's face, but the kindly nun's presence offered us hope. I stayed close in case she needed me. Her presence calmed Mama and Papa as well.

Sister Gertrude applied smelly poultices to Roger's chest and fed him medicines with an eye dropper. She stayed by his bedside until late in the evening, and Roger actually slept for a half hour.

She visited him daily for the next week, applying poultices and giving him tea and medicines. Roger finally began to make progress in dealing with the illness. His vomiting became less frequent and eventually stopped. He began to take small amounts of milk from his bottle again. His coughing diminished and then disappeared altogether. After a few more days, his appetite returned. His normal color came back, and he began to regain his strength.

After checking on him during her next visit, Sister Gertrude told us Roger would get well. "My work is done."

Mama's eyes filled with tears as she answered. "Thank you, Sister. We were at our wits end, and you saved him. We'll be forever grateful."

Sister Gertrude smiled and gathered her long skirt to leave. "We all try to do the Lord's work. May He bless Roger and his entire family."

With the crisis over, Roger's spirit and energy returned. He resumed his place as the healthy, loveable baby we cherished, and the freedom from our fears allowed all of us to regain our normal life.

With Roger's frightening illness behind us, Mama pointed out what day it was on the calendar. "Only three more days until your birthday. You'll be six years old."

My chest swelled with pride. Six was old enough to start school in the fall. I'd be a lot closer to being a grownup. I felt taller already.

When the happy day arrived, we couldn't manage much of a celebration. Everyone wished me a "Happy Birthday," and Mama made a cake to observe the event. My present was a pencil and tablet to write on.

She pulled me close in a big hug. "If you want to learn, I'll teach you to write the alphabet."

I beamed with excitement over all the things I could do if I learned my letters. “Will you teach me how to write everyone’s name?”

Mama laughed. “That takes a long time, but we’ll make a start. You’ll be well prepared when school opens next fall.”

I still had to wait for months before the teacher would let me go to school, but I was anxious to learn in the meantime. Mama promised to teach me all the letters and how to write my name when she found time.

My parents hadn’t talked much about the war since the holidays, but a big airplane flying low over the village the next day got my attention. Then it turned around to come back again. What was it doing here? Were the Nazis attacking? Would it harm us? My heart beat faster, and I held my breath as a feeling of panic settled over me.

Thoroughly frightened, I ran inside. “Mama, I saw a German airplane circling over the village. It had with an iron cross painted on both wings. Why did the Nazis come here? Will they drop bombs on us?”

Chapter 10

My hands gripped the armrests as the big Lockheed Electra Airliner surged into the Paris sky on a cloudy August sky in 1958. This was my first time to fly in an airplane. The cold air made my throat dry, and my queasy stomach reminded me I wasn't as brave as I'd hoped to be. Leaving my family and friends was really happening. It was no longer a fuzzy dream for the future. As I looked out the window on my right, an awesome view of the city lay before me.

The Seine River snaked through a multitude of buildings, wending its way to the Atlantic Ocean. The sight of the Eiffel Tower was incredible. I thought I could make out the Sacred Heart Cathedral and the Arc of Triumph in the distance. They faded from view as we made our way west. I relaxed my grip on the armrests when we reached cruising altitude and the seat belts light went out.

Thoughts of leaving Kaschel to live in Paris welled up in my memory. Mama's head had nodded approval while her thinly pressed lips expressed regret. Papa's eyes filled with tears when I caught the train.

Aunt Lina helped me adapt to city life, but the transition hadn't been easy. Parisians sniffed when talking about people from Alsace who they generally considered to be hard workers but not very bright. Since I didn't start to study French until I was eleven, my limited command of the language and my regional accent was a dead giveaway.

Leaving France scared me, but I eagerly anticipated learning about a new life in America. Some of my friends said everyone there was rich.

Dale chuckled when I told him. "I don't know any rich people, but we won't need to fear being hungry."

My tiny man-child slept peacefully in a hammock the airline had provided. He would have no memory of my troubled life during the Great War. I took my first deep breath since the aircraft had surged forward on its takeoff roll.

The lady sitting on the aisle seat beside me smiled, leaned forward and said something to me in English.

I returned her smile, but I hadn't understood a word she said.

She tried again.

I finally used up about half of my English vocabulary. "No speak English."

She nodded and settled back in her seat to close her eyes.

My thoughts returned to fear of the Nazis that dominated my young life even before their dreaded army arrived. Leaving Kaschel and coping with the new environment in Wolfskirchen had been a challenge. The sight of an airplane with the Iron Cross painted on its wings had struck terror in my heart and sent me scurrying for shelter. I'd miss my mother and father who'd been so brave and resourceful during those terrible years.

* * *

Mama's fingers squeezed and stretched the moist ball of dough she kneaded and pounded it on the counter top. She rolled and twisted the big lump before placing it on the bare table dusted with flour. After tearing it in half, she put the two pieces in separate pans to bake in the oven. Then she looked down at me and responded to my question.

"Don't worry. The airplane won't drop bombs here. When the Nazi's bomb a town, they come with lots of planes."

Her calm explanation didn't keep me from worrying for the rest of the day. The airplane might drop a bomb just because they didn't like us.

Later, Mama caught two more mice in the hayloft, and I clapped my hands and squealed approval. I forgot about the danger from airplanes for a while. Maybe we had caught all the nasty little critters by now, and I'd be able to sleep without worrying about mice in my bed.

When Papa came home from work, Mama rushed to tell him the news. "A German airplane flew right over town today."

He hung his coat on a peg by the door. "I'm not surprised. They've been flying reconnaissance flights over Strasbourg and the entire *Bas Rhin* for several weeks."

I twisted a lock of my hair. "Why, Papa?"

"They are looking to see where the French and British troops are stationed." He sat down to take me on his knee. "British airplanes are scattering propaganda leaflets in Germany telling everyone the Nazis are bad and people shouldn't support them. There were several battles with British and French planes fighting the *Luftwaffe*. The Nazis could decide to attack France at any time, and they want to know where our troops are located."

My shoulders slumped. Imagination conjured up all sorts of weird things that could happen to us. "I'm scared."

He gave me a reassuring hug. "They don't usually attack civilians. Just remember to stay inside if they come."

After the welcome scent of baked pork and cabbage drifted from the kitchen, Mama called us to dinner. We dug into the good food and stopped talking about the airplane.

When I woke the next morning, snow halfway to the top of my boots covered the ground. A cold wind bit me when I stuck my head outside to look. I ran outside to play after eating, but Mama soon brought me a small shovel.

"You and I need to make a path to all the animals and to the outhouse so we don't have to wade through snow." She took the big shovel and started cleaning the path to the outhouse. I cleared a path to the shed.

It didn't take me long to decide that making snowballs was a lot more fun than shoveling snow. My face and hands felt frozen, and my arms ached from lifting the heavy snow-filled shovel. After Mama finished clearing her walk, she went inside to fix lunch. Eager to finish my chore and go inside, I struggled to shovel faster.

Finally she stuck her head outside and called, "Lunch is ready."

My path was almost clean, and I was inside in a flash. "I'm hungry, Mama."

During the afternoon, she let me play outside. I made a snowman and watched the yellow sun pierce thinning clouds as it sank toward the horizon while I waited for Papa to come home.

It was almost dark when he arrived, and he sat twisting each hand as it gripped the other. His face wrinkled when he looked up at Mama as she set the table. "I met the mayor at the station when I got off the train. He said several men from the village have received their notices to report for military service."

"Don't worry, dear. We knew some men would be called for the army."

"The mayor said they leave next week."

I listened to them discuss the draft until Papa went outside after dinner to check on the livestock. I had just settled into my bed when he brushed snow from his hat and coat before entering the room. “It’s snowing like crazy again. I hope it quits soon.”

I snuggled under the covers and agreed with Papa. Shoveling those paths again wouldn’t be much fun.

* * *

Papa’s stomping feet and the slamming door woke me before daylight. His voice roared as he entered the room. “A rotten rafter in the cattle pen broke under the weight of this snow. The roof is sagging. It must be twenty-five centimeters deep outside.”

Mama had flour on her chin as she rushed out from the kitchen. “We need to clear it off the roof before the pen collapses completely.”

“I’ve tethered the cows against the side of the house to offer them some protection. Go see if Mr. Merkle will help.”

When our landlord returned with Mama, Papa had already fashioned a tool to clear the roof. He’d nailed a short board across the end of a long pole. “If we pull the wagon beside the shed, I can stand on it to clear away the snow.”

I joined the grownups as they pushed the heavy farm wagon into place. My light weight didn’t add much, but I gave it my best. Papa climbed on the raised seat. His tool reached the peak of the roof, and he pulled it toward him to scrape the snow off. Cold, heavy cascades showered around him as the snow tumbled from the roof. Mr. Merkle checked the damaged structure inside.

Since I wasn't tall enough to help clear the roof, Mama sent me in the house to care for Roger. I ran inside without hesitation and escaped to the warmth of our room.

Later, Mr. Merkle went home to find a heavy plank and a long post to prop up the broken rafter. After the support was in place, Papa nailed the plank to the broken beam.

When he finished, Mr. Merkle looked up to inspect their work. "Should be strong enough now."

The cows moved quickly when Papa led them back to their stall. They didn't seem to like standing outside in the cold. After a few bites of hay, they appeared to be content.

After the work was finished, Mama called everyone in for a big breakfast. We were all hungry and ate like we were starved. We cleaned the plates of porridge with chunks of pork in gravy, and being warm with a full stomach made me feel better.

Mr. Merkle leaned across the table and smiled at me. "That old wagon was heavy. We might not have been able to move it without your help. Thank you."

I felt my face flush as I leaned against Mama for support, and she gave me a hug. It was good to know someone approved of my effort.

After we thanked Mr. Merkle, Papa hurried to catch the next train to Kaschel. "I'll be late, but my boss should understand we had to deal with an emergency."

My rest didn't last long. The flakes had barely stopped falling, when Mama handed me the shovel. "We need to clean all the paths one more time."

After a late lunch, Mama waded through the snow to go to the post office. Her face was drawn when she returned with another government letter. She dropped into a kitchen chair, her rigid back touching nothing. She didn't move for a long time, staring at the unopened letter on the empty table before her.

"What's wrong, Mama?" I asked.

"We'll find out when Papa gets home. Maybe they've granted him a deferment from military service." Her eyes shifted from the front to the back door.

I pulled at the hem of my dress. "Will they tell us he can stay home?"

"We don't know, dear. Look after the baby. I need to tend our livestock." She slipped out the back door.

I paced around the room, glancing at the cheerful flames in the fireplace. Most of the time I enjoyed the scent of burning wood, but now the room just smelled stuffy. Roger woke and fussed a bit, but he didn't demand immediate attention. I gave a deep sigh as horrible thoughts of what might be in the letter flitted through my mind.

Mama returned from outside bringing the lingering smell of cows with her. She sat staring out the window until Roger's cries of distress finally roused her. She changed him and held him to her breast without speaking. As darkness fell, she told me again to watch the baby while she prepared our evening meal of potatoes, sausage, and cabbage. She didn't set the table until Papa came home.

"Why the long face?" he asked as he took off his coat.

Mama cast her eyes downward as she handed him the envelope.

I held my breath as I waited.

Papa's brow creased, and he dropped onto a chair to open it. His face darkened while he read the contents, and he sighed deeply as he looked up at Mama. "They didn't accept the request from my stationmaster stating that my work here is essential. I'm to report for military service in two weeks."

Chapter 11

The morning after Papa received the awful letter telling him to report to the army, I woke early and sat on the edge of my bed. My shoulders drooped, and my eyes stared at the floor. The house seemed colder after Papa closed the door to leave. Mama came to sit beside me and hold my hand.

She looked into my eyes and spoke with a soft voice. "We'll have to be strong. Your father will need all the support we can give him."

I nodded and sat without moving for several minutes until Mama rose and went to prepare breakfast for the two of us. Roger slept. He was too young to understand the tragedy that threatened our family.

After we'd eaten, I helped Mama with the dishes, and then she brought out the tablet and pencil I got for my birthday. With her help, I soon wrote my letters from A to J several times.

"What comes next, Mama?" I asked.

She gave me a hug and stood. "I have work to do. You can copy your letters again without me. Tomorrow, we'll learn to write the alphabet from K to Q."

She spent the morning doing laundry and cleaning the house. After lunch, she fed our animals and took up her knitting needles. Watching my baby brother kept me busy, but I found time to copy my letters again.

When evening approached and Papa came home from work, Mama served slices of ham they had salted away to go with potatoes and cabbage. We ate dinner in near silence. Nobody knew what to say. Roger made gurgling sounds and waved his arms, looking in vain for someone to play with him while we ate. He had started to pull up on the sides of his carriage to look at the world around him.

Eventually, Papa broke the silence in a flat voice. His expression didn't show any emotion. "I gave my notice today. The boss didn't have much to say. They will need to find someone to replace me, and they wished me luck in the army."

Mama responded with a nod and ran to the kitchen to hide her tears. Not knowing what to do, I slumped in my chair.

Later, I went to bed and lay still, listening to Mama and Papa discuss what she must do to manage the household. The frosty wind whistled outside my window, and icy fingers of cold found their way into the room. Fear of what would happen to us with Papa gone haunted me. The night seemed to last forever, and I woke frequently from bad dreams.

Papa came home from work early for the next several days. He spent hours repairing things around the house, and he showed Mama what to do while he'd be gone. He sat down with me to explain that I'd have to be a big girl and help my mother.

* * *

Two weeks flew by, and the cold wind battered us as we accompanied Papa to catch the train on the fateful day he had to leave. A few snowflakes fell to add to our sadness. My parents walked side by side, and Mama pushed Roger's carriage down the rocky path to the station. I followed them with faltering footsteps.

"We'll pray for you," she said. "Don't worry about us. We'll manage while you're gone. Be sure to write every chance you get."

Papa glanced from Mama to the small bag of belongings he carried. "Life may be difficult for you while I'm away. Don't get involved with politics if the Nazis come. Do what they tell you, and try to shield the children. You can count on your neighbors if you really need help. Concentrate on putting food on the table. Stay safe."

She took his hand. "We'll miss you every day."

"I may not become a great soldier, but I intend to survive this war and come home to you and the children."

The conductor was yelling "All aboard!" and ringing his bell when we arrived at the platform. After kissing us all and holding us close, Papa climbed the steps to the railcar. He stopped at the entry for a final wave. Within minutes, the whistle blew and black smoke puffed from the smokestack. I cried as the train began to move away from the station, its iron wheels clanking on the rails. The icy breeze made me shiver as the last car disappeared behind a screen of bare trees. We were left to survive without Papa being home to care for us.

We worked our way back up the rocky hillside with downcast eyes. The weight of fear depressed me. I understood that Papa faced danger, and our life would be difficult in this strange village. Thoughts of what might happen to us in the future frightened me.

At the end of the day, Mama stayed up late reading her bible at our dining table, and I climbed into bed where sleep was slow to come. Her light bothered me, and I tossed and turned. After a short nap, I woke to find her still reading. The clock struck one as I fluffed my pillow and tried to find a comfortable position. It must have been much later when I finally slept.

Mama was up and moving about the kitchen when I woke and sat up in bed, trying to wipe sleep from my droopy eyes. We ate a breakfast of bread and cheese with a glass of milk.

Neither of us talked much. When Roger let out a loud yelp, she went to change his diaper and give him a bottle.

Later that morning, someone knocked at our door. Mrs. Koeppel offered a plate of freshly baked rolls when Mama asked her to come inside.

Her face brightened as she made the effort to entertain company. "Thank you so much. Come and sit down. May I offer you some tea?"

Mrs. Koeppel shook her head and glanced toward me. "No, thank you. I need to get back home. I thought Irene might like to come over to play with Maria. I'll keep an eye on them, and I have a piece of chocolate they can share."

Mama turned to me. "Would you like that?"

A part of my gloom evaporated. "Yes, ma'am. I'll bring my doll."

Maria and I spent the rest of the morning getting acquainted and having fun with our dolls. We dressed them and gave them a make-believe tea party. The time passed quickly, and the thought of having a new friend made me feel better. I regretted not spending more time to play with Maria. Her mother brought each of us a small piece of chocolate. It had been months since I'd tasted this delicacy. I took small bites and held them on my tongue until they melted. The tiny morsel was delicious.

Mrs. Koeppel gave us lunch before she sent me home. "You must come play with Maria more often."

During the afternoon, Mama taught me to write the rest of the alphabet. My letters weren't pretty, but I was thrilled to learn how to make them. I'd be ready to surprise the teacher when she let me go to school in the fall.

At bedtime, the reality of our situation really sank in. Papa was gone, and he would be in danger far away in the army.

Sobs racked my body as I clung to Mama. My whole world had crumbled. What would we do without my father at home? The Nazis might hurt him, or he could be killed in the war.

I'd lain awake nights listening to my parents discuss his absence. Mama said she needed him to help with the work at home, and his salary bought our food and paid the rent. His strong presence protected us from harm.

What would we do if the Nazis came? What would happen to us if Papa didn't come home from the war?

I needed my father.

Chapter 12

Loneliness took hold of me. Papa's absence left me feeling lost. Wind and snow battered our house. A frosty draft seeped through cracks around the windows as the cold grew more intense. I bundled into my coat and scarf to help Mama feed the chickens and gather eggs while she tended the cows. We cleared the walkways of snow again, and the icy breeze bit my hands and nose. Sinking into self-pity, I pouted.

Mama gave me an impatient look and pointed at the walk. "Get busy and shovel faster."

A new litter of rabbits was born, and Mama killed one of the big ones to eat. I was glad. The baby rabbits were cute, but the big ones tasted better than pork. She cooked it with homemade noodles, and I ate too much.

During the next few weeks, I practiced writing the alphabet, and my chest swelled with pride in writing my letters from A to Z. After I learned to write them from memory, she taught me to write the numbers from one to ten, and then I started learning to write whole words. Soon, I could write all our names and several common words like pig, cow, dog, and cat.

I couldn't wait to start school. *I'll show that teacher how much I already know.*

The cold weather stayed with us, and the fluffy white snow turned dingy without melting. Weeks passed, and we spent most of our time inside. We didn't hear from Papa. Roger learned to sit up and wave at us with a big smile when we clapped our hands. I learned to write more words, and my tablet was almost filled with dozens of repetitions.

One Sunday morning, Mama took us to church. The minister said a long prayer that the war would end. After the service, a group of women whose husbands had been drafted gathered outside the building which blocked some of the harsh wind. I pushed Roger's baby carriage next to the wall to protect him while I listened.

One of the women asked, "Has anyone heard from her husband since he was drafted?"

A neighbor answered her question. "My husband only wrote a few lines. He said he didn't have time to write. They work day and night."

The other women nodded agreement. One of them turned to Mama. "How do you cope? You've been forced to leave your home, and your husband is in danger, far away. You can only wait for the Nazis to invade us here."

Mama looked at the ground and then back up. "We do what we have to do."

I wiped a tear from my eye. Coping with the waiting was a skill I hadn't yet learned.

None of the women were able to think of any good news, and the cold wind succeeded in forcing the gathering to break up.

As we trudged home after the service, Mama told me, "I need to go check on our house. There's no telling what the soldiers may have done to it."

The next morning, she bundled up and climbed the hill at daybreak to leave Roger and me with Mrs. Koeppel.

"I'll check your house while I'm there," Mama said. "I hope the soldiers didn't wreck it."

Mrs. Koeppel brushed back a lock of hair. "I don't think the soldiers have occupied it. Our house is too far from their fortifications, but I'd appreciate you checking it for damage."

Then Mama walked to the station to catch the train.

Mrs. Koeppel cocked her head at me. "You can teach Maria to write her name while you're here." She handed me a tablet and pencil.

She spelled Maria's name for me, and I soon taught my friend how to write it and a few other words also. Learning to write a new word made me proud as well.

After lunch, Maria went to her room for her afternoon nap. Since I was much too old for that sort of thing, Roger and I played together. His brown eyes sparkled as he threw his toys on the floor. My job was to retrieve them and praise him for having such a strong arm.

Mrs. Koeppel laughed. "Looks like this game could last for a long time."

I agreed. "He starts to cry if someone doesn't bring the toys back."

Dusk had gathered when Mama returned. She pulled off her coat and sat down to rest for a moment and talk to Mrs. Koeppel. "It's been a busy day. I hope the children behaved well."

Mrs. Koeppel nodded a cheerful response. "We enjoyed their company."

"Your house was in good condition. The soldiers haven't occupied it. It does appear that some of your furniture is missing."

Mama soon took us home and started to prepare dinner. "Our poor house is dirty as a pig pen. The soldiers don't clean it. A lot of the furniture is missing, and several pieces are broken. The soldiers don't seem to mind."

"Did the Nazis come?" I asked.

She shook her head. "Not yet. The French Army is doing enough damage. They've wrecked the house and burned some of our furniture. The village is torn up with trenches and barricades. There's not a chicken or a bottle of wine left in Kaschel. I'm not sure a battle could be much more destructive than what they've already done."

* * *

Mama didn't talk much over the next few days. I felt helpless. After asking her for bread to eat with my porridge one morning, her answer shocked me.

"I didn't buy bread yesterday. The rent is due next week. We need to ration our spending."

She did her best to avoid buying anything that wasn't absolutely necessary. The war threatened everyone. Prices rose. She put off buying a young pig to butcher in the fall because we couldn't afford to feed it.

A few days later, Mama brought home another letter from Oma and Opa. After she finished reading it, she turned to me and reached out to stroke my hair. "Your grandparents are doing well. The weather is starting to warm, and everything is peaceful. If they wouldn't listen to news reports, they wouldn't even know there was a war."

"What do they do there?" I asked.

Mama reached out to touch my arm. "They go to church on Sunday, and Opa works every Saturday when the greengrocer needs extra help. Oma keeps their house looking nice."

I went outside to sit on the steps and think about how lucky my grandparents were. The threat was much closer here. Everyone believed the Nazis would come soon. I wondered what they would be like. *Will they harm us?*

The next day Mama came home from shopping in the village with a big smile. "The baker offered me a job. The lady who works in the kitchen broke her arm, and he asked me to bake for him until she can return to work."

My lip quivered. "Who will take care of Roger and me while you go to work?"

She pulled me close against her side. "I talked to Mrs. Koeppel before coming home. She said the two of you can stay with her while I'm at the bakery. Maria likes to play with you, and Mrs. Koeppel says two more won't be much trouble."

Relieved, I returned Mama's hug. Mrs. Koeppel was a nice lady, and I would have fun playing with Maria. I'd bring my doll.

The next morning, an hour before daybreak, Mama shook me from a sound sleep. "Time to get up, lazybones. I have to be at work, and you have to go to Mrs. Koeppel's house."

She pushed Roger's carriage through the predawn darkness while I stumbled along beside her, still halfway asleep. The biting wind almost woke me as we trudged up the rocky path.

Mrs. Koeppel gave us a wide-awake smile when we arrived. "The children will be fine here. Go on to your job at the bakery. Don't worry about them."

I felt grateful when she let me finish my night's sleep on her divan. I was ready to face the day when she woke me again at half past seven. Good smells came from the kitchen, and we enjoyed a breakfast of cheese and sausage on a fresh roll washed down by warm milk. Roger was learning to eat solid foods, so she gave him some mashed peas and potatoes.

Roger had already finished his bottle, so she put him on a blanket spread across the floor. He squirmed on his stomach and made progress with learning to crawl. After breakfast, Maria and I watched him while we played. Our duty was to drag him back to the middle of the blanket when he crawled past the edge and reached for things to stuff in his mouth.

Later, Mrs. Koeppel sat down to watch Roger while we amused ourselves with our dolls. After we tired of playing with them, she brought me a tablet. "Irene, would you teach Maria how to write all her letters? She's eager to learn."

"Yes, ma'am." I felt grown up in my role as a teacher.

I taught her more of the alphabet and several simple words. She jumped up and down when she showed her mother.

"Look what I did."

Mama came to take us home before lunch time. She spoke to Maria's mother. "I hope the children were good while you kept them."

"They were well behaved," Mrs. Koeppel said. "Watching Roger learn to crawl is good entertainment. He's very determined. The girls had a lot of fun. Irene is a good teacher, and Maria is learning how to write."

"Thank you so much. I'll bring them at the same time tomorrow."

Back home, Mama fixed lunch and told me about her job. "I help the baker prepare all the bread and pastries each day. We start early and finish before lunch. The work isn't hard, but it doesn't pay a lot. It will be enough, though, to help pay the bills."

She pulled a long baguette of bread from her bag and laid it on the table. "The baker gave me the day-old bread. I didn't have to buy it."

Over the next few weeks, Maria and I became good friends. Roger learned to crawl faster, and I stayed busy keeping him out of trouble.

When the regular cook returned, Mama lost her job and stopped to tell Mrs. Koeppel. "The lady came back with a sling on her arm, but she was ready to go to work. I didn't make a lot of money, but it's enough to help us get by for a while."

Back home, Mama told me more. "I earned enough to pay this month's rent, pay Mrs. Koeppel, and buy food for a few more weeks."

Later, Mama returned from the post office with a letter from Papa. I stood silently behind her while she read it at the table. After waiting for what seemed like forever, she told me what he'd written. Her face was pinched and her lips compressed as she explained Papa's situation.

"He's in training to serve in the infantry and is likely to stay in Soissons when he's assigned to a unit. What they put him through is hard work and different from anything he's done before, but your father is big and strong. He tolerates the hard work better than most. The food is terrible, and he misses my cooking."

"Can he come home to see us?" I asked.

Mama shook her head. "He didn't say, but I'm sure the army won't allow it."

I was still frightened by what I imagined army life to be like. "Does he shoot guns?"

She rested her chin on a hand. "He didn't know much about weapons when he first got there, but he has learned to hit targets when he shoots his rifle."

My stomach started to squirm. "Will he have to fight the Nazis?"

Mama chewed her lip. "He says he'll do what he has to do. He sends his love and hopes we stay safe."

Mama told me she felt reassured by the letter, but icy fingers of fear made me shiver. Papa might have to fight in the war.

People got killed in wars.

Chapter 13

I began to relax when the big airliner reached cruising altitude, and the pilot announced we could move about the cabin. The takeoff hadn't been as terrifying as I'd anticipated, and the other passengers failed to show fear. Flying might not be as dangerous as I'd thought. My infant son didn't experience the worry that plagued me as he slept soundly in his nest.

A patchwork of small farms and villages passed beneath my window as I recalled events that changed my life as a child. Adapting to our sanctuary in Wolfskirchen had seemed difficult at the time, but I made friends and learned to cope with our cramped quarters. Friendly neighbors allowed my family to live in security, and Papa had been able to keep his job with the railroad. We worried about the scraps of news of occasional military confrontations and the real war which could begin at any time.

My family enjoyed the security of Papa's job until he was drafted into the French Army. Money was scarce, but Mama did what was necessary to manage alone. We weathered a hard winter and worried about the dangers Papa might face.

The Nazi invasion changed everything.

* * *

The warmth of a sunny day gave us the chance to venture outside, and Mama took Roger and me to shop in town. She wore a light sweater over her threadbare brown housedress and pushed Roger's carriage as I followed behind. She made me wear a sweater too, even though I wanted to believe spring had arrived.

"I'm not cold, Mama."

She handed me my sweater. "You'll wear this anyway."

Before we started home, a dozen potatoes, a bunch of carrots, two bunches of leeks, and a large onion filled her bag. On the way we met Mrs. Bauer. She looked pale, and her face wrinkled at the corners of her mouth.

She told us the latest war news. "We listened to the BBC broadcast in French on the radio last night. The Nazis bombed the British naval base at Scapa Flow in Scotland yesterday. They hit a British warship and killed a lot of people."

Mama tugged at her lower lip and breathed a deep sigh. "It appears they're building up to an invasion. We could be next."

I felt the hair raise on the nape of my neck. "Why, Mama? Did they drop bombs on France, too?"

"No, dear, but I'm afraid the war may really start now, and your father hasn't even finished his training."

"I'm scared."

She took me in her arms with a reassuring hug. "We'll be safe here."

When we got home, she set her purchases on the dining table and put Roger on his blanket on the floor. "Take care of your little brother while I start dinner."

I sat on the blanket beside him and watched as he tried to crawl off and stuff anything he could grab into his mouth. Frustrated, he fussed at me when I put him back in the center. He'd have to crawl to the edge again. We repeated this scene about a dozen times before he decided to take a nap.

Two weeks later, another letter from Papa told us he had completed his training and was assigned to a unit that would defend Soissons. Mama read most of it to me. If the Nazis invaded through Holland and Belgium, Papa's unit would block any German advance toward Paris. Most of his days were spent digging trenches to stop German tanks. They weren't fighting, but the days were long, tiring, and boring. Papa said after they were released from work, everyone ate a frugal meal and fell asleep.

Early April brought a few mild days, and new buds appeared on the trees. Green grass poked through the dead stubble in places. I looked forward to warmer weather so I could play outside. The Koeppels invited us to listen to the news on their radio.

"We usually tune in to the BBC broadcasts in French," Mr. Koeppel said. "They are the most reliable source we can find."

Maria and I played while the adults talked. When the news broadcast began, the adults crowded close to the radio. Maria and I watched Roger try to pull himself up on a chair. After succeeding, he turned to wave at me and promptly fell on his backside.

Mr. Koeppel's booming voice startled us after an announcement. "The Nazis invaded Denmark and Norway."

Mama lifted both hands in a helpless gesture. "Haven't they conquered enough countries already?"

The announcer continued. "Denmark consists of flat lowlands with few natural barriers. The small Danish army is not likely to slow Hitler's advance."

The next morning Mr. Koeppel stopped by our house with more news of the German invasion. "The Danes were forced to surrender. The Nazis took control and established a new government that will support the Fuehrer."

Mama rubbed a sleeve across her face. "Can anything stop those monsters?"

He slammed a tight fist into his left palm. "Those bastards. They'll try to take France next. The British and French armies will damn well stop them."

Within days we learned Hitler had been less successful in Norway. The powerful Norwegian army and the rugged terrain slowed the Nazis. However, massive German airpower gave them an advantage. Everyone predicted Norway could not hold out for long.

At bedtime, Mama tucked Roger away for the night and asked if I would join her in a prayer for Papa's safety.

The tears I'd resisted shedding during our prayer came in a flood after Mama tucked me in bed and turned out the light. She gave me a final hug when she heard my sobs. Then she went to her bed without saying anything. How could the Nazis be so mean? We hadn't done anything to them. I stayed awake a long time. Bad dreams interrupted my sleep.

* * *

Mama started to plant a garden. Mr. Merkle agreed to allow our cows to graze in his pasture, so they wouldn't destroy the crops we planted. It became my job to drive the cows to a nearby field each morning and bring them home when it was time for Mama to milk them. A few weeks later, the weather turned warmer. Spring had finally arrived.

She harnessed the cows to pull a plow and turn the ground to prepare it for planting. We dug shallow rows in the soil and sprinkled seeds for food crops on our rented land. Rows of potatoes, carrots, lettuce, leeks, cabbage, onions, radishes, beans, celeriac, and corn for the cows soon filled our small field.

The next day, Mama asked me to join her with a fun job. "Would you help me make a scarecrow to frighten the birds away from our garden?"

That sounded exciting. "Oh, yes."

Mama made a cross of two long sticks and covered it with one of Papa's old shirts. I helped her wrap the top with hay to form a head, and she wrapped a bright rag around it to resemble a hat. An old pair of gloves made realistic hands. After looking at the scarecrow, I daydreamed it might scare off Nazis like it would the crows.

I didn't get to finish the scarecrow because Roger woke from a nap, and Mama sent me to care for him. Keeping him out of trouble had become a full-time job. The lively youngster got restless in his carriage, and I put him on a blanket spread on the ground. His crawling speed had become too fast to leave him for an instant. He learned to pull himself up on the sides of his carriage and soon toddled around if I held him upright.

That evening, we returned to the Koeppels' house to hear more news. Luftwaffe bombers attacked London inflicting terrible damage on the city and British air bases. The radio also reported British fighter squadrons destroyed many of the bombers. The Brits had proved they would fight.

"Will the Nazis bomb Wolfskirchen?" I asked.

Mama shook her head. "We're not important enough for them to notice."

A few nights later, the BBC announced that British and French troops had landed in northern Norway to help their besieged army fight the Nazis.

At home, buying plants for the garden took most of our money. Mama was barely able to pay the rent. Oatmeal showed up more frequently on the table. She found a little work cleaning city hall after events, so we didn't go hungry. At mealtime, she gave thanks for our food, and I learned not to complain about missing my favorite dishes.

Papa was able to earn a little money doing extra duty for other soldiers and sent us a few francs. Mama put the money away to pay next month's rent. She always worried about paying the bills. At mealtime, she would remind me, "Clean your plate. We don't have food to waste."

During the next few weeks, the weather continued to warm, allowing me to play outside until Mama needed me to care for my little brother. He began to risk turning loose from whatever he pulled up on and walked with wobbly steps. He didn't control his direction very well and usually fell after he crashed into something.

"You need to go slower," I told him.

Then his lips pinched and he grunted as he pulled himself up to try again. He didn't act tired when he tried to walk, but he usually took a long nap afterwards.

Days later Roger turned one year old. Being able to walk allowed him to get in more trouble quicker. His antics kept me busy. His brown eyes lit up when he saw the cake Mama pulled from the oven. With rationing, sweets had become rare. I rushed to hold him back so he wouldn't burn his hands.

Mama laughed and wagged a finger at him. "It's hot. You'll get to taste it later. We are going to have a party to celebrate your birthday."

I felt sure he didn't know what a party was, but he recognized the sweet smell of the cake as something that promised to be good. Eager for a taste, he squirmed to reach it and protested as I held him back.

After dinner, the Koeppels showed up with Maria leading the way. She and I tried to distract Roger, but his eyes were fixed on the cake. Finally, I rolled a ball across the floor, and he scrambled to chase it. This game kept him occupied for a few minutes.

The Bauers were next to arrive followed by Mrs. Merkle. We'd never had so many people in the room before. We only had chairs for the adults. Roger made the rounds and babbled a greeting to our visitors, but his eyes kept returning to the cake.

Soon, Mama brought out a small package and helped Roger pull the newspaper wrapping away from the box inside. He managed to remove the lid without help. The box held a pair of big-boy shoes with hard soles. They would make walking outside easier for him. He wiggled as Mama tied them on his feet and quickly stood to try them out.

His face lit up as he heard the clomping noise they made walking across the floor. After stooping to get a better look at the shoes, he stamped his feet to make more noise.

Mrs. Merkle clapped her hands to applaud his reaction. “It’s obvious your mother chose the perfect birthday present for you.”

Mama asked everyone to gather around the table. Lacking chairs, Maria and I had to stand. Mama held Roger in her lap. She lit the single candle and held Roger back to keep his fingers out of the flame. I had to blow out the candle on his cake. Mrs. Bauer held the birthday boy while Mama cut it, and we all enjoyed the rare treat. With sugar rationed, she didn’t often bake sweets. Roger grabbed at his piece with both hands. Cake crumbs soon littered the floor and table around him. Icing covered his face and hands. We all laughed at the scene. Mama had to wipe him off with a damp towel before she let him touch anything else.

Then Maria and I grabbed his hands and held him up as the three of us danced around the room. Roger didn’t appear to understand what all the fuss was about. He tried out the new shoes again and grinned at the noise they made as he stomped across the floor. He was still celebrating when our company said good night and left.

* * *

Two days later, Mr. Koeppel knocked on our door as we were finishing our breakfast. When Mama asked him in, his voice wavered. “The Nazis have invaded Holland and Belgium. They attacked with hundreds of airplanes. Tanks and artillery are crushing everything in their path. The real fighting has begun.”

She gasped. “That’s how they will invade France, just like 1914.”

He nodded. “Nothing seems to slow them down. They are moving across Holland like they didn’t have an army opposing them.”

I slumped in my chair. The Nazis were coming. My heart seemed to sink in my chest as I realized Papa would have to fight them. Too shocked to cry, I choked at the thought we might never get to go home.

Mr. Koeppel frowned, his eyes downcast. “I’ll bring you more news when we hear it on the radio.” He closed the door and walked slowly up the hill.

Mama dropped to her knees and held Roger and me in her arms.

Chapter 14

I'd already gulped down most of my breakfast when I looked out our window. Mr. Koeppel clomped down the hill wearing his scruffy boots, work-stained trousers, and a clean but neatly patched shirt. He knocked on the door, and a broad smile appeared on his face when Mama invited him inside.

"We have good news today," he said. "The British people were getting desperate. They named a new prime minister who has a backbone. Winston Churchill will replace Neville Chamberlin."

"How will that change anything?" Mama asked.

"Chamberlin was a weakling, but Churchill will fight. He'll be the British Bulldog we need to confront those Nazis."

Mama took a deep breath and expelled the air with a whoosh. Her eyes looked hard, like they did when a cow didn't do what she wanted. "We could use good news."

I sat there confused. Who were all these people? I'd never heard of them.

Mama clasped her hands together and looked directly at him. "We need someone who will stand up to Hitler's gang of killers. Nobody—Danes, Norwegians, Dutch, Belgian, British, or French-has stopped the Nazis so far."

Mr. Koeppel waved his clenched fist. "Churchill won't stop fighting. He doesn't know how to quit."

I nibbled at the last of my bread and cheese and finished the bowl of warm milk Mama insisted I drink. "Is Mr. Churchill in the army?"

The adults had a good laugh as I felt my face grow red.

Mr. Koeppel smiled again when he answered. "You could say that. He's their leader.

At twilight Mama carried Roger, and we climbed the hill to the Koeppel's house so she could hear more news of the war. The room grew stuffy as the adults gathered around the radio. We heard only static until Mr. Koeppel tweaked the controls. I'd planned to play with Maria, but the broadcast scared me. I couldn't pull myself away from the radio. Maria listened for a moment, then she moved back in the corner of the room to change her doll's dress.

After the static disappeared, we heard the announcer say, "German tanks have broken through the French lines in the Ardennes. Their army is advancing through the gap."

Mama's jaw dropped. Her face showed lots of worry lines. "Did anyone talk about fighting at Soissons?"

Mr. Koeppel shook his head. "Some troops are pulling back to defend Paris."

The announcer's voice sounded gloomy, and he said he didn't know any more details. Everything was happening too fast.

After Roger started to fuss, we made our way home in the darkness.

Later, Mama tucked me in. I lay in my bed tossing and turning. The Nazis were getting closer, and I still couldn't understand why they wanted to fight with us. Unable to sleep, I wondered what a Nazi would look like if they came here.

The next morning, I asked Mama, "Where are the Nazis? Will they come to Wolfskirchen?"

Mama wiped a hand across her brow and bit her lip. She hesitated before speaking, and her voice sounded sad. "The Nazis attacked Belgium first, then they turned to attack France."

I was still confused. "Is Belgium close to Kaschel?"

After she failed to make me understand, Mama took Roger and me to city hall to see the big map in the hallway by the mayor's office. She showed me where all these strange places were located on the map. It was a big piece of paper filled with different colors, strange words, lines, and squiggles. She waved a finger over the map to point out Germany, Belgium and France. "This is Alsace. We live here. This is the Ardennes, a big forest where the Nazis broke through the French army that protects us. They are still a long way from Kaschel or Wolfskirchen."

Trying to understand the map confused me. "Where is Papa?"

Mama pointed to a big word on the map. "This is Soissons."

"Will the Nazis go there?"

"We don't know, dear. We must pray that Papa stays safe."

* * *

During the next two weeks the weather warmed, and green sprouts in the garden pushed their way through the ground. Mama cared for the young plants and the cows. I fed the chickens and rabbits to do my share. She made a game of my work by teaching me how to count the eggs I brought in each day.

All the adults in the village talked about the Nazi advance as they drew closer to us. I didn't always understand. I wanted to be brave, but bad dreams filled my head.

Mama tried to explain what was happening, and I could tell by the sad look on her face that everything she heard was bad. The radio announcer said the Dutch Army gave up without much of a fight. The German Army quickly broke through the Belgian lines and defeated them as well. British and French forces were surrounded and fought their way back toward Dunkirk so they could escape to the British Isles. Hundreds of boats came to rescue them. Thousands of British and French troops fled across the English Channel to seek safety in Great Britain.

In Wolfskirchen, frightened families crowded onto trains heading for the south of France to escape the Nazis. Maria told me her family knew some of the people. They were too scared to stay here.

I ran to Mama. "Maria told me their neighbors left on the train. Will the Nazis kill us if we stay here?"

Mama sat down and pulled me onto her lap. "The Nazis may not be nice, but I don't think they will harm us. We are civilians, and we can't fight them."

I wanted to believe her, but some families were leaving their homes and running away. "If there's not any danger, why are they leaving?"

"Some of the people are Jews. They are afraid the Nazis will take them away as prisoners to live in big camps to hold people they don't like."

"Why do they want to harm the Jews?" I asked.

Mama held her hands out to the side, palms up. "I don't know."

The war news got worse in the days that followed. The French army couldn't stop the Nazi forces, and they soon reached Alsace. Mama spent most of our money to buy food and items we might need during an occupation. She climbed to the hayloft and hid a box filled with sugar, coffee, white flour, spices, and other hard rations under the hay.

"You must never tell anyone about the box," Mama told me when she came down the ladder. "The Nazis might take it and punish us. We would have nothing left to eat."

I shivered at the thought of Nazis stealing our food. "I won't tell."

The next day Mama returned from the post office with a letter from Papa. "I'm amazed it was delivered. The Nazis have overrun everything in that part of France."

My knees felt too weak to hold me up. "What did he say? Read it to me."

She opened the letter and read a few lines before looking up. "Your father sends us his love. His unit was held in camp as reserves. They had received orders to go to the front when a big group of Nazi bombers attacked their base."

"Did they fight?" I asked.

"He only had time to grab his rifle and dive into a shallow trench he'd dug beside his tent. He hid in it to escape the bullets and bombs."

My chest felt like someone had tied our clothesline around it and squeezed it tight. My voice trembled. "They dropped bombs on him?"

Mama's finger moved farther down the page. "Papa says dozens of bombs fell on his company. He clung to the bottom of his shelter as they exploded around him. The earth shook like an earthquake had hit. Clouds of black smoke made it hard to breathe. He says the noise was deafening, and he lay in his trench, too frightened to move. Everyone hid in their shelters. Nobody had weapons to fight the airplanes. He's thankful to be alive."

I felt like a bomb had crushed my heart. Sobs racked my chest.

Mama squeezed my hand. "He's fine, but most of their equipment was destroyed. Too many people were hurt and too many of their guns were damaged for them to fight the invaders. They were ordered to fall back. He doesn't know where they will go."

I tried to dry my tears, but they wouldn't stop. The Nazis would surely chase after them. "Will Papa have to fight again?"

Mama's lip trembled. "I hope not, dear."

News of the war grew worse. Nazi troops occupied Metz and rolled into Alsace. British and French armies were fleeing at Dunkirk. Radio broadcasts from Germany said Allied Forces were retreating everywhere, and the Nazis would soon become masters of all Europe.

* * *

A few days later, Mama took Roger and me to town to buy bread. We had just left the bakery when two large noisy trucks filled with German troops rumbled into the village and stopped in front of city hall. Several soldiers climbed out of the lead truck. One man wore an officer's cap, and he led several of them as they stormed through the door to enter the mayor's office. A dozen more men carrying guns jumped out of the trucks and formed a circle around the building. Several stood guard at the front door.

Two of the soldiers rushed to the flagpole and pulled down the French flag. They left it lying on the ground while they raised the Nazi flag. An older boy wearing a white shirt ran to pick up the blue, white, and red banner of France and started to brush off dust clinging to its fabric. When a soldier walked up from behind and clubbed the boy with his rifle, it fell to the ground again. The boy tumbled face down across the flag and lay still. Blood from a big cut on his head stained the fabric of the flag and his shirt. Nobody went to help him.

People in the area ran away or hurried inside buildings to avoid the frightful scene. The street fell silent, and merchants lowered their blinds.

Watching what happened, I felt cold all over. My voice turned suddenly shrill. “Is he dead? Why doesn’t someone help him?”

Mama held me close. “I think he’s still alive. Everyone is afraid the Nazis will hurt them if they try to help the boy.”

Her face turned pale as the soldiers pointed their rifles at people on the street like they were waiting for someone to resist. I clutched Mama’s hand and breathed in big gasps of air as I watched the Nazis take control of the village.

My voice trembled as I asked, “Will they shoot us?”

Mama bent to hug me again. “No, child, but we’ll have to do what they say. We have lost the war, and Nazis will control our lives.”

Then Mama hurried to push Roger’s carriage over the cobblestone street and moved us away from the soldiers. She stopped in the next block to look back. “Everything will change now. We’ll go home and wait to see what the Nazis do.”

I stayed close to Mama as we made our way slowly down the rough street toward our house. Would the Nazis hit me if I angered them?

Roger slept soundly in his carriage while the Germans took control of the village.

Chapter 15

The next morning at breakfast, Mama said, "Mr. Koeppel told me the mayor cleaned out his desk and abandoned the office during the night. The Nazis appointed his replacement. The new mayor will do whatever the Germans tell him."

I slid off my chair at the table. "Will they hurt us?"

"The war is over for Alsace. Germany has taken control of our government. We are now occupied by the Third Reich, and the Nazis say we must be loyal subjects of the Fuehrer. They claim Germans are the superior race, and they rule. The Wehrmacht will enforce their laws. We must obey or we will be shot."

My chin sank to my chest. I didn't want to be a Nazi.

Mama tugged at the scarf covering her head. "Our lives have been turned upside down. The schoolteacher left without notice. The new one will teach children that Jews must be eliminated to purify the population. Each day, all the students must pledge allegiance to Adolph Hitler. Every child must participate."

When we attended church on Sunday, a young Nazi in a crisp military uniform of perfectly creased gray wool, medals hanging from his chest, and wearing shiny boots, occupied the first pew. When we entered, I noticed he sat alone. *He must not be too bad if he wants to attend church with us.*

Mama leaned down and whispered to me, "He's here to spy on us and ensure no words are spoken against the Fatherland. They won't even leave us in peace at church."

The gloomy congregation left a large empty space around the Nazi. Most people sat silently and avoided looking at the invader as they filled the quiet sanctuary.

Father Zimmer's face was stern when he came to the pulpit. His sermon was short and blunt. The main topic was a warning. Everyone must accept the political reality of our situation and try to live in peace. His closing prayer left a lasting impression.

"May God have mercy on this congregation and guide us to find a swift end to this terrible war. Amen."

The somber crowd shuffled out of the church without the normal friendly conversations among the churchgoers.

That afternoon, we learned the Nazis forbade any display of French flags. They visited merchants and intimidated them into flying the swastika to show their loyalty to the Third Reich. The plaque on the front of city hall that read, "Liberty Equality Fraternity" had been ripped from the building and replaced with the Nazi version, "Work Family Country."

Nobody dared to complain publicly. The wrong person might hear.

In spite of the war and the Nazis, ordinary life continued. Mama worked long days to do Papa's work as well as her own. She fretted about how we would feed our cows and approached Mr. Merkel. "The cattle will need hay this winter. Could you spare any? I can pay."

He agreed to set aside another hectare of his meadow for hay to feed our cattle. He cut it with his mowing machine and left the rest of the work for us. After it cured for a day, Mama turned it over with a pitchfork to make sure it would dry. Green hay might start a fire so it couldn't be stored. The job kept her busy all day, and I looked after Roger while she worked. He was walking now, and keeping him safe had become a full-time challenge. I almost panicked when I ran to stop him just before he tried to catch a bee in his hands.

It rained that night. The hay was soaked, and we couldn't store it wet.

The next day, Mama trudged to the field and turned it again. After it dried for two more days, she hooked the cows to the wagon and loaded the dried grass to bring home and pack into the rooms upstairs. Three trips were needed, and Mama had to lift it from the wagon with a pitchfork to fill the space above our living quarters.

After she finished, she wiped sweat from her brow. "We could have used your father's help for this job."

I raised my eyes to hers. "Is Papa still fighting the Nazis?"

"I don't know, dear. He's probably waiting to stop the Germans from entering Paris. We can only pray he is safe."

The afternoon had slipped away by the time she finished, and her steps began to falter from fatigue. Her breathing came in gulps, and sweat soaked her dress after she put away the wagon and released the cows to their pasture.

When she returned, I sniffed the fresh hay in the loft. "It smells good."

She ruffled my hair. "The cows will think so, too."

* * *

After Mama returned from a visit with the Koeppels and the Bauers, she shared more war news. "The British and French troops that landed in the north to help the Norwegians weren't strong enough. The Nazis beat them back. Norway finally surrendered, but many of their troops escaped to England with the British and French armies."

I choked up again when I thought about Papa. "Are they still fighting in France?"

A corner of Mama's mouth twisted down. "The Nazis have overrun half of the country, but some of our troops escaped to Great Britain. I don't know where your father is. Our army in North Africa hasn't been attacked. General De Gaulle promises to fight even if the French government surrenders."

Thinking about war made me dizzy, as I tried to understand the puzzle of this changing news. *Why did grown people want to fight?*

Confused and fearful, I escaped the stuffy old house to enjoy the sunshine outside. Kicking my ball around the yard worked off some of my frustration.

Later, Mama thought of another chore for me. "Some of the garden vegetables are ready to harvest. Bring me a dozen carrots, some lettuce, spinach leaves, peas, beans, radishes, and a few green onions. I'll make soup and a salad for tonight."

I felt sorry for myself as I spent the next hour pouting and digging with the trowel, pulling up plants until my basket was filled with vegetables. I picked lettuce and spinach leaves by hand. The hot sun made me wet with sweat. Dirt caked under my fingernails. My legs began to cramp before I finished. Finally, I delivered the overflowing basket to Mama.

That afternoon, the scent of fresh vegetables filled the kitchen when Mama started cooking. The soup was delicious, and I took pride in my contribution.

* * *

A few days later, Mr. Merkel stopped by our house while we were eating breakfast. He removed his floppy straw hat. "Smells good."

Mama smiled. "We can probably find another bite or two."

After finishing a slice of bread smothered with strawberry jam, he told us, "General De Gaulle formed a Free French government in exile. Our troops in North Africa are intact and ready to confront the Nazis. I'm glad someone has the courage to resist this *master race*."

Mama sighed. "I'm not sure what he can do, but I'm glad someone will be able to fight those devils."

Watching a butterfly sample the nectar from Mama's flowers, I struggled to figure out how the general could help us. "We are already occupied by the Nazis."

Mama bit her lip. "I'm glad he didn't surrender, but the Germans are sure to be furious. It might make things worse for us here."

Later, she bought a copy of the local newspaper and took it to the Koeppel's house. I followed with Roger. The huge headline screamed, "FRANCE SURRENDERS." A picture of Hitler gazing at the Eiffel Tower appeared beneath the bold words.

On the inside page, a short article announced that Italy had attacked along their border with France. French forces stopped them after a short advance.

Farther down, in small print, an article reported General DeGaulle's holdout. He promised the Free French Army in North Africa would continue to resist the Nazis.

A dark cloud soon swallowed the bright sun overhead. The distant rumble of thunder promised our cheerful day would change to storms.

Mr. Merkel ran a callused hand across the page. "Germany occupies the north of France and the entire Atlantic coast. Paris has been spared for now."

Mama read further. "What is left of France will form a government at Vichy, certain to be friendly to the Nazi regime."

Mr. Merkel raised his eyes to the ceiling. "The France we knew and loved is gone."

I listened without speaking. The Nazis were here to stay.

* * *

A few days later, Mama ran an errand in town. The gray sky threatened rain, but she wore a cheerful smile when she returned with another letter from Oma and Opa. "I took a quick look in the post office, but I want to read it again."

She studied the single sheet of paper for a moment and explained the reason for her good cheer. "They've decided to return. Opa says they have been well treated in the Haute Vienne, but life with the Vichy government won't be any better than living under the Germans. Their roots are in Kaschel, so they're coming home."

"Can we go home?" I left Roger holding the bottle as I ran to her.

Mama reached for my hand. "We can go when all the violence ends."

I went back to help Roger with the bottle when his loud voice demanded help.

During the evening, we were visiting with the Bauers when the BBC announcer interrupted a program on their radio. "The British navy attacked the French port in Algeria, sinking and damaging a number of French warships.

Worry lines appeared on Mama's forehead. "Why?"

Mr. Bauer shrugged his shoulders. "The British feared the Vichy government would give the ships to the Nazis."

Mama held both sides of her face with her palms. "They were probably right."

* * *

Several weeks passed before Mama decided it would be safe for us to make the trip home. The fighting had stopped, and most of the trucks and tanks stayed off the roads and in their bases.

She announced we were ready to leave after we'd eaten our breakfast of bread and milk. "With the Nazis in control, the roads appear to be open for travel. The fighting has ended. I've made arrangements with Mr. Merkel to help me load the wagon. The hay and our garden will pay for our last month's rent."

I hugged my doll to my breast and did a happy dance. We were going home. Maybe Papa would be there.

We packed clothing, bedding, dishes, food and filled boxes and bags with small items until bedtime. The next morning, Mama pulled me from my bed when the rooster crowed. After a bowl of oatmeal, I helped her pack the rest of our belongings that fit in boxes. Clothing and linens stuffed the drawers in our few pieces of furniture. By bedtime, we were exhausted and fell into bed to rest for another busy day.

The next morning, Mama told me to take care of Roger when he woke. "Mind your brother while I finish packing."

Roger's eyes lit up as he watched Mama rush around organizing our things for travel. I struggled to change his diaper while he tried to pull free, eyeing the pile of furniture, beds, clothing, and kitchen ware. Even after I fed him a bowl of porridge and gave him his bottle, his head swiveled to keep track of what Mama did. He could see something was happening, and he didn't want to miss anything.

Mama sighed when she looked at the stack of possessions covering the center of the room. "If we load the furniture and beds first, this is more than enough for a wagon load. We still have things from Opa and Oma's house plus all our farm tools, chickens, and rabbits to haul. We'll need two trips. Mr. Merkel will look after our animals while we're gone."

She sent me to the garden to pick all the vegetables that had grown large enough to eat. "We may need the food until we can grow more."

Mr. Merkel helped us load the wagon after we'd finished lunch. "Be careful what you take with you. The Nazis still have checkpoints to look for contraband."

Mama set down a box and straightened her back. "What do they consider contraband?"

Mr. Merkel shrugged. "That's not yet defined. It probably means anything the soldiers would like to keep."

Mama tapped her foot. "We're only taking our belongings."

His eyes narrowed. "Several people have been arrested for having things they don't allow. You don't want any trouble with our new rulers."

After he'd taken a quick look at the big stack of our possessions, he shook his head. "You'll not be able to haul all this stuff in one trip."

Mama pursed her lips and shrugged. "I'll come back for the tools and farm equipment, plus any of the things which don't fit on this load. Cages for the chickens and rabbits can ride on top of our second trip."

After we loaded the wagon, we said goodbye to the Bauers and the Koeppels.

Mr. Koeppel wished us a safe trip. "We'll be home in a few weeks."

Tears filled my eyes when I gave Maria a final hug. "Come visit me when you get home. We'll play together."

Back at our rented house, Mama set aside food for breakfast and sent me to bed early. "Sleep well. We'll leave at sunrise tomorrow."

Roger enjoyed the comfort of his carriage during the night, while Mama and I shared a pallet on the floor. Fatigue sapped my energy, but anticipation kept my eyes wide open for a time. I'd be going home.

Would my friends be there? Would the Nazis take our things at the roadblocks? Would our house really be as dirty as Mama had described? Had the Nazis dropped bombs on Kaschel? Would they allow us to live in our house? Would they arrest us when we went through their checkpoints?

Sleep didn't come easy.

My eyelids got heavier, and I remembered my father hugging me at bedtime as sleep was ready to claim me. Then I heard the skittering of tiny feet across the rough cement floor. A mouse. They liked to run beside the walls where we lay. Visions of those nasty little vermin crawling under the covers to share my blanket kept me awake long into the night.

I dreamed of sleeping in my own tall bed in Kaschel.

Chapter 16

I stretched my legs to shove my feet beneath the seat in front of me as the peaceful French countryside slid beneath the airplane. After wiggling my toes, I lowered the tray on the seat back and picked out a magazine tucked in the storage pouch. It was written in English, and I couldn't understand the words. Dale spoke French, and he'd tried to teach me his native language, but I hadn't made much progress.

As a child, I learned to speak the Alsatian patois at home. The Nazis taught me to speak true German. I heard French on occasion but didn't study it until the war ended. Living in Paris offered very little need for speaking English in our daily life.

The Normandy coastline passed under the wing and disappeared behind us. We'd have another ten hours cooped up in the noisy Lockheed Constellation before we reached New York. Little Paul slept soundly in his cradle beside me. The trip didn't worry him.

The flight attendant stopped at my seat with a tray of refreshments. "Would you like something to drink?"

"Non, merci."

I replaced the magazine in its pocket and leaned back to think about the events that led me here. Living in Wolfskirchen to avoid a Nazi invasion had been a terrifying experience for a five-year-old child. People were nice to us, but I'd never felt like it was home. My father's absence, to serve in the French Army, had been a difficult time for the family. We'd lived in constant fear he'd be hurt or killed in the war.

We returned home to a village that was no longer like the one we'd left. Mama told me how badly our house had been ransacked by the soldiers, but actually seeing it had made my stomach turn. Fear of the Nazis dominated our lives. In spite of our efforts to adapt, living as captives under German rule presented problems. Becoming German citizens made life even more difficult because most of our men would be drafted into the German Army. A large portion of the food we produced was taken from us to feed that army.

Neighbors trickled back to their homes. We were all afraid someone would tell the invaders about a rule we'd broken or some remark they deemed disloyal to the Third Reich.

Dale assured me that life in America would be free of those worries. He'd have a good job, and we'd have a nice place to live. I was already homesick, but he promised I'd be able to return home for a long visit after we lived there for three years.

* * *

When we left for Kaschel, Mama harnessed the cows to the wagon before daybreak. Excited about leaving to go home, I got dressed and gobbled down a quick meal she'd prepared the previous evening.

A sudden thought jolted me. "Mama, you forgot the box of hard rations under the hay."

Her hand flew up to cover her mouth. "Thank you, dear. I hid some of our money with the food." She climbed the ladder and brought the package down from its hiding place. Her panicked look disappeared as she tucked it into a bag of clothing.

She had prepared a bed for Roger behind the driver's bench. My job was to sit with him to keep him from climbing out and getting hurt. Mama tapped the cows with the reins, and we started on our journey. Wolfskirchen was barely awake when we passed through the center of town. Roger was hungry, and holding the bottle still was difficult as we bounced over the rocks. He fretted when he lost contact with the nipple. I took one quick look at the hilltop village that had been our home for so many months. Trying to remember what Kaschel looked like yielded only fuzzy images. After we arrived at the main road, Mama pulled on the reins to turn the big animals onto the road toward home.

The ride was smoother on the pavement, and the plodding cows made steady progress. Evidence of the war was scarce. The only thing I saw was a small military truck that passed us. Most of the land along our way had been planted, and the crops pushed their way out of the fertile soil. We saw several farmers working in their fields. No signs of war.

Another thought struck me. “Mama, we didn’t plant anything at home. Will we have anything to eat?”

She reached back to touch my arm. “It’s not too late to plant most of the crops. We may not have everything we usually do, but we won’t starve. I’ll bring everything you picked from our garden on the next trip.”

Roger fretted about having to stay in his cramped space, and I tried to amuse him by teaching him to play “pat a cake” during the ride. We came to a road barrier a short distance before we reached Sarre Union.

A German soldier carrying a rifle held up a hand and said, “Halt.” Two other soldiers with guns slung on their shoulders stood beside their truck.

Their stern looks and the ugly guns made me wish for some place to hide.

“State your name and what your cargo is.” The man’s voice sounded harsh, and he clipped his words like he was barking at us.

"We are the family Reeb, returning to our home in Kaschel," Mama said. "We were evacuated from the village when the fighting started."

His eyes shifted to examine the wagon. "What are you hauling? How much contraband do you have in the load?"

She straightened her back and looked directly at him. "We have our clothing and household goods. Nothing more. We are bringing them home."

An older soldier waved to our questioner. "Have a look."

The soldier motioned me to take Roger and sit beside Mama. Then he circled the wagon pawing and poking through our belongings. My heart froze when he shook the bundle where Mama had hidden our hard rations and money. The sudden trembling in Mama's arm betrayed her fear as well. It felt like an eternity before the soldier moved on. After finding nothing unusual, he motioned for us to proceed.

He gave the Nazi salute and grumbled, "Heil, Hitler."

I realized I'd been holding my breath and exhaled a blast of stale air to refill my lungs.

Mama waited for me to move Roger and climb back to our little nest in the bedding. After we settled in, she snapped the reins to start the resting cows moving again.

We passed through the town of Sarre Union without stopping. I noticed a pair of army trucks parked downtown. Several German soldiers wandered the streets. A red and white flag with a black swastika in the center flew over city hall. The normally lively town was quiet, and most of the residents went about their business without stopping to talk to neighbors.

I'd seen fear in Wolfskirchen, but it was more intense here. People looked over their shoulders like they were afraid a soldier would take them away.

The temperature rose during the afternoon as occasional sunlight peeked through the growing cloud cover. I was soon sweating and glad Mama brought a jug of water with us. A couple of healthy swallows soothed my parched throat.

We came to another checkpoint before we entered Kaschel. The German soldier waved us on when Mama explained where we were going. He carried a gun like the others who stopped us before we'd reached Sarre Union.

As we approached the village, we saw deep ditches on both sides of the pavement. In places, the trenches had been cut through the highway. Dirt filled the cuts where they crossed the road. The ground had settled, and the wagon jolted me when it bounced across the hasty repair.

Mama's brow furrowed as we crossed the makeshift surface. "They need to fill the ditches and repair the pavement."

As we drew closer to the village, trash appeared along the sides of the road. Many houses stood vacant. The stink of rotting food and manure made my nose wrinkle. Odd pieces of French army gear lay abandoned along the roadside. We passed houses with lots of missing shingles and broken windows. Empty buildings and piles of trash didn't look like the village I remembered. Kaschel appeared to have been deserted for a long time, but some people had returned. One house had a stone wall caved in and a big hole in the ground bedside it.

I pointed to the broken building. "What happened to the house, Mama?"

She leaned forward for a better look. "I'm not sure. An artillery shell may have exploded next to it."

As we entered Kaschel, we passed more rubbish and damaged buildings that had been deserted. Only a few people were visible in the streets. My feelings resembled the now overcast sky, gray and troubled.

Mama glanced aside, then faced straight ahead. "Those pigs."

The village looked shabby when we entered the main street. Trash and garbage was piled everywhere. Weeds grew tall in the tiny yards. When Mama made the final turn toward home, I recognized our house. Even the piles of rubbish surrounding our kitchen door could not disguise the familiar old building.

Our friendly home still stood, its huge grapevine clinging to the rocks around two sides. The massive stone walls, reaching uninterrupted from the ground to the tile roof, hadn't changed. The sturdy building had endured for almost three hundred years. Even the soldiers hadn't managed to destroy it.

A shutter over the kitchen window dangled from one hinge, and the pit filled with cow manure hadn't been emptied since we left. Trash and spoiled food containers covered the area along both sides of the house. The bad odor made me hold my nose. Mama stopped the cows, and we climbed down from the wagon.

Across the street, two men who worked at Mr. Schmidt's cement factory were busy repairing woodwork adjacent to the stone walls of his spacious home. I didn't see any of the family.

Mama entered our house first. Her sharp intake of breath should have warned me something was wrong. I followed her inside, holding on to Roger. Empty wine bottles, soiled dishes, and discarded paper bags covered the floor of our summer kitchen. Light coming through the filthy windows revealed the damage. Baked-on grease covered the top of the stove. It ran down the front and onto the floor. A rancid odor of decayed food and filth almost caused me to vomit. Roger covered his nose with a tiny hand and tried to escape from the room. I gritted my teeth and held him close to keep from crying.

Mama waved us on. "We might as well see the rest."

We passed under the low doorway to our winter kitchen. It didn't look any better. Dirty dishes covered a small table, and broken china given to Mama by Opa and Oma Lang as a wedding present crunched beneath my feet as we entered. The cabinet we used to store cooking utensils and dishes was gone. I hesitated to look when we entered the living room. The torn and filthy couch smelled of spilled food and wine. The floor looked like it hadn't been swept since we left. Two of our chairs and a bookcase were gone as well. Tears crept into my eyes as I looked at the horrible mess that had been our home.

The dining room that held our table and chairs was bare, and we found dirty serving bowls stacked in a corner. The sight of all the destruction left my stomach feeling sick.

Mama paused to give me a hug before continuing her search. "Don't worry, dear. We'll clean up the mess."

I stayed with Roger while she climbed the steep steps to the upstairs rooms. Her face was pinched and her eyes looked hard when she came back down. "The beds in all our rooms look like pigs slept there. Two of our wardrobe cabinets are gone, and they left the storage room filled with junk and trash."

She sighed. "We'll have to sleep in the wagon tonight. It will take a couple of days to get the house clean enough to unload our belongings."

Mama drew a tub of water from our well and the cows drank it immediately. She nodded to me. "They made the trip without anything to drink. They were thirsty."

I waved my hand at the house and yard. "Why did the soldiers do it, Mama?"

Her head jerked with an angry shake. "I don't know. Animals couldn't have done worse."

The outhouse needed attention, also. The door latch was broken, but the small stone building had survived better than the house.

Mama wiped a sleeve across her eyes. "Everything is in bad shape, but we can make it fit to live in if we work hard enough."

After looking at the woodshed, she chewed her lip. "Our firewood is gone as well. The soldiers must have burned everything, including most of the furniture."

For dinner, we ate cold ham and potatoes Mama brought from Wolfskirchen. Then she drove the wagon into the open shed our woodpile normally occupied. We shifted the cargo to give us a large enough space to sleep.

After glancing around Papa's shop and the stalls used for our animals, she said, "Most of our farm implements are still here. I'm sure the soldiers didn't use them to do any work."

She unhitched the cows from the wagon and allowed them to graze in the tall grass for a time. Later she milked them and closed them in their stall for the night. A cool wind whistled through the open sides of our shelter, but we had a roof overhead. After the day we'd lived through, I was too exhausted to complain and slept without waking until daybreak.

When the rising sun cleared the treetops, Mama gathered enough sticks to build a fire in the dirty stove. Then she cooked a bowl of oatmeal, and we ate breakfast in the clean air outside. Leftover ham and bread, along with fresh milk, completed our morning meal.

Later, she lifted the baby carriage from the wagon and set it on the ground. "Take Roger for a walk to look at the village. I'll start cleaning up this mess."

Chapter 17

Roger babbled lively sounds nobody could understand as his carriage started to move. I pushed it along the street toward Opa and Oma's home. Next door, Mrs. Rolf was busy making dust clouds, sweeping the walk in front of their house.

She smiled at me and came over to give me a hug. Then she picked up Roger and held him at arm's length. "My, you've turned into such a big boy."

He squirmed to get down and explore on his own two feet.

Mrs. Rolf looked at me as she returned Roger to his carriage. "I saw your wagon arrive last evening. Tell your mother I'll be over shortly to help her get organized."

"Thank you," I attempted a smile, and we continued our tour. Several of our neighbors had already returned to the village and cleaned up the mess around their homes. When we reached my grandparents' house, I spotted the same sort of abuse we'd seen at home. My knees felt weak as I imagined Oma's reaction when she confronted the mess the French Army left.

We returned home to find Mama carrying a few pieces of moldy furniture outside along with a big box of shattered dishes the soldiers had ruined. Mrs. Rolf came to help, and the box soon overflowed. Then Mama filled a tub with water from our well and stirred in flakes of yellow lye soap. The smell burned my nose. The two women slid the tub inside and started to scrub the floors. Later, Mrs. Rolf invited us to lunch.

I was hungry, and the chicken and dumplings tasted good.

"When did you get home?" Mama asked.

"About a week ago," Mrs. Rolf said. "Our place was in almost as bad shape as yours. We're still cleaning and mending."

"Was there any fighting here?" Mama asked.

Mrs. Rolf shook her head. "A few buildings were damaged by artillery shells that landed here when the Nazis made a trial attack on the Maginot line. There was no confrontation in the village. The French troops loaded their equipment and pulled out before the Germans arrived. Someone said they had orders to fall back and defend Paris."

Mama crossed her arms and gazed at the ceiling. "We must not be important enough for the army to defend."

Mrs. Rolf rolled her eyes. "Obviously."

"Have the Nazis caused much trouble?"

"Only by strutting around the village and being insolent. Most of our troubles come from the new mayor's edicts. The Nazis removed the mayor we elected and appointed Mayor Spengler to replace him. He's one of them, and he will report anything you do or say against the occupation. He keeps his cows in the field by the river and passes by our houses every day to care for them. He's worse than the Nazis."

Mama nodded. "He's got a lot of power, and he'll be eager to please them."

* * *

Back home, Mama brought in more sticks and built a fire to heat water. We gathered all the bedding and some of our clothes that hadn't disappeared during our absence. She spent the rest of the day doing laundry, and I was able to sleep soundly in my own bed when darkness fell. I didn't have to worry that a mouse might climb under the covers with me.

Mama spent two more days cleaning and putting the house in order, and it took on the fresh smell of soap and water. Then she prepared to leave for Wolfskirchen to bring the rest of our belongings. Mrs. Rolf invited Roger and me to stay with her until Mama got home.

After the cows had been harnessed and hooked to the wagon, Mama slapped their backsides with the reins. The animals made their way slowly down the street and took the highway leading south. The trip there and the return would take two days.

Feeling deserted and frightened about Mama making the trip alone, I waved a timid goodbye from the Rolfs' front yard.

"You can shell some peas while you watch your little brother," Mrs. Rolf told me. "I have an errand to run in town."

I'd hoped to play outside and explore more of the village, but Mrs. Rolf kept me busy. All the troubles I'd seen recently had me worried. Would Mama be safe on her journey? Would the soldiers allow her to pass their barricades? Would she really be home tomorrow night? I sat down to strip peas from their long pods. After several interruptions to tend my restless little brother, I filled the bowl with fresh green peas.

Later Mrs. Rolf found more chores for me. "You can fold the laundry after you give Roger his bottle and feed him some oatmeal."

It became obvious I wouldn't have any free time to play outside. My gaze was directed at the floor. "Yes, ma'am."

The following day, the setting sun had already cast long shadows across the village as I watched Mama turn the wagon into our street. Forgetting my duty to look after Roger, I ran to meet her, shouting, "Mama."

She raised her eyes and awarded me a smile as the cows maintained their slow advance. "You look well. Where did you leave your brother?"

"Oops."

I collected Roger and hurried home. Mr. and Mrs. Rolf helped Mama unload the heavy farm equipment. After it was stowed in the shed, we turned the chickens loose in their run. The rabbit cages returned to their place against the back wall of the building.

Mama brought two large boxes of produce I'd picked from our garden in Wolfskirchen. "Most of the plants aren't ready to harvest. I took a little more and brought what we could use."

Mrs. Rolf stayed to help Mama arrange the rest of our household goods. I would have been happier if Papa had been there to take charge of the work.

When they finished, Mama wiped her brow with the tail of her apron. "We can start planting our late garden tomorrow morning."

Mrs. Rolf straightened suddenly and looked at Mama. "Just be careful with our new mayor."

Mama lifted her head to stare off into space for a long moment. "I suppose we must learn to live with a spy in our midst."

* * *

Mama had just finished washing the dishes from our evening meal when she heard a soft knock at our back door. She opened it a few inches to peer outside, and Papa's seventeen-year-old brother stood in the darkness. Her back straightened, and she moved quickly to fling it open. "George!"

When she reached out to hold him in a long hug, I saw tears run down her face.

Uncle George's body was thinner, and he'd let his cropped blond hair grow longer while we'd been away, but his smile hadn't changed from the teenaged boy I knew.

Uncle George slipped inside and pulled the door closed before dropping a filled pillowcase on the floor. "I just stopped in to say goodbye. I've already picked up some of my things from Mama's house. The Nazis plan to make Alsace part of Germany, and they will draft young men into their Wehrmacht. They are sure to take me even if I don't believe in their cause. I'm on my way to the south of France to wait for the end of this war. Fighting for Hitler is not something I plan to do."

"How will you travel?" Mama's voice faltered. "The Nazis are everywhere."

Uncle George's face turned serious. "I'll start out walking after dark and hiding during the day. I brought a change of clothes and some money from home. With any luck, I'll be able to slip into a boxcar heading south when I find a switching yard."

"Do you have warm clothes for staying outside at night?"

He pointed to the pillowcase. "I have enough."

"What will you do when you get there? The Vichy Government may treat a stranger as bad as the Nazis."

George's lips tightened and he shook his head. "I have to try. I'll change my name and pretend to be a native. I think I'll be able to find work on a farm. If I stay here, the Nazis will make sure I wind up in their Wehrmacht or worse."

I stood back in a corner of the room and listened in silence. If Uncle George went in the German Army, he might come back to fight us.

Mama got busy at the stove preparing food while Uncle George sat at the kitchen table and talked to me. “You’ve grown into a big girl while you were in Wolfskirchen. Be sure to take care of Roger and help your mother. Life will be hard with the Germans controlling everything here while your father is gone.”

I managed a nod, but I couldn’t find my voice.

Mama soon brought him a plate filled with potatoes and dumplings. “Eat. I’ve made more you can take with you. Don’t trust anyone. The Nazis have spies everywhere.”

Uncle George paused between bites. “I’ll be careful.”

A half hour later, he hugged each of us and shouldered his meager belongings. Then he slipped out the back door to disappear into the night.

Chapter 18

After two weeks of hard work, our house finally looked clean. At least clean enough that Mama wasn't afraid to live there. Repairs to mend doors and windows broken by the French soldiers could be made as time permitted. Papa could do it when he came home. The stale smells of spilled food, dust, and mildew had been chased away with soap and water.

The animals were settled and had enough food for a month or two. Our garden was not complete, but we had a good start. The plants maturing early had taken advantage of the sun and rain to sprout and grow. Beets, turnips, potatoes, and kohlrabi would ripen later. Mama used a hoe to clean weeds from the rows of rhubarb and asparagus planted along the side of the house. They came back each summer.

She bought a pig to butcher in the fall to provide us with meat during the winter. She also bought a young sow to produce a litter of pigs the following year. Our chickens were laying eggs, and two of the hens were brooding. If everything went as planned, we would soon have a flock of baby chicks.

"We shouldn't starve this winter," Mama said.

When she found an hour to spare, she walked up the street to start cleaning the mess in my grandparents' house. She didn't have time to repair things that were broken, but she cleaned most of the clutter and made sure the door locks worked. The place looked better after she'd swept and mopped all the floors.

Trying to make the house truly ours again took a lot of time. The biggest problem was not having a couch and a China cabinet to store the dishes. Most of the chairs and two oil lamps were gone as well. Some of the broken glass we swept from the floor might have been our missing lamps. Two of the wardrobe cabinets where we kept our clothing were missing. From looking at the scraps of hardware thrown in the corner of the kitchen, it appeared they had been burned for firewood. Most of our furniture had been ruined by our French defenders or stolen by looters.

Mrs. Rolf came to visit and remarked, “It smells clean in here, but you need furniture to replace the things you lost.”

Mama motioned for me to take charge of Roger. “I need several things, but we don’t have the money now.”

“That’s one way the Nazis have actually been helpful. The Jewish population in Sarrealbe all fled to the south of France before the German army arrived. Nazis collected all the goods they left behind and stored them in a big warehouse. We can go there and select anything we lost during the hostilities. Take what you need, compliments of the Third Reich.”

Mama shook her head. “I wouldn’t feel right taking anything. It seems like stealing from unfortunates who were driven away by these horrible people.”

Mrs. Rolf reached out to touch Mama’s arm. “Mayor Spengler assured me the Jews will not be coming back. Their belongings are already lost to them.”

Mama motioned Mrs. Rolf to sit down and took a chair opposite her. “How can he be sure they won’t return?”

“Because the Nazis would haul them off to concentration camps if they tried to come home. They would almost certainly be killed in the camps. The mayor told me Germany has no place for Jews.”

Mama’s brow wrinkled, and she wiped away a tear. “It still doesn’t feel right to take things from people who fled the Nazis.”

Mrs. Rolf continued. “Everything in that warehouse will go to someone. The Nazis own it now. The French army looted the things you’re missing. Replacing what you lost is your right under German law. The previous owners will never be allowed to reclaim anything. If you don’t take advantage of this offer, someone else will.”

Mama looked at the floor. “I’ll have to think about it.”

Mrs. Rolf cocked her head and wagged a finger. “Don’t think too long. Things you need will be gone.”

The next morning I tagged along leading Roger when Mama stopped Mayor Spengler as he walked past our house to tend his cows.

She spoke to him in a faint voice. “Some of our furniture is missing and the soldiers ruined a lot more. Mrs. Rolf told me we can recover the things we lost.”

The mayor’s fat body jiggled as he straightened to his full height, thumbs hooked under his suspenders. “The Third Reich has already solved your problem. Most of the undesirables ran like rats from a hungry cat when the German Army approached. They left most of their belongings behind. This province will soon become part of Germany.” He pointed a finger in the direction of the Jewish quarter in Sarrealbe. “I can assure you those people will never return to claim ownership of anything.”

Mama glanced toward our house. “If they do come back, they’ll need their furniture”

“The Wehrmacht collected things the riff raff left behind and stored them. The Jews are gone for good. You can take what you need.”

Mama shook her head and frowned. “But the things don’t belong to me.”

The mayor sweated in the warm sunlight and wiped his brow with a handkerchief. "The previous owners lost any claim to goods they owned when they ran away. You can't steal what belongs to nobody. The French Army looted the things you're missing. They are no longer here. You have the right to replace what they destroyed or stole from you."

Back inside, Mama told me, "I feel sorry for the poor people who left everything behind to escape the Nazis."

I thought about the Jews who ran away. "Why do the Nazis want to hurt people?"

Mama grimaced. "That's who they are."

Her explanation didn't make sense at first, but after I spent some time thinking about it, I understood.

The next day she took the wagon to Sarralbe to select a couch, a China cabinet, a small table, four kitchen chairs, a chest of drawers, two wardrobe cabinets, and two oil lamps to replace things our French soldiers had broken or looted. We needed the lamps to supplement our fifteen watt light bulbs upstairs if we wanted to read something at night. She brought along a small tablet to make notes of anything that might identify the owner if they ever returned.

Some of our clothing had been stolen, but she turned away from piles of everything from socks to overcoats. "I'll not dig through personal items. We'll make do with what we have."

After she returned home and arranged the new furniture, our house began to look almost normal.

I sat on the soft, clean couch we'd brought home, looking at our living room the next day. The new things filled the empty space, but I couldn't help feeling sorry for the people who lost everything when they ran from the approaching Nazis.

Mama came to stand beside me. “These nice things must have belonged to families that cherished them. We need to care for them like their owners did.”

She sat beside me and wrapped an arm around my shoulder. “The Jews fled the German Army to save their lives. Taking their furniture isn’t right. Unfortunately, we have no power to keep these people safe here. The Nazis would persecute them. We can only pray they find happiness in their new homes in the south of France.”

Chapter 19

During a spell of warm weather in late July, the Schmidts came home to their big house across the street. We considered them to be rich people because Mr. Schmidt owned a cement casting factory. Several of his employees had spent weeks cleaning and repairing the dwelling. They had repainted the outside woodwork, trimmed the lawn, and pulled weeds. The Schmidts' yard now rivaled the village soccer field.

Roger and I followed as Mama crossed the street to greet our wealthy neighbor, Mrs. Schmidt. "Welcome home."

She came to their gate to meet us with a smile. "Thank you. It seems like we waited forever while our workers got the house ready for us to move in. It's clean, but we're missing a lot of furniture and china."

Mama nodded. "I think everyone suffered damage and lost furniture. We're just glad we were able to come home."

Mrs. Schmidt lifted her hands and shrugged. "It's not a big problem, except we'll surely spend a lot of time finding suitable replacements that match our décor."

As we returned home, Mama shook her head and smiled. "It must be nice having someone else clean your house and put things back in order."

* * *

Our hay crop stood tall, well past due for harvest. It rose to my waist when I walked through the field. Mr. Rolf agreed to cut it with Papa's mowing machine. It took him a half day to mow the tall grass and leave it lying on the ground. Mama spent the next three days turning it over to dry. Feeling more secure now that she was back home, she paid a neighbor boy to help her load the wagon and bring it in. When they finished, our loft over the stables was filled with sweet-smelling hay that would feed our cows during the long winter months.

Several days later, a returning neighbor limped up to our door to see Mama. The sleeves of his faded shirt had been cut off above the elbows. Both knees of his trousers had been patched with fabric that didn't quite match. He held a ragged cap in his hands. "We are short of food, and our money is gone. I still have time to plant vegetables, but I need food for my family now."

Mama stood silent with downcast eyes. "We have the same problem. We've planted crops, but most things aren't ready to harvest. I'm not sure we have much help for you."

The neighbor tugged at his cap. "We don't ask for much, but my family is hungry. I can pay you back with labor."

Mama cupped her chin in her hand. "We might be able to spare a few things. I have some early vegetables we can share. Turnips and beets won't be ready to harvest until fall, and I'm not sure if we'll be able to dig the potatoes before cold weather kills the plants."

His hands shook when he lifted them. "Vegetables would be wonderful. What do you need done?"

Mama looked at the empty space in our shed. "I'm about out of wood for my cookstove, and we have nothing to heat the house this winter. If you can bring us some firewood, I'd consider the debt paid."

When he left, I asked Mama, "What's wrong with his leg?"

"His foot was crushed under a wagon wheel. It hurts when he stands for more than a few minutes. It's hard for him to keep a job. He is often out of work."

I helped Mama gather the vegetables and filled our wheelbarrow with what we could spare. "It doesn't look like much for a whole family."

Mama nodded. "I'll give them a chicken and a young rabbit as well. They will need some meat."

I held Roger's hand as he toddled along beside me while Mama delivered the food. She helped the man carry everything into the house and offered a smile to his thin, plainly dressed wife and three small children.

When the wheelbarrow was empty, Mama said, "Come back in about two weeks. I may have more by then."

A few days later, two rows of firewood filled our woodshed. Mama sent me to deliver another bag of snap beans and half-grown beets plus a dozen eggs.

* * *

While I ran an errand in the village, a big bus rattled to a stop in front of city hall. Several people, most of them elderly, struggled to descend from the big vehicle while carrying their bags. I moved closer and couldn't believe my eyes when I recognized the couple trying to climb down the steps. They were helping each other with several pieces of luggage.

"Oma!" I screamed as I ran to hug her.

My grandmother dropped to her knees and held me close. "I'm so glad you're safe, child. We've not been able to hear news of what's happening here."

Opa laid his hand on the top of my head. "It's good to be home. You've grown so much taller. We can't wait to see your parents and baby brother."

My curiosity to hear more about their adventure and my happiness at their arrival had me dancing in the street. The somber sky and gathering storm clouds failed to cast gloom on the joy of having my grandparents safely back in Kaschel.

I hugged each of them again. "We missed you so much."

Others poured from the bus. Most of them stood bewildered, looking at changes to the village they called home. One by one, family and friends welcomed them back from their exile.

Word spread quickly, and Mama came on the run, carrying Roger. She released him to me and tried to hug both of my grandparents at the same time.

Tears welled in my eyes as I watched the three of them hold each other and cry. I wondered why we all cried when we were so happy they had returned safely from a faraway place such as Haute Vienne.

Mama helped carry their luggage home while I led Roger. "Be ready for a shock when you see your place. The soldiers weren't kind. I cleaned it, but we have a lot to do."

* * *

Within days, the familiar "Welcome to Kaschel" signs placed at several entry points to the village had been removed. Signs reading "*Welkommen im Duetche Elsess,*" meaning Welcome to German Alsace, had replaced them.

"Why?" I asked Mama.

She raised her palms. "They want to remind us we are no longer French."

Later Mayor Spengler posted a notice at city hall. It started with a reminder that we were the benefactors of Nazi goodwill and had been awarded our rightful place in the Third Reich. As German citizens, we were expected to appreciate being in the movement that would rule all of Europe. The notice ended with a reminder. "Protests against German rule or any disloyal speech are strictly prohibited and will be punished."

Almost immediately, a group of citizens appeared at city hall to voice their disapproval. I went with Mama and Roger to listen. The men and women looked like farmers dressed in work clothes that had gathered dirt from tilling the soil. None of them seemed to be among the few prosperous farmers who owned larger tracts of land. The leader seemed to be agitated by changes to his way of life and voiced his loud objection. "We are French. Even if we've been conquered, that doesn't make us Germans."

The mayor raised both hands above his head and waited for quiet. "There will be no further discussion of this matter. We are loyal citizens of Germany, and rebellious talk will not be permitted."

The outspoken farmer continued. "We have a tradition of free speech. You can't end it by decree."

Raised fists and loud shouts of agreement erupted from the crowd of protesters.

The pudgy mayor motioned to a Wehrmacht sergeant standing with him. "Sergeant Schnabel, this man and his family are banished from German Alsace effective immediately. See that they cross the border before sunset."

Sergeant Schnabel pointed to the man and waved him toward the street. "Come! Bring your family." He shoved the man's wife and made spanking motions to the children.

When they turned the corner, Mama's shoulders drooped as she faced us. "We won't see them again."

Others who had joined the protest stood mute, their faces drawn and fearful. When the mayor returned to his office, they disappeared without saying anything more.

Mama's jaw hardened as she watched the crowd slip away. "This is the end of any public protest in Kaschel."

Later she told me, "Everything has changed. You must always be careful what you say. The Nazis will punish us if we don't obey their orders and show respect."

The next day, we received a notice from city hall that all French street names had been changed to names that honored Germany. It reminded us that speaking French was prohibited and would be punished. French names for people were no longer allowed as well. My name, Irene, pronounced E-RAIN in French, would now be Irenee and pronounced E-RAIN-UH. Mama's name, Mina, was acceptable. Papa's name, Adolph, was perfect. Roger's name couldn't be made to sound German, so he became Rudiger.

Mama clasped her hands together and leaned forward. "They're trying to steal our souls."

I bit my lower lip. "I don't want to say my name in German. Roger is Roger. It's not right to make him change his name because the Nazis don't like it

* * *

I ventured outside on a sunny afternoon to enjoy the warm weather and gather eggs from the chicken shed. A strange man turned at the corner of the street and walked toward our house. He wore a wrinkled, dirty French Army uniform and carried a large canvas backpack. A wide brimmed cap obscured much of his face, but I could see he had a scraggly beard. Something about his walk reminded me of Papa, but Papa was away in the army. Frightened as the man continued to approach our house, I hid behind the rows of firewood. When he reached our door, he pushed it open with a shout.

"I'm home!"

I heard Mama's scream as she rushed to meet him in the doorway. She wrapped him in her arms so tightly he couldn't put the backpack down.

His voice sounded exactly like Papa's. "The army discharged me. I'm home to stay."

It couldn't be true. Papa had been gone more than six months. He didn't even come home after France surrendered. Streaks of gray had invaded his shaggy brown hair, but I could see it was truly him. With shaky knees, I crept out from my hiding place and approached them.

He turned to me with a broad smile and knelt to take me in his arms. Suddenly I felt safe. Papa was truly home. He had returned to protect and provide for us. Tears filled my eyes as I clung to him. Neither of us spoke.

He rose again when Mama returned from the kitchen, leading Roger outside to greet his father. After bending to lift the toddler, he held his son at arm's length to get a good look at him.

Roger let out a startled yelp and started to cry.

Papa laughed as he held the youngster close. "I'd cry too, if someone who smells as bad as I do grabbed me. You're getting to be a big boy. We'll have to spend some time getting to know each other. I won't look so frightening after I get a bath and clean clothes. Then we can get better acquainted."

Mama heated bath water and found clean clothing for Papa. He dragged a tub plus soap and a razor out to the shed. Mama filled the big tin vessel with warm water and left his clothes on the woodpile. Papa's bath took a long time. When he returned, his whiskers were gone, and his face looked gaunt. He smelled a lot better, but he still needed a haircut.

We filed inside and sat around the kitchen table. Roger stopped crying and stared wide eyed at this stranger. Mama carried in glasses and the single bottle of good red wine she'd bought after we returned home.

She handed the wine and a corkscrew to Papa. "It's time we opened this."

Chapter 20

Papa opened the wine, and Mama filled two glasses. She also poured a thimbleful in a glass half-filled with water and set it before me. Then she proposed a toast to his return. This was the first time I'd been allowed to drink wine. I was proud to participate and eager to sample it. Since my glass was mostly filled with water, it didn't have much taste.

After Mama poured the last of the wine, we all sat around the table. Roger recovered from his fright and climbed on Papa's lap to investigate him. He was soon trying to talk and quick to accept Papa into the family.

I stayed close and snuggled against Papa's warm wool shirt as my parents brought each other up to date about things that happened while they were separated.

"I made some good friends in Wolfskirchen," Mama said. "We were eager to come home, but the Nazis are arrogant and demanding." Her lips thinned, and her jaw firmed. "We're not allowed to be French anymore. We are forced to show loyalty to Germany."

Papa ran fingers through his long hair. "After Soissons, my regiment did nothing but retreat. We deployed to defend Paris, but the Nazis never attacked."

Mama reached to take his hand. "I'm glad they didn't."

"Germany annexed most of our industry and the entire Atlantic coast. The French government at Vichy is a virtual slave to the Third Reich. They will be independent only as long as they obey the Nazis. Leaving Paris and the southern part of France with a separate government run by the French was no better than throwing a small bone to a starving dog."

"Why did the army keep you so long?" Mama asked. "The war was over. France surrendered."

Papa shook his head. "Nobody knew who was in command. The army was paralyzed. We had no leadership and no mission. All the officers were confused and most were afraid to make a decision. It took a couple of months for someone to figure out they wouldn't need to feed what was left of the army if they sent us home."

"How did you travel?" she asked.

Papa chuckled. "I didn't have money for the train, so I caught rides and walked. A friendly truck driver bought me a meal when we stopped at Metz."

* * *

The next day Papa went to see the stationmaster at the rail road and returned with a smile on his face. "I have a new boss, but he gave me a job starting the first of the month. I'll be doing maintenance work and setting signal lamps."

Mama wiped a hand across her forehead. "Did you tell him about your difficulty distinguishing red from green?"

Papa licked his lips. "I didn't say anything, but the old station master let me keep the lanterns in different places so I wouldn't hang the wrong one by the track."

Mama said, "The Nazis may be stricter. They're sticklers for rules."

Papa's voice firmed. "They need workers. The factories are hiring every available person they can find."

"They are also preparing to draft more men." Mama leaned closer to him. "I hope they don't take people from Alsace."

I cringed. Papa could lose his job. Even worse, he could be drafted into the German army. We needed him at home.

Later Papa killed and cleaned a rabbit for dinner, and Mama splurged on a round of cheese that cost a lot and had been hard to find. I spent an hour in the garden, weeding and gathering vegetables for a big meal. Papa spent most of the afternoon helping my grandparents with some repairs and invited them to dinner. When we all gathered around the table, Opa gave thanks we were together again. I began to feel safe after months of scary things happening. Papa would take care of us.

Mama had prepared a feast, and Opa brought two bottles of red wine. Papa told us stories about his time in the army. The adults all tried to talk at once, and I kept Roger amused while I listened. A warm and secure feeling surrounded me. Our family was together and safe. Midnight approached as my grandparents left, and I climbed the steps to tumble into bed.

After sleeping late the next morning, I joined my parents when they attended another town meeting called by Mayor Spengler. There wasn't enough room inside, so everyone gathered on the lawn. I sweated under the bright sun and fanned Roger as we waited for what felt like forever until the mayor appeared. Finally, he sauntered out of his office to stand before us. Sergeant Schnabel stood beside him.

The mayor spoke to the crowd. "I have good news for the village. Several houses were burned or badly damaged by the French Army who occupied the village before we were liberated. Further destruction happened during military skirmishes at the Maginot Line. Neither Germany nor our residents were responsible for this regrettable opposition. The needless damage was caused by the stubborn and mindless French."

A shout came from the assembled residents. "It happened. What can we do about it?"

The mayor lifted both hands with a broad smile. “Sergeant Schnabel can address that. He represents the Third Reich, and they are attentive to our welfare.”

Papa shook his head and leaned toward Mama. “The Third Reich couldn’t care less about our welfare.”

Sergeant Schnabel stepped to the front and cleared his throat. “The French Army ignored the needs of our residents and allowed this damage to occur. My superiors in Berlin have authorized me to remedy this injustice. Don’t spend your resources trying to repair the damage. If your home is unfit to live in, take one of the houses left by people who ran away from their homeland. Many of the deserted homes are not badly damaged.”

He paused to show a fake smile to the gathering. “The Third Reich will rebuild all your homes when the situation stabilizes.”

The mayor made a few more vague remarks and dismissed the crowd.

As we walked home, Mama turned to Papa. “You don’t believe the mayor and the sergeant will keep their word?”

Papa kicked a pebble into the gutter. “I’ll believe them when our chickens grow four legs and the rabbits fly.”

* * *

Papa took a long look at the garden. He returned with a frown marring his face. “I don’t think we have enough planted to get us through the winter.”

Mama flinched. “We had so many things to do at once. I guess I overestimated what we’d harvest, and I gave some to a family in need. It’s not too late to plant more.”

"We can still plant cabbage," he said. "It will keep in cool weather, and we can make more sauerkraut."

Mama turned to look out the window. "I'll plant kohlrabi, beets, and some celeriac as well. We'll need to buy more potatoes because ours will be small when we harvest them."

Papa nodded agreement. "It will soon be time to gather wild plums. I need them to make another batch of schnapps. The soldiers drank it all. You can cut up some of the plums to dry on the roof with the apples. They'll make good tarts during the winter."

"That will help," Mama said. "We'll also have your salary to buy a few things."

Papa shook his head. "That will help unless something happens or I lose my job. I could still be drafted into the German Army."

During the next week, Papa made our garden bigger. Another of Mama's hens was brooding, and Papa let the buck breed our two adult female rabbits. He also planted more carrots to feed the expected litters. Later I took a basket and picked up plums that had fallen from the trees, bringing home a new basketful each day. Mama sorted them. Good ones were cut up and dried with the apples to be eaten during the winter. We stored the rest in a big vat Papa used to ferment them and make a plum wine. He would distill the wine to make his schnapps. The end product was a crystal clear and potent liquid. His schnapps was renowned as the best available in all of Kaschel.

When I asked to taste it, Papa said I was too young. Still curious, I waited until he was gone and sneaked a taste. Then I spit and gagged as it burned my mouth like liquid fire.

Papa had been right.

* * *

Gray skies and frequent rain signaled summer was coming to its end. The temperature dropped, and I needed to wear my sweater during the mornings. Our baby chicks thrived, and another hen brooded on a cluster of eggs. We'd need several more chickens and plenty of eggs to get us through the winter. Papa and Mama assured me we wouldn't go hungry even if food from our garden ran a little short.

We were all surprised when an inspector who worked for the Nazi commissioner in Sarregemines knocked on our door. "I'm here to count your livestock. If you have more than you'll need, you are required to deliver the surplus to the Wehrmacht.

Sudden fear gripped me. Would the Nazis take away our food? Mama and Papa had already said we could run short of garden vegetables.

Papa accompanied the inspector as he carried his clipboard around the building to count our animals. The man wrote several words and hesitated as he looked in the pig pen.

After he'd counted the rabbits, he stopped to push back his cap. "I didn't find that you have more than your family needs for the present. However, when your young sow delivers her litter of pigs next spring, you'll be authorized to slaughter only one of them for your own use. The remainder must be delivered to the authorities to feed the loyal soldiers who protect our homeland."

After the inspector left, Papa added his feelings about what the Nazi official said. "He didn't mention payment. They'll take the product of our labor to feed our oppressors. We get the privilege of helping them force us to live as subjects of the Third Reich."

Chapter 21

When September arrived, I was ready to start school. It was scheduled to begin in early September, but a German teacher wasn't available. When she finally opened, I began first grade. The schoolroom was located in a wing of city hall. The walls needed paint, and the floor creaked when we walked on it. We all shared the lone teacher. Younger students attended morning classes and older students met in the afternoon. Catholics went to a separate school in a building beside their church.

On our first day, the school had a lot of changes from previous years. Our teacher, Mrs. Eva Hauser, was from Heidelberg, Germany and a loyal Nazi. Her gray-streaked black hair was pulled into a tight bun. Metal-rimmed glasses framed the sharp features of her wrinkled face. A plain black jacket and full cut gray skirt gave her a no-nonsense look. A swastika adorned the wall behind her desk. She sat erect and still, lips pressed firmly together. Her cold eyes watched each student as they entered the room and found a seat.

When the classroom was filled, she stood to gaze at us. "Good morning. I am your new schoolmaster. You will address me as Mrs. Hauser. I will expect silence in the classroom unless you are responding to a question or I give you permission to speak. Do you understand?"

She nodded permission when one of the boys raised his hand.

The boy stuttered and cleared his throat before finding his voice. "Will we still learn the lessons we've missed by starting late?"

Mrs. Hauser crossed her arms and stared at the boy. "You will learn what you need to know. Your previous school was run by the stupid French. They taught you a lot of frivolous notions. Here you will learn how to conduct yourselves as good and productive citizens of the Third Reich. After that, we will concern ourselves with the material you have missed."

I sat in the back row, wondering what she wanted to change. I sensed she didn't want to hear any more questions about it.

Finally, the teacher clapped her hands. "All first graders will find a seat in the first row. Second grade will be in the second row, and third grade in the back."

After everyone found a place, she pointed to the large swastika draped on the front wall. "Our first lesson is to learn proper respect for the Fatherland and the Nazi Party. "You will start each day by giving the Nazi salute in unison and singing the 'Horst Wessel' song."

Mrs. Hauser made us all stand straight and still behind our desk. My knees felt weak when she passed by and stopped to stare at me. Someone in the second row wasn't as lucky.

The teacher's sharp voice sounded. "Don't touch the back of your chair. Put your hands by your side and face the flag."

She continued down the aisle, scrutinizing each of the students and correcting some. After she was satisfied, she returned to the front.

"When I start the music," she said, "you will stand and salute the flag. Keep your right arm straight with your palm facing forward. The hand must be level with your eyes. When the music stops, you will drop your hands to your side."

We repeated the salute until everyone could do it properly. The room felt stuffy, and my arm began to cramp, but I stood straight and did as she told us until she was satisfied. Then she spent the rest of the day teaching us which political views were acceptable to the Third Reich.

After we mastered the Nazi salute, Mrs. Hauser told us the latest news. “Japan has signed the Tripartite Pact. Germany, Italy, and Japan are now united. This axis will rule the world.”

Biting my lip kept me from answering. A world ruled by Nazis would be a terrible place. I felt liberated when it was time to go home.

During the next several days, she taught us that Germans were the master race and French culture was inferior. Germany would rule all of Europe, and we were fortunate to be among the people allowed to become part of Germany. We spent hours learning the proper way to greet Nazi officials and how lucky we were to be granted German citizenship.

At the end of our indoctrination, Mrs. Hauser announced we would learn to read and write in proper German the following week. “Your patois is crude and contains a lot of French words. You may not speak it in school.”

Three weeks spent learning how to be a Nazi appeared to be more than enough, and I was ready to learn something useful.

On Saturday morning, I didn’t have to go to school, and Mama let me sleep late. I had just finished breakfast when Opa came by to visit. He wore his rumpled work clothes and a broad smile.

Mama was quick to greet him and called Papa in from weeding the late crops in our garden. She motioned my grandfather to sit at the kitchen table. “Would you like some coffee?”

“No, thank you.” He pulled an envelope from his vest pocket and smoothed it on the table. “I have a letter from someone whose name I didn't recognize. It was postmarked in Marseilles, and it's obviously from George."

Mama released a long sigh. "It means he arrived safely in the south of France."

Opa nodded. "It says he found work on a large farm and intends to stay there. He wrote nothing that would indicate who he is nor where he lives. He sends his love to the family, but he didn't mention any plans to come home. If the Nazis were to read this letter, it doesn't tell them anything that would help them locate him."

I shivered from fright. "What if the Nazi's do find him? They might put him in jail."

Opa reached out to pat my hand. "The Nazi's don't go there. His only worry will be the Vichy government, and I don't think they'll look very hard."

* * *

October arrived with morning frost. The leaves changed from green to red, yellow, and brown. They soon covered the ground. A final cutting of the hay crop yielded enough to fill our hayloft to the rafters. We gathered most of the food in the garden, and vegetables we'd planted late could wait a few more weeks. The work went much faster with Papa home.

He wiped his brow with a shirt sleeve when he stored our harvest in the closet-like room beside the kitchen. "We should have enough to make it through the cold weather."

During the night, a violent storm rumbled through the village with rolling thunder and constant lightning. Wind-driven rain rattled against the windows. "Everybody up," Papa shouted. "Get behind the couch in the living room." Our stone walls and tile roof were strong, but that didn't appear to be good enough for him.

We pushed the big piece of furniture away from an inside wall and crawled into the space behind it. Papa was the last to settle into the narrow opening. "The couch will protect us if the roof or walls collapse."

Roger started to cry, and Mama rocked him in her arms. "Don't worry little one. This will end soon."

He hiccupped a few times and settled down to sleep.

I was more sleepy than worried. We'd done this in the past, and nothing bad ever happened. Papa was being too careful. Our house was surely strong enough to withstand a storm, but I didn't want to bring down his wrath by protesting.

A howling wind and heavy rain battered the building for a few minutes while we huddled in our narrow little hideaway. The wind calmed, and I waited for Papa to let me go back to my cozy bed. He made us wait until the rain diminished.

The next day, the mayor posted a notice at city hall, and Papa came home after he read it. "Sergeant Schnabel will provide rolls of black paper for each home in the village." He explained that British air raids were becoming troublesome. "They are concentrating on industrial sites that support the Nazi war effort."

"Why does that affect us?" Mama asked. "We don't have any industry."

"The mayor said the Luftwaffe is making a valiant effort to stop the raids and shooting down most of the bombers, but some have succeeded in dropping their bombs on German cities."

Mama interrupted. "The neighbors told me the BBC reports they lost very few bombers. They come at night, and Nazi interceptors can't find them."

Papa continued. "We are required to have a complete blackout during the hours of darkness. All windows and openings to the outside must be covered if an inside light is illuminated. Kaschel is not a likely target, but it might be used as a navigation waypoint. A blackout will prevent British bombers from finding the village at night."

He covered his eyes with his hands and then wiped back his hair. "The war is beginning to find us."

Chapter 22

We didn't have to wait long before the Nazis used their power. I went with Papa to listen to the news at Mr. Schmidt's house. "A large number of politicians, journalists, professors, religious leaders, and any remaining Jews have been expelled from Alsace. The victims were forced to leave their homes with only the belongings they can carry. Their houses stand vacant, and their fields are left fallow."

Papa commented during a pause. "Sergeant Schnabel is always present to make sure that exiles from Kaschel are really gone."

Rationing cards were issued to everyone. Bread, meat, milk, sugar, butter, and potatoes disappeared from stores. Fewer choices in clothing were available, and finding shoes became nearly impossible. People stood in lines, sometimes for hours, to buy food, and it was not usually very good. Farmers suffered less because they could grow much of what they needed.

A developing black market gave us another choice. Those willing and able to pay more or those who had goods to barter could avoid the lines and find better quality.

I wasn't sure how a black market worked. "Everyone complains, Mama. We find things we need. Why do other people have so much trouble?"

She sat on a kitchen chair and paused before answering. "We grow most of our food, and we have a better rationing card because Roger is under three. Your father's job at the railroad gives him easier access to the black market. He gets better prices because he meets people with goods for sale at the station, and they can avoid the risk of peddling their wares in town."

"It's a way to avoid the restrictions of Nazi rationing." Mama paused and knelt in front of me. She took my chin in her hand and looked in my eyes. "You must never say anything about the black market to others."

I still didn't understand how all that worked, but I knew not to tell the Nazis anything. It was comforting to know we had enough food so we wouldn't go hungry.

***

At school, Mrs. Hauser finally started teaching us to read and use numbers, but she still spent a lot of class time teaching us how to be good little Nazis. After we sang the anthem and saluted the swastika each morning, our teacher usually told us news about how Nazi forces were driving back the British and Russians on all fronts.

"German superiority is winning. The Fatherland is destined to rule the world. *Deutschland uber alles.*"

When I complained about her Nazi talk at home, I didn't get much help.

Papa listened and exhaled a deep sigh. "You must not argue with her. She is wrong, but the Nazi regime gives her the power. Just be silent and learn to read."

I didn't like the idea. "Why does she tell us things that are not true?"

"She believes what the Nazis want her to believe. But Churchill won't surrender, and Hitler might have problems with the Russians. He and Stalin both want to rule Europe. I'm not sure the German army is really prepared to deal with Russia."

During the evening, Mama asked me to watch Roger while she washed the dishes and cleaned house. He was able to run now, and keeping him safe became a challenge.

Sometimes we played with a ball on the floor. He would sit in a corner, legs splayed, and I'd roll the ball to him. He could grab it without moving and fling it back. His aim was terrible, so I wound up being the one to chase the ball. I'd be the tired one when Mama came to put him to bed.

It seemed like I'd just gone to sleep on a night the air raid siren sounded. The insistent wail frightened me without even considering it meant we might be bombed. I pulled the covers up over my head and waited for what would happen.

Papa stormed into my room. "Air raid. Get up. Now! Go downstairs to the living room and sit behind the divan."

Frightened and not fully awake, I hesitated to move. "Will the airplanes drop bombs?"

"I don't know. Get moving!"

I scrambled downstairs and ran to the divan. Mama was already there, holding Roger in her arms.

She pointed to the space beside her. "Here. Hurry up."

Papa was right behind me. He dropped onto the floor at my side and pulled the heavy divan close against us. "Now we wait."

The floor felt cold, and the slight movement of air from an open window made me shiver as we crouched in our makeshift shelter. Roger was tucked into Mama's arms. He was warm and relaxed there, but his eyes were wide open.

A half hour later, we heard the all clear.

After that first episode, the alarms came frequently during the nights. I lost sleep each time sitting on the cold floor, hiding behind our divan. No bombs fell on our village.

Papa wouldn't relent. "Better safe than sorry."

* * *

Winter arrived, snow and ice covering everything, but we had food and shelter. We celebrated Christmas quietly by inviting my grandparents for dinner on Christmas Eve. Kris Kringle left a few presents under the tree. The smell of lighted candles cheered me, but the grip of the Nazi regime didn't leave us much to celebrate. Papa gave thanks that we had plenty of food and all our animals were healthy.

I still had one big problem. My shoes were worn out. I covered the holes in the soles with cardboard. Seams were ripped, and we couldn't find a pair to replace them.

Papa took a close look at the worn shoes and how they fit my growing feet. "I know a man who repairs footwear. He might be able to do something."

He took me to see the cobbler who shook his head at the sight of my tattered shoes. I could hardly squeeze my feet into them.

"I can put on new soles and splice a piece of leather in the uppers to make them longer. I'll have to stretch them to give you a little more width."

It sounded to me like he would tear them up to fix them. "Will they be ugly?"

He twisted the corner of his mouth and chuckled. "They won't look like new shoes, but they'll fit your feet and keep the snow out. I can stain the leather all one color."

I walked home in my stockinged feet. Fortunately, the streets were almost snow-free, and I stayed inside at home. Two days later, I had my shoes. When I put them on, the patchwork looked terrible, but they fit. They would protect my feet from the cold weather. Knowing that getting new ones was unlikely, I'd wear the patchwork shoes and try to take good care of them.

We celebrated my seventh birthday in February. Mama baked a small cake and gave me a pair of long wool stockings she'd knitted to keep my legs warm when I walked to school.

"Your rebuilt shoes are part of your present," Mama said. "We were fortunate the cobbler could save them."

I hugged her and said, "Thank you," but I struggled to hide my disappointment that my birthday hadn't brought me any new toys.

* * *

The winter finally warmed in fits and starts, and the arrival of spring brought pleasant days. On a Monday morning, Mrs. Hauser waited until all the students were present and had us stand to sing the Nazi anthem and pledge allegiance to the Fuehrer.

Then she kept us all standing for an announcement. "We have a duty to render a service to the Fatherland. Certain plants that grow in the fields can be processed and used to make medicines needed by the Wehrmacht. After you are released from class, you are to gather these plants to aid the Third Reich in its struggles. Mr. Reinhard has volunteered to lead you. He has agreed to make sure you do the job properly."

I bit my lip to keep from protesting. It didn't feel right that school children would be forced to help the army that was holding our country captive.

After school Mr. Reinhard waited outside and led us to a meadow bordering the forest. When we got to the field, he parted the grass with his fingers to find the plants we would gather. "This is nightshade in my right hand. My left holds foxglove. It is important that you don't pick anything else or mix these two. I'll check your bags before we store the plants."

He handed each of us two paper bags marked with their names. "Make sure you pick only those we want. When your bags are filled, we'll take them back to your classroom and spread them on the attic floor to dry."

A chill breeze made me wish I'd worn a jacket as I searched the meadow for the proper plants. They looked like weeds to me. The work wasn't hard, but my back began to hurt from the constant bending. I started to daydream about playing with my doll when someone screamed.

"Snake!"

Everyone stopped work, and some let out frightened squeals as we searched the ground around our feet. After I recovered from my fright, my curiosity was aroused. I'd never laid eyes on one of those fearsome serpents.

Mr. Reinhard came running to find the little creature. After a careful look, he reached down and picked up the snake. It was as long as my arm and wiggled to free itself.

None of the students came close enough to take a good look.

"It just came out of its snug den to catch some sunlight," Mr. Reinhard said. "It's not warm enough for it to be as active as it would be in the summer. No poisonous snakes live this far north, so it won't hurt you. Take a good look, and I'll release him in the forest."

I found enough courage to move a little closer, but not too close. The snake looked long and slippery, too scary for me to approach it.

We returned to picking the weeds. After a few hours, our bags were filled, and Mr. Reinhard led us back to school. "The lower grades can hand up the bags and clean up the dirt you've tracked in. Third grade boys will climb to the attic and spread them out to dry."

I noticed he checked each bag before it was passed up to the attic.

He sent us home late with news I didn't want to hear. "All students will be present tomorrow afternoon to gather more of the medicinal plants."

We spent each afternoon filling our bags with more of the plants for the next three days. My back hurt, and dirt packed under the broken fingernails on my grubby hands. Mrs. Hauser allowed the students to leave at noon on Friday, but I wasn't there to celebrate. I'd stayed home pretending to be sick.

* * *

Our sow produced a litter of a dozen little pigs, and she kept them safe and warm in her sheltered pen. The pigs were cute, and I enjoyed playing with them after I convinced the sow I wasn't a threat to her litter. They were a healthy and lively lot, and Mama told me they would be in demand when they got bigger.

She brushed back her hair and grimaced. "We'd have a good profit if the Nazis allowed us to keep them."

"They're our pigs," I protested. "How can the Nazis take them from us?"

"They tell us we have to be loyal citizens, and it's our duty to give them to the government to feed the army. We don't have any choice."

Later I asked Papa. "Will the Nazis really take our pigs?"

He puffed out his cheeks and expelled a long breath. "An inspector will come by to count them. The mayor told us we could keep one for ourselves. The rest of the litter belongs to the Third Reich."

"That's not fair."

"It doesn't have to be fair. It's their law."

I wasn't ready to give up that easily. "Can't we hide the pigs?"

Papa shook his head. "Some people have turned their pigs loose in the forest, but they go wild. It's difficult to find and catch them later. Besides, the mayor walks by every day. He knows we have a litter of pigs, and he'd report us to the Nazis."

We discussed it during dinner. Neither of my parents wanted to let the Nazis take what we'd worked to produce. We depended on selling the pigs to buy things we needed.

Finally, Mama offered an idea. "We could probably succeed in hiding one or two if we knew when the inspector was coming."

Papa nodded. "He rides the train when he comes to Kaschel, and I'd be sure to see him arrive. We might hide a pig for the day. I know his usual route, and we could ask a neighbor to warn you when he's on his way."

He directed a stern look at Mama. "Don't forget we'd be in a lot of trouble if the inspector found a pig we'd hidden."

Chapter 23

Papa prepared our fields for crops after the danger of freezing weather passed. He turned the land and planted several hectares in wheat along with a large potato patch. I helped him plant the garden at home after I got out of school.

Soon after, Sergeant Schnabel delivered another surprise to the villagers. He brought in a new organization to plague us. The *Hitlerjugend*, the Hitler Youth Group, had come to Kaschel. We learned about it from a neighbor.

Tears glistened in Mrs. Hoffman's eyes when she came to see Mama. "The Nazis forced my daughter, Elke, to join the *Hitlerjugend*. She's a child, only fourteen. She's not involved with politics."

Mama motioned her to take a seat at the kitchen table. "May I fix you a cup of tea? What on earth is the *Hitlerjugend*? I've never heard of it."

Waving away the offer, Mrs. Hoffman said, "It's an organization of young people who are forced to cultivate land abandoned by the Jews and others who fled. Everything they produce will go to the state to benefit the Wehrmacht.

Mama poured the tea the lady had refused. "That's terrible. At least she'll be safe in the village, but it's not right to force her to work for the Nazis."

After she mindlessly sipped from the cup, Mrs. Hoffman said, "The real reason for the activity is to indoctrinate our children to become Nazis. It prepares them to serve in the military or work in industries that build Hitler's war machine."

Mama slumped into a chair. "Why pick on Elke? She hasn't done anything wrong."

"They're forcing young people who are not in school or working to join. Elke's not idle. She took a year away from school, but she works on our farm. The commissioner says she must do this as her duty to the Fatherland."

I listened from the doorway. Elke was a quiet girl who had always been nice to me, and I knew she wanted to go to the secondary school at Sarregumines in the fall. I wondered if the Nazis would make me join the *Hitlerjugend*. The thought scared me.

"Isn't there anything you can do?" Mama asked.

Mrs. Hoffman shook her head. "My husband requested an exemption from the sergeant because Elke has already applied for enrollment when school starts. He said it would be disloyal to question the wisdom of an official representing the Third Reich."

After Mrs. Hoffman left, I went to Mama and asked, "Why?"

She pulled me close and hugged me. "They are Nazis."

* * *

I felt more grown up when my school term ended, and I was promoted to the second grade. At home, Mama kept me busy working in the garden. This spring, we had planted a larger crop than normal, and she carried water from the well to keep the plants growing. I pulled weeds and gathered the food we ate. I often wished for Roger to wake from his nap so I could sit with him while Mama worked.

By late spring, our garden began to yield fresh vegetables. Lettuce, spinach, radishes, and green onions, showed up on our dinner table. The whole family welcomed this change from our bland winter diet.

A few weeks later, we were all seated at the table after eating our Thursday evening meal when Papa spoke up. "We planted enough extra this year to take our excess produce to the Saturday market in Sarrealbe. People in cities have a hard time finding food, and it would bring in extra money."

Mama nodded, but she twisted her mouth like she was thinking about it. "We have work to do here. We haven't time to spend our Saturdays at the market."

Papa crossed his arms and turned to face her. "We could send Irene with Oma to sell our surplus. They could share the space, and Oma can look after her. The extra money would come in handy."

Mama frowned, but, after hesitating, she nodded agreement.

I spent most of the next day picking and washing vegetables. Mama separated them in bundles for display. By evening, we had loaded Oma's handcart to take to market the next morning.

Papa told me what prices to ask for our produce. "You can allow a small discount if they buy a lot, but don't let anyone bargain you down to a foolish price."

"What if nobody buys it?" I asked.

"If something doesn't sell, bring it home."

Then he handed me several different coins and made me learn how to make change for customers. I knew about numbers, but Papa made me practice for a long time counting out coins to make change.

When the sun peeked over the line of trees by the river on Saturday morning, Oma and I were already on our way. She pushed the handcart, and I walked beside her. The cool breeze felt good, and we made the trip to market in less than an hour.

Oma selected a spot and laid a blanket on the ground in line with several others. We spread our bundles of fresh vegetables on opposite sides.

Shoppers soon appeared. Several paused to look at my display, but nobody stopped. Then Oma sold a bundle of spinach to a well-dressed young lady. I watched in silence as people passed me by. After Oma made another sale, I wondered why they didn't buy from me.

My grandmother leaned across the blanket and patted my knee. "You need to smile and greet people when they approach. Talk to them. Everyone thinks all the goods are mine and you're just tagging along."

I spent a long moment thinking about what she said. I needed to work harder at getting people interested in buying from me.

When an elderly man approached a few minutes later, I looked up at him and smiled. "Good morning, sir."

He stopped and returned my smile. "Good morning. You're a very young merchant. What have you to offer?"

Shyness almost stopped me, but I pointed out what I had for sale. "I picked all of this just yesterday."

He bent down for a closer look and nodded. "How much for a bundle of onions?"

I told him, and he paused to consider the purchase. Then he pulled a wallet from his pocket and handed me a large coin.

"You drive a hard bargain, but they look good."

I handed him the bundle and counted carefully before giving him change. Oma watched me count and nodded approval before looking away.

"Thank you, sir." I breathed a sigh of relief that I made change correctly and watched my first customer leave happy.

By midday, Oma and I had sold most of the produce we'd brought to market. We were both sweating from sitting in the sun all morning. Oma had started to gather things that hadn't sold when a tall lady paused to look at what remained of my goods.

"How much for the radishes?"

I smiled and gave her the price.

She sniffed and speared me with a haughty gaze. "The market is closing soon. I'll give you half price."

Clearly, she was correct. I'd soon have to take the unsold produce home. Papa's instructions welled up in my memory. "I'll reduce the price by one fourth if you buy all of them."

She persisted. "You'll get nothing if you don't sell them."

My face warmed. This woman thought she could push me around because I was just a child. My answer came without thinking. "I'll take them home to feed the rabbits before I give them away!"

The lady huffed and started to walk away. Then she turned back. "I'll take them."

Chapter 24

Papa had just left for work when Mr. Rolf knocked on our door. "Adolph," he shouted. "Hitler's gone crazy. He invaded Russia."

Mama seemed to wilt in the doorway. "Adolf already left for work. That's terrible news. Doesn't he have enough trouble fighting with England?"

"Fighting in Russia will put a big strain on his army. Feeding all those troops will make it worse for us. That's a sure thing."

"Will the Nazis draft our men?"

Mr. Rolf threw his hands up. "They'll draft our men, and they'll force us to produce more food for the army."

"What will happen to us if he loses?"

Sweat beaded on Mr. Rolf's forehead despite the cool morning. His voice trembled when he answered. "The Russians might murder us all. Stalin's as bad as Hitler."

I listened from a corner of the kitchen where I was trying to spoon mush into Roger's mouth. *Who were these Russians? Would they attack us now? Would the Nazis protect us?*

Roger slapped the table and yelled when I failed to give him another bite on time.

After Mr. Rolf left us, Mama came inside and sat at the dining table for a long time holding her head in her hands.

I reached out to touch her. "Will the Russians fight us now?"

She looked up and wiped tears from her eyes. "I don't know. Russia is an ally of Great Britain, but we've been annexed by the Germans. Our family is loyal to France, but we can't say it in public. We don't know what Russia will do."

* * *

During the afternoon, Mrs. Rolf sounded out of breath when she stuck her head in our kitchen doorway. "Mina, the inspector who counts our livestock is on his way. He'll be here soon."

Mama wiped her flour-covered hands on her apron. "Thank you. We need to prepare."

As Mrs. Rolf turned to leave, Mama motioned to me. "Bring me one of the little pigs. Be careful not to upset the sow when you take it from her. We need to hide him from the inspector."

I wrinkled my nose at the smell when I entered the sow's pen. "I need to borrow one of your babies. Don't worry, I'll bring him back safe and sound."

The sow and her brood knew me because I fed her, and I petted several of the playful pigs before I picked up one of them. Taking him in my arms, I moved slowly and scratched his back to make sure he wasn't frightened. The big sow grunted and didn't appear to notice as I backed out and closed the gate to her pen. Once outside, I ran to the kitchen to deliver the little animal to Mama.

She pointed to the cupboard under the sink. "Put him in there. I've poured milk over some leftovers from breakfast. I gave him plenty, so that should keep him happy and satisfied until the inspector is gone. Make sure you don't say a word."

She closed the cupboard doors and listened. The pig was silent. Then she motioned me outside. "He should be happy and quiet with all that food. We'll work out here and wait for the inspector."

Mama cleaned the chicken run while I pulled weeds in the garden. Fear of the Nazis made my knees tremble and feel weak. The minutes we waited felt like hours.

When the inspector arrived, he was accompanied by a young Wehrmacht soldier who stood by in silence, holding a pen and clipboard while the official talked to us.

"I see you've added a number of chickens, Mrs. Reeb. I suppose your family can use that many eggs?"

He glanced quickly at the hayloft and walked toward the rabbit cages at the back of the building. "It appears your rabbit population has grown as well. Does your family really consume so many?"

Mama's voice sounded thin when she responded. "My husband's parents are old, and we must give them meat and eggs."

The inspector nodded and continued on to the cattle and pigs. "Two cows. You'll need them to work the land." Then he looked at the sow and her litter.

Mama pointed to the pigs. "She has a litter of eleven. We work hard in the fields, so we eat a lot of meat."

The inspector turned to the young soldier. "Make a note. These people need only one pig to butcher. They will deliver ten grown pigs to the authorities in November."

Mama's voice firmed. "We worked long hours and spent money to feed those pigs. Our cost is more than one pig is worth."

The inspector smirked. "Consider it a donation to the Fatherland." Then he speared Mama with a hostile stare. "What have you hidden from me? The penalties for evading contributions to the Third Reich are severe."

Mama took a short step toward the man. "Nothing."

He motioned to the soldier. “Take the child with you to inspect the house.”

My stomach tightened like I might be ill as I followed the young soldier inside to search all the rooms. He poked and stretched to see everything. He was a pleasant young man, tall and thin. Blond hair peeked from beneath his military cap. What would he do if he found the little pig? When we got back to the kitchen entry, he smiled at me and wrote something on the clipboard.

I had just begun to relax as he prepared to leave. A sudden sound from the cabinet under the sink sent chills through me.

Oink.

The soldier started at the sound and glanced at the cabinet. My whole body froze. What would happen to us now? Would the soldier shoot us? I couldn’t move.

He took a step toward the cabinet and stopped. Then he turned back with a smile for me and walked to the door. “You should tell your mother to fix that noise under the sink before it causes a lot of trouble.”

Then he stepped outside and reported to the Inspector. “Nothing inside.”

Tears of relief flooded my eyes. I’d met a Nazi who could be kind. I ran to clutch Mama’s skirt as the pair moved up the street to inspect another house.

* * *

We seemed to be getting our life under control as July approached. Our flock of chickens grew to provide two or three dozen eggs more than we would need each week. Papa frequently took a basket of them to work and sold most of them to people who passed through the train station. Ration stamps weren't used, so he got a good price. City people didn't ask questions. They were happy to find fresh eggs.

"Why don't we sell them at the market?" I asked as I brought in the basket of eggs I'd gathered.

Papa tugged at his ear. "Because the Nazis might decide we have more chickens than we need. They would force us to give them to the authorities. I keep the transactions secret because they are considered black market. You must never tell people about this"

Our rabbit population grew and the large garden provided food for them. I was happy when one of them showed up on our dinner table on Sundays.

I continued to sell our produce at the market. Every Friday was spent gathering the fresh vegetables, and I accompanied Oma to the marketplace on Saturday mornings. When they ripened, I added currants and gooseberries to my offerings. By the end of summer, I had beets. kohlrabi, apples, pears, and plums.

After a few weeks, Oma spread another blanket beside hers. "You're selling enough to need more room. Put your wares here. I'll still be close by"

Customers already recognized me, since I was the youngest vendor at the market. I swelled with pride when they stopped to buy my produce. Sales increased and I rarely had to ask Oma for help. We soon had to bring bigger loads of produce, and I stretched to stand taller when I gave the money to Mama.

* * *

When the wheat was ready to harvest, Roger spent the day with Opa. Papa used the mowing machine with a catch plate behind the blade. The cows pulled the machine, and he enlisted

Mama to sit behind him. The machine cut the stalks. When enough wheat accumulated, Mama dropped it on the ground.

Oma and I followed on foot to pick it up and tie it into a shock. We used heavy twine to wrap around the wheat and hold it together. Then we stood the bundle on end so it could be easily gathered and loaded on a wagon.

"The mill needs them presented this way to glean and separate the grain from the straw," she explained. "All the farmers do it the same way."

The hot weather tormented us while clouds of dust from the dry wheat straw made me sneeze. Sweat dripped in my eyes, and my dress was soon soaked. My back hurt from bending to pick up the loose wheat stalks. Oma appeared to have the same problems, but she didn't complain as much as I did.

When we tied the bundles, the strings broke frequently, and I had to replace them and tie the bundle of wheat again.

"Why does it break so often?" I whined.

Oma shrugged. "The strings are old and rotted. We need to buy new ones."

I didn't say anything, but it occurred to me it would have been better to think of this before the harvest.

Oma must have read my mind. "Your father said he would buy new strings next year."

When the field was bare, we loaded the wheat on our wagon. I accompanied Papa to the mill. Each shock was placed separately on the broad conveyor belt, which carried the bundles into the machine. Inside, it separated the grains of wheat from the straw and yielded several bags of grain. Papa loaded the straw on our wagon to use at home. It made good bedding for the pigs and rabbits.

The mill took one bag as tariff for separating it, and a Nazi official took half of what was left. They used the Catholic Circle Hall to store the share they took from the farmers as a tariff to repay the cost of "liberating" us from France.

Papa took what remained to a mill in Sarre Union and had it ground into flour to make bread. We'd always had enough to last for the next year.

He returned with less, and his shoulders slumped when he brought the small bags in. "The Nazis are trying to starve us."

He hung his cap on its peg. "This won't last until next year's harvest. We'll have to eat less bread."

Chapter 25

September arrived, and the school year started. Nazis had been busy messing up our lives over summer. Everything changed. Separate Catholic and Lutheran schools had been abolished, so we attended classes together. The first three grades met in the Catholic building, and the upper classes met in a room at City Hall. We would have full days of instruction this year.

Papa pushed back his chair with a loud scraping noise when we finished breakfast. I'd be in second grade, and it was time for me to leave for the first day of school. He waggled a finger at me. "Don't let them make you a Catholic. They believe their pope is like God."

Mama reached across the table and laid a hand on his arm. "I don't think they'll teach religion. Nazis don't seem to care much about that."

Papa glared at her. "They cared enough to stop paying pastors and priests. They want us to be like Hitler. I don't want my children taught what Catholics believe. It's not right."

I looked at the clock. "I'll be late."

Papa's chair crashed against the wall as he rose. "Don't play with any Catholic boys. The neighbors will talk about us."

Mama shook her head, her lips pressed shut.

I ran all the way and arrived just before the bell rang. I knew my classmates from the Lutheran school and recognized most of the Catholic students but didn't know them well.

We had a new teacher who looked old, and his hair needed to be combed. He walked with a limp as he passed down the aisle to stare at each of us. Then he returned to his desk and introduced himself.

"You will address me as Herr Klein. Your previous school year was cut short, and you didn't have time to cover everything you needed to learn. We have a lot of work to do, so let's get busy."

He separated us by grades and assigned seats for all the students. My desk was on the aisle in the second row next to a Catholic girl named Annette. She stayed quiet and paid attention to the teacher.

Annette and I talked during recess. She told me her family had sought refuge in Domfessel when we were evacuated. She'd attended the Catholic school last year and hoped Herr Klein would be nicer than the lady who taught there.

We were both a little standoffish because we'd each been taught to beware of the other's religion. Still, we made an effort to become friends.

During the afternoon, one of the boys used a few French words to answer a question. Herr Klein called him to the front of the room. "This village is now part of Germany. We are all citizens of the Third Reich. We will not allow the pollution of our language by the use of French words. Now, answer me again using proper German."

We got the message. We must learn to be good little Nazis.

* * *

On Saturday, I accompanied Mama to pick blackberries and boysenberries. My bucket was almost full by the time we started home. "It's heavy, Mama."

She flashed me a sideways glance. "It would be heavier if you hadn't eaten so many."

Since I was all too guilty, I avoided looking at her.

Back home, she cooked the berries, adding sugar and spices. The sweet smell of simmering fruit soon filled the kitchen. Heat from the stove and steam from the berries had Mama wiping sweat from her forehead with the tail of her apron. The mixture went into jars as delicious jelly that would last through the winter and beyond. I stayed close to lick the spoons.

Roger stood beside me, so I was forced to share with him.

Later Mama made a trip to the bakery. Since we were trying to make our flour last longer, she bought bread. When she returned, her happy mood had vanished. "The baker told me the Nazis decreed all Jews must now wear a yellow Star of David sewn on their outer garment. That makes them easy to identify if the government wants to harass them."

"Why, Mama?" I asked.

"The Nazis hate all Jews. Papa heard it on BBC at Mr. Schmidt's house. They're already sending Jews in the east to camps. They will become slave laborers for Germany."

I still didn't understand why the Nazis hated Jews and had bad dreams about Jews becoming slaves.

A few weeks later, Papa announced during breakfast how we would spend our Saturday. "The potatoes are ready to harvest."

My heart sank. I'd planned to go play with Maria.

"Mina, gather the baskets and trowels," Papa said. "Irene, put some old clothes on Roger. He can go with us to the field. I'll harness the cows and load the plow."

A half hour later, we climbed on the wagon, and the cows made their way out of the village to our fields.

Papa unloaded the plow and hitched the cows to pull it. The patient animals plodded along each side of the row, the plow ripping a trench in the soil and uprooting the potatoes.

Mama and I followed, stooping to put them in our baskets. The plow hadn't succeeded in exposing all the potatoes, and we used our trowels to dig out those hiding under the dirt.

Roger tried to help us dig. He put a half dozen potatoes in the basket before he lost interest and started to throw dirt clods.

Bright sunshine had driven away the cool morning, and I started to sweat. Dirt from digging potatoes out of the soil filled the space under my broken fingernails. I wanted to rest, but Mama said no. A short break at our two-liter water jug gave me a little relief. Mama always put a cup of coffee in the big jug to make the drink taste better after it got warm.

Papa waved a hand and aimed a stern glance at me. "Hey, back to work."

Roger ran away, and my feet dragged when I had to go catch him and bring him back. Then I tried to convince him. "You have to stay here."

Papa finished plowing the rows and came to help with collecting the potatoes. He patted me on the back. "Good job. Go take care of your brother before he finds more mischief."

After an outdoor lunch, I kept Roger out of trouble while Mama and Papa gathered the rest of the crop. We worried the Nazis might take half of our harvest, but Papa took a back road, and the cows pulled the loaded wagon home without being seen.

The sun sank toward the horizon as Papa stopped the wagon next to our kitchen door. "We need to hurry. If our luck holds, we can hide them and avoid the Nazis taking our crop."

We could lock the storage room. Its sunken floor would stay cool but not freeze for the entire winter. Root crops would be edible well into the next summer.

* * *

Cool gray skies gave way to colder temperatures and sunshine. A hard freeze appeared to be imminent, so Papa decided to harvest the remainder of our little plot of ground by the house. He dug a pit under the shed beside the wood pile and covered the bottom with straw.

At breakfast, he announced, “It’s time to harvest our garden.”

The whole family spent two days collecting vegetables to store in the pit. Then Papa covered them with another thick layer of straw for insulation. Next he added more dirt to hold the straw in place. He left a large hole in the center so we could reach the vegetables when we needed them. A heavy wood block covered the opening. Our food would stay cool and dry and protected from freezing during the winter. We left a row of Brussel sprouts in the garden that could be harvested in cold weather, even after it snowed.

Several big jars of dry beans already rested on our kitchen shelves along with two large crocks of sauerkraut preserved for the winter months. Mama shredded and pickled a basket of turnips. They’d spice up a meal.

We were all tired from our long day’s work, but it wasn’t finished. Papa walked to the center of the village to buy a few bottles of wine, and Mama went to milk the cows.

While Roger took a nap, I slipped outside to feed the rabbits. Coming back, I stopped to watch Mama sitting on a stool with her head pressed against the cow’s flank, stripping milk from its udder into a bucket she would bring inside to strain through a cloth and feed the family.

She looked tired, and I felt sorry for her. “Why do you always have to milk the cows? Doesn’t Papa want to help you?”

Her chin raised and she let out a long sigh. “Your father is too gruff and impatient. He frightens them, and they won’t give milk.”

“How do you make her stand still?” I asked.

Her shoulders sagged. “It takes patience. Don’t ever learn to milk a cow. If you do, you’ll be doing it for the rest of your life.”

Chapter 26

One cold November morning, Papa rode his bicycle to Sarrealbe and returned in a bad humor. “There’s no real coffee to be found, so I bought ersatz coffee instead. It’s made of chicory and roasted barley.”

Mama rolled her eyes. “The Nazis have taken everything. Chicory and barley doesn’t sound good, but we can see what it tastes like.”

After the pot had boiled, I asked to try it.

“You may as well. It’s not real coffee.”

She poured me a half cup, and I took a sip. It was bitter, so I made a face.

Mama nodded. “I thought so.”

We learned to drink it. Making do would soon be necessary for other necessities as well.

After the first hard freeze, it was time to slaughter and put up the meat from the hogs. The Nazis had allowed us to keep one, and we’d hidden another. Papa wanted to have both of them cut up and out of sight before the Nazis came to collect the rest of the litter.

“Everyone to bed early,” he commanded. “We start work two hours before daybreak so our nosy mayor sees nothing amiss when he comes by to tend his cattle.”

I wasn’t sleepy, but I knew there was no sense in arguing, so I went to bed.

Opa and Oma came to help the next morning. By sunrise, we had two carcasses hanging from hooks in the shed. Papa dismembered one first, and we brought it in the kitchen to be ground into sausage or to be salted or smoked. With only one pig visible, the mayor wouldn't notice anything wrong if he got curious and stopped to chat when he came by our house.

A skim of ice covered the cattle's water trough when we started work, and I shivered in the cold breeze. Oma and I dragged the offal down to the tree line bordering the river to get it out of sight. Then I carried the chunks of meat into the kitchen. I got a short break to tend Roger, but it didn't last long.

"You can turn the crank to grind sausage while you watch your brother," Mama said.

An hour after daylight, Papa decided it would be safe to allow everyone to rest for a few minutes. "Mina, put food on the table, and we'll eat something."

We ate, but we didn't stop work long enough for me to feel rested.

Shortly after we resumed, the mayor strolled down the path and came over to see the carcass hanging in the shed. My knees felt weak, and my hands shook as I recalled my terror when our hidden pig had grunted while the soldier stood nearby.

He tugged at his wool cap. "Looks like hog-killing time. You'll have plenty of pork to last through the winter."

"We'll have all the inspector allowed us to have," Papa said. "It's not enough to last a whole year."

The mayor's fat belly jiggled when he chuckled. "Ah, yes, but you can feel satisfaction that you're helping to feed our noble troops that defend us from the Red Horde."

Papa's voice was firm when he replied, "I'll do my duty, but you can't blame me for being concerned about my family suffering from the loss of food we normally eat."

The mayor's response sounded stern. "We must all suffer a little to support the German state."

Papa turned back to the carcass hanging from the big hook. "Guess I need to get him cut up. We must save what we have."

The mayor turned away, and I cringed when he looked as if he might enter our kitchen where Mama worked to preserve the other hog. I exhaled when he walked away to the pasture where he kept his cattle. Hopefully he hadn't noticed anything that would lead him to believe we had butchered more than one hog.

Later Papa hauled the hams and sides of bacon to Opa's smokehouse. He kept the rest at home so the meat wouldn't all be in one place if the Nazis decided to take it. By nightfall the whole family was exhausted, but the job was done. My arms cramped and felt like they were ready to fall off from turning the grinder.

"At least we'll have meat for the coming year," Mama said as she slumped into a kitchen chair.

The conversation continued without me. I fell into bed and slept.

* * *

After a few clear days, the rains came. The temperature dropped, and the moisture turned to light snow. During the evening, Papa visited the Rolfs to listen to the news on their radio. I heard him kick the step at our kitchen door to remove snow from his shoes when he returned with a newspaper tucked under his arm.

He took a seat on the couch. "The German Army is advancing across Russia and destroying the Red Armies as they go. The Nazis are congratulating themselves on Hitler's decision to invade. It seems nothing can stand up against their *blitzkrieg*."

Mama pointed to the newspaper. "I thought the Germans closed all the French papers."

Papa held it up. "They did. This is an underground publication from the French Resistance. It's written in German. It doesn't say the same things as the Nazis try to make us believe. It says Nazi casualties are high in their march across Russia."

"I feel sorry for the poor soldiers," Mama said.

He ran a finger down the page. "It also says British raids are disrupting manufacturing. That's not what the Nazis claim."

She sighed. "The Nazis only tell us what they want us to hear."

Papa pointed to the paper. "The publishers would be sent to one of the camps or shot if the Nazis found them. We would be punished for reading it." He looked directly at me. "You must never tell anyone we saw a newspaper like this. We would be in bad trouble."

"What is the Resistance?" I asked.

"Groups of French citizens who don't want to be ruled by Nazis," he said. "They call themselves *The Maquis*. They do things to make trouble for Germany. The Gestapo makes an example of them when they're caught. They do it to frighten others into accepting German rule. We do not want them to make an example of us."

After two weeks of relative calm, Mr. Rolf practically jumped with joy when he rushed into our kitchen. "The Japanese have launched a raid on the United States at Pearl Harbor, Hawaii. Their attack came as a complete surprise, and they sank a large number of navy ships. Several were battleships. The devastation was terrible. The Americans lost a big part of their fleet, but Roosevelt will fight back."

Papa jumped to his feet. "Germany and Japan are allies. This could change everything."

I sat in a corner of the room puzzled and unnoticed. Who were these Americans? Where did they live? Why would they want to fight Germany? I knew Japan was on the other side of the world, but the Japanese hadn't attacked France.

The next day Papa's eyes glowed when he came back from visiting neighbors. "America declared war on Germany. They joined Great Britain and the Free French to fight the Nazis."

Mama's words tumbled out. "That's wonderful, but they're all the way across the ocean. It could take years before they send an army to fight Germany."

"Hans Koeppel says President Roosevelt has been preparing to enter this war for a long time. He's been giving ships to the British and building an air force at home. Now it appears the Japanese have made the decision for him. The United States is a huge country. They will make a difference in the war against Germany."

Mama wiped her hands on her apron. "I wonder what they'll do about us."

Later Papa removed part of a row of firewood and dug another pit to hold our cured and salted pork. After covering it with layers of straw, planks and dirt, he replaced the firewood. "This will be our reserve."

Mama ran a hand through her hair. "In the meantime, we still need to survive while the Nazis try to take everything we have."

Chapter 27

I had dozed off momentarily when the airliner hit a patch of rough air. Little Paul was awake and starting to fret. After I yawned to overcome the drowsy feeling, I fed him a bottle. Outside my small window, layers of clouds filled the sky. The baby finished his milk, and I took him to the bathroom for a diaper change. Then he slept again.

My thoughts touched briefly on what promised to be my exciting future before returning to the war-torn years of my childhood.

Soon after Pearl Harbor, the Nazis published an announcement requiring all young people to report to the authorities for enrollment in the *Reichschaftsarbeit* when they turned eighteen. They would work in Germany for a six-month term either in a factory making war materials or on farms. Left unsaid was they would receive training that would make them better soldiers when they were taken by the German Army or when they were forced to work in factories to produce materials for the war effort.

Many evaded this service with the help of their parents. They made their way to Vichy France to hide, often under assumed names. If they were caught, the Nazis sent some to work as slave labor in German industry. Some were shot. I prayed that Uncle George stayed safe.

Unfortunately, many young men complied with Nazi orders. Their future proved to be even more difficult. Most of them eventually served as cannon fodder on the Russian front.

A determined few made their way into the French Underground. The organization helped them find ways to remain hidden, and they became part of an important movement to cooperate with the British and work toward liberating France from the Nazi yoke.

* * *

As the year 1942 dawned, winter hit Kaschel hard. Heavy snow blanketed the village. Continued cold weather prevented it from melting. Then, even more of the white stuff fell on us. Playing with my sled was fun, but the dirty, trampled snow made chores more difficult. Walking through this mess back and forth to school became treacherous.

Mr. Klein made my days difficult. He seemed to have taken a dislike to me. My grades were good. I was the best student in my German language class, and my performance in mathematics was near the top. Nevertheless, he found reasons to single me out for criticism.

His brows furrowed when he speared me with a harsh look. "You don't sound enthusiastic when you sing our national anthem."

Unable to think of a suitable answer, I shrugged.

Mr. Klein frowned and pursed his lips. "Your salute is sloppy, and I can barely hear your voice when you pledge *Heil Hitler*."

I stammered before I found an answer. "I'll try to say it louder."

He ended the conversation, but he continued to direct unfriendly looks at me.

One morning I forgot to bring part of my homework, and Mr. Klein refused to accept my excuse. "Perhaps an hour of detention will help you remember in the future. I'll expect you to finish the work and hand it to me after school."

I fumed, but I made the effort to sound meek when I delivered the assignment.

Back home, Papa made my upcoming birthday an excuse to heap more responsibilities on me. "You'll soon be eight. It's time you learned to cook. Your mother will be working in the fields with me when spring arrives, and you're old enough to have dinner ready when we get home. Mama will teach you."

I should have been happy to learn something new, but I'd already figured out cooking was a lot of work.

Mama tried to go slow and teach me a little at a time. "You have to knead the bread dough until it is smooth. Have your oven hot when you put the pan inside."

I hadn't mastered how to start the fire in its box yet.

"There's a lot to keep track of," Mama admitted.

I learned to peel potatoes, trim wilted leaves from the cabbage, and put the chunks of pork Papa had cut to size into a skillet with melted lard to give it flavor and prevent sticking. My first try at cutting up potatoes and cabbage to the right size didn't turn out well.

Papa frowned when he looked at his plate. "Too much lard in the skillet. The potatoes and cabbage should be cut to bite size."

At least he hadn't complained about the way I'd boiled the field peas. "I'll try to get it right next time."

Mama didn't comment, and Roger ate his portion without complaint.

After I'd made several attempts, Papa finally admitted his meal was edible. I took that as a compliment and kept secret my pride in having mastered the task.

When my birthday finally arrived, Mama baked a cake with the last of our monthly sugar ration. The simple pound cake made the whole kitchen smell good. It was delicious, and I smacked my lips over each bite. Oma and Opa were invited, and everyone enjoyed a small piece of the rare treat. Sweets had almost disappeared from our table.

After we finished the cake, Opa waved a hand at me. “Come with me. There is something in the woodshed you need to see.”

Puzzled, I followed him outside. When we reached the woodpile, he pulled away a piece of canvas covering something. A bright green bicycle leaned against the stack of wood.

Opa grinned at me. “Happy birthday.”

I didn’t know what to say. It was so beautiful. I reached out to touch it then pulled back my hand.

Opa laughed. “Go ahead and push it inside. Oma and I figured a big girl like you needs a bicycle to get you around the village.”

I took the handlebars and pushed it inside while Opa held the kitchen door open for me. Mama and Papa were momentarily unable to speak when they saw it.

Finally, Mama reached out to touch the metal frame. “Where did you find it? I haven’t seen one for sale since we returned to Kaschel.”

Opa took his seat at the table. “The preacher had it since his son left home. It was starting to rust and needed some work. He sold it to me cheap. I lubricated and adjusted the moving parts and sanded off the rust. I’ve had the green paint since before the evacuation.”

I came down from the clouds long enough to give each of my grandparents a hug. “Thank you. I love it.”

I had to wait for the snow to melt before I tried to ride my new bike. Papa volunteered to hold it upright while I learned how to balance and pedal.

“No,” I insisted. “I’ll learn by myself.”

I pushed the bicycle around the corner to the next street where I found a small hill with a gentle slope. After sitting on the seat and placing one foot on a pedal, I pushed off to coast down the grade. The bicycle promptly turned over. I sprawled on the ground and collected a few bruises.

My first several tries were failures. Then I managed to balance it to coast down the slope for a few meters. It overturned again when I tried to stop. After each fall, I'd push the bicycle back to the top of the hill.

When I'd been gone for a half hour, Papa came to check on me. "Sure you don't need any help?"

I shook my head. "I can do it myself."

He shrugged and left me alone.

It took me a few days to learn how to mount, coast, stop, and dismount without falling. Then I'd push the bicycle back uphill to try again. Finally, I learned how to pedal without overturning. Riding was more fun after I didn't have to push the bike up the hills.

Toward winter's end, I'd worn out another pair of shoes, and my parents didn't act very happy.

"You are a shoe murderer," Mama said.

Soon Papa came home from a trip to Sarre Union with a new pair of shoes for me. They were a size too large, allowing my feet a chance to grow into them. Their high tops made them suitable for walking in the snow. "You'd better take care of this pair," he said. "I was lucky to find them. The Nazis won't give us another ration stamp for shoes until next year."

The following day, Mama returned from the bakery, shaking snow from her boots and carrying a loaf of black bread. "We're running low on white flour, so I bought bread from the baker. This was the only kind he had. He says it's popular in Germany. It tastes good and keeps for a long time."

Papa shook his head. "I heard about it. It's what they feed the troops these days. The stationmaster says someone told him they mix in ground up bones to make the flour go further."

"Since I didn't have a choice," Mama said. "We'll eat it for dinner tonight.'

Later we gathered around the table, and she served baked pork ribs nestled in a bowl of sauerkraut. She gave me a glass of water with a little bit of wine in it which made me feel almost grown up. My favorite meal. A small plate held thin slices of the black bread.

Papa tasted it first. He wrinkled his nose like it smelled bad. "I've tasted worse. It's not as good as our French bread, but it looks like we'll have to get used to it."

Roger reached to grab a slice and munched it while waving his hand toward the sauerkraut. He tried to say something I couldn't understand because his mouth was full.

Mama slid the bread plate to me. "Try some."

My jaw hardened. "No, thank you."

"You need to eat bread," she said.

"No, thank you," I answered. "I'm not going to eat ground-up bones."

Mama's voice softened. "That's not really what's in it."

I squared my shoulders and leaned toward her. "I'll do without bread."

She said nothing, and we ate our dinner in silence.

After the meal, Papa told us more news of the war. "German broadcasts continue to claim Nazi forces moving toward Moscow are meeting only light resistance. The underground papers tell a different story."

"What's the real story?" Mama asked.

"The Wehrmacht is suffering casualties at an alarming rate. The Russians fight like devils to protect their homeland. Neither side appears to let casualties affect their strategy."

Papa went to work at the train station each day, and Mama continued her struggle to care for Roger and me and to keep food on our table. Approaching three years old, Roger filled the house with energy and curiosity. Nothing worried him.

I just wanted to be carefree, play with my friends, and ride my bike. But I worried about rationing, cold weather, the mayor, Sergeant Schnabel, and my Nazi teacher.

In addition to all that, I couldn't shake the fear that a stray bomb might fall on us.

Chapter 28

Snow and cold wind gave way grudgingly to warmer air and showers. With the arrival of spring, Papa told us we'd need to make full use of our fields this year. He figured the Nazis would demand a bigger share to support their troops in Russia. Also, the United States entry into the war posed a threat of more fighting in the west.

My family made changes in our duties to fulfill Papa's plan. He spent the daylight hours in the fields after his work at the station, and Mama helped him most of the time. I took over caring for Roger, cooking, and doing the housework. As an active three-year-old, Roger required a lot of looking after.

The task of preparing meals for the evening fell to me. It didn't always go well. I learned by making mistakes.

One evening, Papa's voice thundered, "You forgot to add salt."

The next evening, he complained, "This tastes terrible. You must have salted it twice."

I couldn't think of a satisfactory answer.

My cooking didn't measure up to the meals Mama prepared. Frequently, something burned while I was distracted by rescuing Roger from trouble he'd found. Given all his uncontrolled energy, it happened often.

Even if I felt sorry for myself, one chore never fell to me. Mama found time to milk the cows every day. She evidently meant it when she'd told me, "Never learn how."

As the weather warmed, Mr. Schmidt brought us more news from the hidden radio in his basement, telling us what was happening in the world. He always pulled the blackout curtains and locked the doors before tuning in to news from the BBC.

People who were caught listening to foreign broadcasts had their radios confiscated. Some had been sent to work at forced labor in Germany. I understood why we must never talk about this in public and kept it secret. Roger was too young to understand, so we didn't speak of it in his presence.

Papa came home with surprising news of the war one evening. "The British bombed Cologne last night with a force of a thousand airplanes. The city is at a standstill with massive damage to their war industry. The bombing covered most of the city, the commercial center and even residential areas."

"Where did you hear this?" Mama asked.

"Two different stations," Papa said. "Nazi radio reports light damage with dozens of bombers shot down. BBC reports minor aircraft losses with major damage to the city."

I wondered where Cologne was. It sounded like a lot of Nazis lived there.

After we finished planting our crops, Mama spent more time at home, and I was relieved of some of my duties. Thankfully, she took over most of the cooking.

During the summer vacation Papa found more chores to fill my idle time. "I want to leave the grass and harvest the hay field where we let the cattle graze. With planting done, I'm not working them. You can take them to the idle fields owned by the village."

"That's almost a whole kilometer away," I protested. "The cows might wander into someone else's fields and eat their crops."

"Not if you stay with them and make them graze where they're supposed to stay."

I found several more reasons why all this effort on my part wasn't needed, but he didn't change his plan. I was stuck watching the cows eat grass each day.

It was a lonely job. They didn't wander very often, and it was easy to drive them away from the crops, but they didn't provide much company. Fortunately, Annette visited me occasionally, and the monotony was relieved. We dreamed up dozens of things we could do when classes resumed. She got a soccer ball for Christmas, and we planned to play with it during the day. I wasn't much good at sports, but it would be a lot more fun than tending cattle.

* * *

A few weeks later, Papa's face was ashen when he came home from listening to forbidden radio broadcasts. He sent me to the kitchen to polish silverware, but I peeked around the door and listened as he talked to Mama.

"The Nazis are rounding up Jews by the thousands and sending them to a concentration camp at Auschwitz," he said. "They said the reason is to give them better accommodations and allow them to work for the Fatherland."

"They certainly need better places to live," Mama said. "I've heard the conditions are terrible where they're at now."

Papa grimaced and shook his head. "You don't understand. They're not going there to live. It's mostly Jews, and a few intellectuals and civic leaders. They're going to Auschwitz to be murdered. The Nazis have built huge poison gas chambers to kill hundreds at a time and ovens to burn the bodies."

I watched from the doorway and saw Mama turn away and swallow hard. Her eyes were closed.

Papa continued. "That's not all. They're also sending anyone the Nazis don't like."

Mama turned back to face him. "German people will never let them do that. It's inhuman. They'll revolt."

Papa made a choking noise. "They're keeping it secret from the people. The camp has a strong fence around it to prevent anyone from entering. We're only able to learn about it through the underground radio."

"I can't believe people won't know what's happening there."

"They live under the same rules we do here. If you ask questions or say you don't approve, you'll likely be sent to join them."

I listened in horror. It was hard to believe anyone could be so cruel. Visions of people being driven into death chambers flooded my unwilling mind. My stomach heaved, and I made a mad dash to get outside before the vomit spewed from my mouth.

* * *

Our family spent several gloomy days trying to rid ourselves of these visions. Keeping up with all the work needed to make our living on the small farm seemed to be the best way to fight the horror. I began to welcome the solitude of herding the cows to graze in their small space. Alone, in this isolated pasture beside the forest, I didn't need to put up a brave front or fool anyone about my true feelings. I brought the cattle home each day when I heard the noon whistle at the cement plant.

A week later, Papa returned from listening to the Rolf's radio on a rainy evening. The news he brought with him lifted our spirits. "American aviators have arrived in Great Britain. Help is on the way."

If the Americans really came, I hoped they wouldn't be mean like the Nazis.

In late August, one of the warmest days of the year, Papa came home with bad news that would directly affect us. Men between the ages of eighteen and thirty-five, who lived in Alsace and Moselle, were subject to being drafted into the German army. Unmarried women could be taken as well.

"No!" Mama cried. "We're not Germans. You already served in the French Army against the Nazis. It's not right."

Papa thrust out his hands, palms up. "We have no choice. Hitler may have bit off more than he can chew. He needs more cannon fodder."

"But you have a family," she said. "They already take half of everything we produce on the farm. We didn't ask for this war."

"He won't ask us if we want to serve. It will be mandatory."

I huddled on the couch, listening to the conversation. Papa was French. He couldn't fight for the Nazis. When I realized they could force him to go in the army, I sank lower on the cushion and held my head in my hands.

The whole family sat silent and subdued for a time. Even Roger seemed to realize something was wrong. Our despair lasted through the evening, and I was unable to sleep.

* * *

We did our second and last hay cutting the next day. Since I was eight years old, I wasn't tall enough to throw the hay onto the top of a stack on the wagon. However, Papa said I was just the right size to climb on the hay to trample and compress it.

Papa cut it, and we spent the next three days turning it to dry, raking it into mounds, and loading it on the wagon. The attic space was crammed full when we finished filling it with new hay.

We spent the next few weeks harvesting other crops and preparing them to last through another winter. The biggest job was digging out potatoes. After two days of bending, shoveling and wiping off dirt that clung to them, we finally finished the harvest.

School started at the end of summer, and I entered the third grade. That made me one of the big kids in our three-grade classroom. I hadn't seen much of Annette during summer, and we had a lot of catching up to do. A new teacher, Mrs. Diedendorph, greeted us. She was a heavyset old woman and wore a black dress. Dark hair sprinkled with gray fell to her shoulders. She laid down the rules we would live by. Any hope we might be spared the Nazi patriotic requirements were quickly dashed.

"Each morning, you will continue with your salute and oath of loyalty to the Fuehrer and the Nazi Party," she announced. "You will show proper respect at all times."

Most students looked down at their desks and listened in silence. All of us were obviously disappointed, but showing it would get us in trouble.

Chapter 29

Papa's face was drawn as he stamped snow from his boots on an early November afternoon. I could tell something was wrong. He didn't say anything to me as he hung up his coat and walked into the kitchen where Mama was busy preparing dinner.

"The Americans and British have invaded at several points in North Africa. The Vichy French forces are opposing them. They're fighting for the Germans."

"The Germans probably forced them to do it," Mama said.

"It's too late to curry favor. The Nazis will surely occupy the rest of France anyway. They are massing troops to move in and take control."

The war was too complicated for me to understand. "We're French, but the Nazis turned us into Germans. Vichy France gave up, and they're still French but fighting for the Nazis. The British are supposed to be on our side, but they attacked our colonies in Africa. Now the Vichy French Army is fighting the British and Americans." Frustration sent my hands flying into the air. "Which side are we on?"

A surprised grin erased the lines on Papa's face. "You seem to understand what's going on better than I do. If we want to be free, we'd better hope the British and Americans win."

Three days later, German troops occupied Vichy France.

"The reason is the French didn't put up a good fight against the British and American invaders in North Africa," Papa said. "The entire country is now controlled by Nazis. But not all Frenchmen have surrendered to their rule. The French Resistance, the *Maquis,* have stepped up their efforts to hurt the Germans."

I still didn't understand this war.

The next day Papa brought home another underground newspaper. It was written in our patois, and I only needed help with a few big words. The front page reported the British had parachuted crates of weapons and communications equipment at prearranged points during a dark night. A British ranger accompanied this latest drop to teach the Résistance how to use the weapons and advise them about targets that were easy to hit and hurt the Nazi war effort.

Papa read over my shoulder. "I'm glad we still have Frenchmen willing to fight. It's been too easy for the Nazis so far. With British help, they might be able to hurt the Germans."

I read farther down the page. "It says the *Maquis* sends information about what the Nazis are doing to the British. It helps both countries."

He scratched his head and stared out the window for a moment. "If they blew a few railroad bridges, the Nazis would have heartburn. They ship a lot of military goods by rail."

"What happens to the *Maquis* if the Germans catch them?" I asked.

Papa frowned and looked at his hands. "Sometimes they torture them to get more information about the others. Then the Nazis kill them."

I shuddered at the thought. "The Resistance must have a lot of brave people."

Mama wrung her hands. "I hope George isn't involved with them."

* * *

Two weeks later, Mama brought bad news after a visit with Oma. "The Reis boy up the street received a draft notice for military service. He has ten days to report. Mrs. Reis begged him to run away to Vichy France, but he told her his family would be sent to a concentration camp in the east if he failed to report."

Papa rubbed his chin with a rough hand. "It's a terrible choice. He has no option. The Nazis would surely do it."

"What will become of him?" Mama asked.

"They'll probably send him to the Eastern Front. Russians are killing German soldiers by the tens of thousands." He exhaled as if he'd never take another breath.

We ate dinner in silence. Hans Reis was a good neighbor. I'd always looked up to him.

We heard of others, two or three each month, which were drafted and left quietly. Family members could only grieve.

* * *

Wind-driven snow flew through the open door when Mama returned from the post office. Her eyes filled with tears, and her hands shook as she laid an official-looking envelope on the table.

A chill fell over me. "What is it, Mama?"

"It's from the Nazi commissioner in Strasbourg. It's addressed to your father. He'll open it when he gets home from work."

"Did he get drafted?"

"I don't know, dear. Your father will open it."

Paralyzed with fear, I hurried to sit down before my legs failed to support me. The memory of our struggle without Papa in Wolfskirchen had scarred me forever, and this felt the same. Germany's war was now huge, and the soldiers suffered.

Everyone talked about the horrible fighting on the Eastern Front. If the Nazis sent Papa there, he might never return.

Mama sat at the table, holding her head in her hands in silence. She made no move to start dinner. When Roger waked from his nap and cried, I went to tend him and bring his small chamber pot. Hopefully, he'd soon be tall enough to use the outhouse. Then I found a few of his toys and played with him. Mama's fear would have disturbed him if she came to him now.

The wood was consumed while we waited, and the room cooled. Mama didn't seem to notice, so I finally dragged in a few big sticks to feed the fire.

We'd been sitting at the table for hours, trying to deal with the frightening possibilities of the letter, when Papa stormed through the door and shook snow from his cap. He pulled off his heavy coat and turned to look at us.

"What's wrong?"

Mama handed him the letter. He swallowed hard and sat beside her before opening it. His face had paled, and his fingers fumbled at the envelope.

I wanted to run to him and tear away the letter, but I couldn't force myself to move.

Finally, he removed a single page and held it up to read. His shoulders sagged as he laid the letter on the table. "I'm to report for induction into the Wehrmacht in two weeks. I'm fortunate it wasn't the *Waffen SS*. Some have been sent to join that gang of murderers."

I slid off the side of my chair and retreated to the corner of the room where I sought refuge when something bad happened. I found myself unable to say anything.

Mama sprang from her chair, her voice rising in pitch. "You can't go. We'll run away to the south of France. They won't find you there."

"The Nazis occupy the whole country. We couldn't avoid them."

"We'll go to Switzerland, then. They're neutral."

Papa shook his head. "The Swiss intend to stay neutral. If they accepted us, the Nazis would accuse them of taking sides in the war."

Mama sank into a chair, hands covering her face. "You can run away by yourself. You'll be able to hide."

Papa began to shake when he spoke to us, his voice barely a whisper. "If I did that, they would send all of you away. You'd probably end up in one of the death camps. I might live, but I couldn't live with myself without you."

Mama's body collapsed into a chair. "We have to do something."

She began to sob, and Roger came to her with big questions in his eyes. I wrapped my arm around her shoulder.

Papa rose and came to kneel beside us, gathering us all in his arms. "We're not beaten yet."

Chapter 30

The next day Papa went to his job as usual. Mama didn't talk much as she made our porridge and cleaned the kitchen. I went off to school feeling like a thick fog surrounded me. The only cheerful member of the family was Roger. He didn't understand what happened.

My mind wandered during math class, and Mrs. Diedendorph summoned me to the front of the room to lecture me. I didn't even try to explain. Her long speeches on why we must do our duty for the Fatherland were fresh in my memory. I wasn't ready to hear it again. Papa didn't want anything to do with the Third Reich. In any case, Mrs. Diedendorph didn't care if I learned arithmetic or not. She just wanted me to be a good little Nazi.

Sergeant Schnabel stopped me on the way home from school. "Tell your father we are proud he has a chance to serve the Fatherland. Remind him that slackers face punishment."

I clutched my book and walked faster. The Nazi sergeant was telling me they were watching Papa. They wouldn't give him a chance to run.

At the end of the day, Papa came home in a cheerful mood. "I have no intention of becoming a new recruit who will end up standing in front of Russian cannons to please Hitler. There might be a way to avoid it."

"What can you do?" Mama asked.

"I have an idea."

On Saturday he made the short trip to Sarralbe to talk to the pharmacist. He returned clutching a small package that he stowed in his duffel bag. "I'll have one chance to avoid becoming a Nazi soldier. The pharmacist hates the Nazis as much as I do."

I started to ask what Papa had in mind, but he shushed me. "We can't talk about this."

My knuckles turned white as I gripped the back of a kitchen chair. Papa planned to do something the Nazis wouldn't like, and I feared he might be caught.

We spent his remaining time at home preparing for what we would do if Papa had to go to war in the German Army. He made sure we had enough firewood to last through the cold weather and food for the animals. When tears appeared in Mama's eyes, she turned away to hide them.

Mr. Rolf offered his support. "If you need help with any of the heavy work, I'll be available."

Two weeks flew by in a rush. I felt helpless as Mama and Papa tried to decide how she would manage while he was away. If his plan didn't work, it could be a long time. Even worse, he might never return.

On the morning he had to report to the induction center in Strasbourg, his bag was already packed, but I watched him tuck in a half-liter bottle of schnapps at the last minute. We were a sad group as we accompanied him to the station. Papa's goodbyes were brief. He kissed each of us as the train ground to a noisy stop. Steam hissed from the boiler as the train waited by the platform. Tears filled my eyes as he picked up his bag and walked to the train. I cringed at the sight and sound of hissing steam. The shriek of the whistle seemed to predict something bad could happen.

At the foot of the steps, Papa turned to look back. "I love you all. God willing, I'll be home within a week."

He boarded, and more black smoke puffed from the stack. Iron wheels clanked on the rails as the string of cars gathered speed. Everything I needed had been torn from me. The train disappeared in the distance, and the dark gray cloud remained.

Mama and I both cried. Roger was too young to understand what was happening, but he held tight to Mama.

Discouraged, we trudged home to face life without Papa once more.

I went to school later, and Mrs. Diedendorph called me to the front of the room to chastise me again for being inattentive. I had good reason to be sad, but my pride wouldn't let me tell her what happened.

At home Mama didn't allow me to mope around feeling sorry for myself. I had to take over some of Papa's chores like gathering firewood to keep the wood box in the kitchen filled. The next day I had to clean the chicken run and the ground under the rabbit cages.

After dinner I thought my work was finished, but Mama had another plan. "If you learned how to iron your clothes, I'd have more time to do everything else."

She showed me how to put the flat iron on the stove and how to know when it was hot enough. "Wet your fingers and tap the bottom of the iron. It should just sizzle. You don't want it too hot. You'll burn the fabric."

After putting a pad on the dining table, she brought one of my dresses she'd washed earlier in the day. "Be careful. Never let the hot iron set on the same spot for more than a second or two. You could ruin the dress."

She watched me as I tried to flatten the wrinkled fabric, correcting me when I did something wrong. After several clumsy starts, the dress finally appeared smooth and neat.

A smile came to my face when I looked at my work. "Can I wear it tomorrow?"

She covered her mouth to mask her amusement as she shook her head. "You need to keep the one you're wearing now for another day. The neighbors will think we're not thrifty if you change after wearing it only once. You can put this one on for church on Sunday."

In spite of my eagerness to show the dress off, I'd have to wait another day before telling everyone I'd ironed it myself.

On Sunday I wore the dress when Mama took us to church. We found seats in a pew near the back of the room and listened to the pastor's message. I joined her in a prayer for Papa's safe return.

* * *

Sadness seemed to hang over us. Mama did her work and took care of Roger and me, but I saw tears in her eyes more than once. We heard nothing from Papa. Opa and Oma came to visit bearing small gifts. It made Mama cry again. I tried to hold back my tears, but worry about Papa hurt me inside. Terrified that he might never come home, I went to school and did my chores in silence. Even Roger appeared to understand we feared something tragic could happen.

Oma and Opa came to visit us again, and Opa had good news. "We got a letter from George. He signed a false name, but he told us he was safe and had avoided the Milice so far. He sent his love to all."

Ten days after Papa left, I stood in the chicken run, handkerchief tied around my nose to keep out the dust and foul odor, raking droppings from our flock into a pile to be added to the manure pit. A biting wind stung my skin through a heavy sweater as I attempted to work hard enough to stay warm. I barely noticed the man who entered our street until he neared the house.

My heart leapt when I recognized him. He still wore the same clothing he had on when he left, but he looked different. He walked with short steps, his feet shuffling on the rough path. A thick smudge of whiskers covered his jaws and chin, and he'd lost weight. I dropped my rake and ran to give him a hug.

"Papa."

He bent down to hold me close. "I'm home. Everything will be all right."

I'd been so frightened he might never return I couldn't believe it was really him.

Mama shrieked as she bolted from the kitchen. Tears streamed down her cheeks as she wrapped him in her arms. Roger was close behind her. He babbled a greeting as he joined our celebration of Papa's return. Finally, Mama led us into the kitchen where she pulled out a chair for him.

When he was seated, she asked, "Would you like a glass of schnapps?"

Papa made his first attempt at a smile. "How about a cup of tea instead?"

While she put the kettle on the stove, Roger drifted off to the corner of the room to play with his ball.

My curiosity bubbled over. "Did the army let you come home?"

Papa's hand rubbed his brow and lifted his wool cap from his head. "They planned to keep me until I failed my physical exam. After that, they didn't want me anymore."

"But you are always big and strong," I said.

He chuckled. "My heartbeat was completely erratic after I swallowed the pills our pharmacist gave me."

Mama frowned. "I'm surprised he gave you something that endangered your health. I'd think it would be against his code of ethics."

Papa reached out to take her hand. "I neglected to tell you it was safe enough until I mixed it with the bottle of schnapps I took with me."

Mama slumped back in her chair. Her face turned almost gray. "You took a terrible chance."

He put his elbows on the table and leaned forward. "The chance I took was better than going to Russia to fight for Hitler."

Papa's decision to fail the army physical examination looked a lot better the next morning. Mr. Rolf came over waving a copy of the Resistance newspaper. The top story told us the Russians surprised the German armies with a massive counteroffensive at Moscow. The Nazi forces were in full retreat, and their pursuers were merciless. Tens of thousands of German troops lay dead on the frozen plains.

Chapter 31

Hard winter with snow and icy weather descended on Kaschel as the Christmas season approached. Papa spent most of his free time taking care of things at home. He packed the rabbit cages with wheat straw to keep them warm. The cows stayed inside their sheltered stalls eating hay. My worn out shoes failed to protect me from the snow, and even my long wool coat didn't keep me from shivering as I walked back and forth to school.

After a few days, Papa began to regain his weight and energy. He and Mama had some conversations I wasn't allowed to hear, but I stood at the top of the stairs and strained my ears to listen. I couldn't understand what they said, but they must have decided something because we all bundled up and caught the train to Metz on an early December Saturday. Papa brought along a bundle inside the sack he carried on his shoulder.

As we settled onto a bench in the railcar, I couldn't wait to ask, "What's in the sack, Papa?"

He smiled. "You'll find out soon enough."

When we arrived, Papa led us to the commercial district. "I think we might do some shopping."

After he asked directions from a shopkeeper, we entered a nearby store to look at the merchandise on display.

A scant collection of footwear sat on a single shelf. Papa examined the choices for a few minutes and shook his head. "These won't do."

He summoned the merchant. "We need good shoes for my wife and children. I can make it worth your while."

The man shuffled his feet and looked away. “I may have a few more choices in the stock room, but they won’t be cheap.”

“We should be able to reach an agreement,” Papa said. “Can you fit my family with solid shoes?”

The merchant nodded and measured our feet. “I’ll see what we have.”

We waited in silence. Even Roger kept sneaking glances at the door to the storeroom.

After I tried to sit still for a long time, the man reappeared carrying three shoeboxes. “Try these on.”

They were made of good leather, sturdy and comfortable. All three pairs fit.

“These aren’t cheap,” the merchant said.

Papa set the sack he brought on the counter and took out the package. He opened it to reveal a whole ham, a rack of ribs, and a large chunk of side meat.

The man’s eyes widened. “These shoes are very good quality. You won’t find better. I’ll need more than that.”

Papa began to rewrap the meat. “We’ll go elsewhere.”

The merchant held up a hand. “Two pairs, and the little boy can choose a pair from the rack.”

Papa continued wrapping. “Good meat is hard to find in the city. Someone else will be glad to have it.”

The merchant wilted. “Don’t go. We have a deal.”

Papa pushed the package across the counter. “Enjoy the food. It was a pleasure to do business with you.”

As we walked back to the station, Mama put her arm around him. “Thanks to your trading skill, *Kris Kringle* will have nice presents for us this year.”

* * *

After we celebrated a joyful Christmas with Opa and Oma, the New Year dawned. We heard more news about the increase in resistance group activities. The *Maquis* had become a major topic of conversation in Kaschel.

I opened the door for Mr. Koeppel when he brought more news to Papa. "They've damaged factories and rail lines and blown bridges all over the country."

Papa scratched the back of his neck. "The Nazis tend to punish us double when they respond to resistance activities. Living near one of those sites can get people killed."

"The *Maquis* tell us it's the only way they can strike back at our occupiers. They say reprisals will stiffen French resolve to throw off the Nazi yoke."

The nighttime chill made me shiver, so I threw another log on our fire. Then I retreated to my corner and listened.

"It's a chance we have to take," Papa said. "How else can we drive the Nazis out of France?"

"There's been almost no activity around here." Mr. Koeppel leaned in closer to the fire. "We have more Nazi sympathizers than they do farther south."

"We did speak a German dialect here before we were annexed. It could make the Nazis consider us German. They might be more reluctant to suspect us."

"More bad news from Russia," Mr. Koeppel said. "The Communist Army murdered tens of thousands of German prisoners during their retreat from Moscow. A lot of young men from Kaschel have been drafted into the Wehrmacht and sent there. Killing prisoners saved food the soldiers would have eaten. They used it to feed hungry Russians."

Mama slumped in her chair. Her lips began to tremble.

Papa looked up with a grimace. “This war will not end well for Hitler. In the meantime, we can expect more harsh demands from the Nazis as they become more desperate.”

When the conversation turned to talk of the planting season that approached, I climbed the steps to my room. In spite of the sick feeling in my stomach, homework needed my attention.

Two days later, we had just sat down to dinner when a man from the railroad came looking for Papa.

“A train derailed between Kaschel and Sarre Union. Several cars overturned, and they need a cleanup crew to gather the scattered cargo.”

“I’ll get my coat,” Papa said. Then he was gone.

We finished our meal without him, and Mama set aside a plate for him when he returned. After putting it back in the oven, she said, “I hope nobody was hurt.”

I’d finished my homework and was fast asleep when I heard the kitchen door slam. I rubbed sleep from my eyes and dressed quickly, grabbed a blanket to protect me from the nighttime chill, and ran down to meet Papa.

Mama added wood in the stove and put the loaded plate back in the oven while Papa unbuttoned his heavy coat and sat down.

“Did you work at the wreck?” I asked.

Papa mumbled something and nodded as he tore off a chunk from the long loaf of black bread. When Mama brought his food, he shoveled in a huge mouthful of sausage and sauerkraut.

His response hadn’t answered my question. “What caused the wreck?”

“Someone loosened the connector plate on a siding junction. The engine made it past the siding, but six cars derailed and overturned. They're badly broken up and scattered across the hillside."

Mama added another stick of wood to the smoldering fire and sat beside him. "What kind of cargo were they hauling?"

"A load of boots from a factory near Paris to a depot for the German Army. Boots were scattered all over the side of the hill. I helped recover them."

"That sounds just like the Nazis." Mama sniffed. "Boots aren't available for us, but they had a whole train load for their army."

"What will they do with all the wrecked cars?" I asked.

"They'll bring in some heavy equipment tomorrow. After they repair the rails, they'll lift the cars back onto the tracks. Looks to me like they'll only be able to salvage two or three. The rest are too badly damaged."

"Do they have someone guarding all those boots?" Mama asked.

Papa spooned down the last of his food and chuckled. "There are more *Waffen SS* and Gestapo there than you can count. They didn't take any chances. Sergeant Schnabel is helping them recover all of the boots."

Mama spread her hands on the table before her. "I still think it's a shame. They're sending boots to the army in Germany while shoes are rationed for us, and the only way we can find good ones is to pay double or even more on the black market."

Papa leaned back in his chair with an amused look on his face. "Somehow, one pair found their way about a half dozen meters up in an oak tree. If they're still there after all the Nazis leave, they may find their way home with me."

Mama made a choking sound. "You didn't! The SS might have shot you."

Papa nodded with a serious look. “When they’ve finished their work and gone, I’ll make a midnight visit to the tree. The boots should still be waiting.”

A week later, Papa came home late at night carrying a new pair of good leather boots.

Chapter 32

An endless expanse of ocean slid past my tiny window. The airliner traveled the same direction as the sunlight, so it would be a long day. There was nothing to see except calm water and a few scattered clouds.

The noisy Lockheed aircraft hit bumpy air and shook for a moment as it droned on toward the strange land where I would start a new life. Thoughts about the Nazi occupation when I was a child welled up in my memory. Life as an unwilling German citizen had been difficult for my family. We didn't like the Nazis, but we tried to avoid controversy and live peacefully. Others were bolder, but we all dealt with the constant threat of reprisals.

Within days of the suspicious train wreck, our local Nazi commissioner had relayed orders from Berlin. The Third Reich issued a mandate for an additional 250,000 Obligatory Work Service enrollees to increase the German labor force. As unwilling citizens of Germany, nobody in Kaschel felt safe. We worried constantly that Roger might say something or the Nazis would notice that Papa wore German Army boots.

The draft had continued and young men from the village disappeared into the gigantic maw of Hitler's military machine. At first they had selected men of eighteen and older, but they soon began to take younger boys.

Some escaped to southern France, but they were forced to evade the French authorities who cooperated with the Germans as well. The Nazis demanded complete subservience, so the Vichy Government supported everything they wanted. If an escapee was caught, he would be punished severely and, most likely, wind up serving on the Russian front. The Gestapo shot a few to make an example of them.

Just recalling the fear we'd lived under made my stomach turn.

* * *

With the arrival of February, the weather warmed for a few days, and a driving rain melted most of the snow. Kaschel was immersed in a sea of cold mud. Mama had stoked the fire to take the chill off the room and used saccharine to make a small cake for my ninth birthday. She invited my grandparents to share it. Everyone voiced congratulations and gave me a hug. Then Mama cut the cake. She gave the first slice to me.

I waited until everyone had a piece before taking my first bite. The chemical taste of saccharine ruined it for me, but I tried to show a happy face. "Thank you, Mama."

Papa didn't show as much restraint. "This isn't fit to eat. If we don't have sugar, don't make a cake."

Mama wilted. I thought she might cry.

Oma cast an accusing eye at Papa and laid a hand on my mother's arm. "You did your best with what we have. We all appreciate it."

This being my birthday, I tried to make it a cheerful gathering. We were all in a good mood by the time my grandparents made their way home.

A few days later, Sergeant Schnabel came to summon Mama. "Since your husband has a job, you have been selected to work for the needs of the Fatherland."

Mama's eyes darted around the room. "But I have small children to tend."

"No matter. The girl is nine. She can manage the house and care for her brother."

I held Roger's hand and shrank into a corner.

"But we have animals to feed and chores to perform," Mama said. "Irene is too young to take care of everything."

"Your husband will care for the animals before he leaves for work. You will report to city hall at daybreak. Your work is nearby, so you'll be allowed to come home at night. We chose a task located close to Kaschel so you will be able to look after your family. You're fortunate. Some have been sent to cities in the north to work in factories." The arrogant Nazi sergeant smirked and stalked out of the room without a backward glance.

Mama made breakfast and milked the cows by lantern light before she left for work. Papa cleaned the stables and fed the sow before he walked to the station. Our house would be my responsibility until they returned. Oma came to watch Roger for a few days, so I didn't miss too many days of school. My stomach hurt, and I felt sad that Mama had to work for the Nazis. Trying to shake off the bad feeling, I washed our dishes and waited for Roger to wake.

The day dragged. I gave my little brother his breakfast and made sure he dressed warmly. We fed the chickens and rabbits, and I brought in the eggs. Roger played with his toys until Oma came to check on us during the morning and invited us to lunch.

During the afternoon, I spent some time trying to keep up with my schoolwork. Knowing I was telling a lie, I wrote a short report about how much my family benefited from the Third Reich. I knew Mrs. Diedendorph would be happy to read that I appreciated my privileged status.

A bored Roger came to look at what I was doing and reached for my pencil. "Show me how to write."

An idea popped into my mind, and I ignored a momentary twinge of doubt and fear. "I'll teach you to write your name in French, but you mustn't show it to anyone outside the family. The Nazis will punish us if we don't use your German name."

After practicing for half an hour, he managed to scribble his name in a form I could almost read.

"Good job, Roger," I told him. "You've earned a rest. Go play, now."

Papa and Mama returned at nightfall, Mama taking short steps and tripping over things when she failed to lift her feet. They found a clean house, a proud Roger showing them his writing, and a dinner of potatoes and pork on the stove ready to eat.

After looking at Roger's work, Papa took the paper from him and put it in the fire. "You mustn't write in French or use your proper name. The Nazis would punish us."

Roger tucked his head and started to cry.

Papa pointed at me. "You should have known better."

Chastened, I waited for everyone to sit down, and then I served the meal. The pork was overcooked, and the potatoes had too much salt, but nobody complained.

Mama pursed her lips and frowned. She looked tired, and her dress was covered with splashes of mud. "The food tastes good, Irene."

Papa wagged his fork at Mama. "What sort of work did they make you do?"

Mama looked up from her plate. "I spent all day digging ditches for an army fortification they're building across the river, on the road to Sarrealbe."

"That's heavy work," Papa said. "Too hard for a woman."

Mama's mouth twisted. "I'm exhausted, my back hurts, and they told me I didn't dig fast enough. I'm taking a hot-water bottle to bed to help ease the pain in my back."

The pride I felt for all my accomplishments during the day faded away. They didn't compare with what Mama was forced to do.

The next day, Oma looked after Roger so I'd be able to go to school. Mrs. Diedendorph scolded me for being absent the day before without a good excuse, but I didn't let it bother me. Nothing was likely to be right as long as we were ruled by Nazis. They only cared about making everyone loyal to the Third Reich.

Mama dug ditches for two weeks. She looked more tired each night when she came home. Papa tried to milk the cows so she could sleep longer, but they wouldn't give milk for him. I made sure all the cooking and cleaning was done before she limped through the kitchen door at night. She didn't talk much and went to bed after eating most of her dinner. I wondered if my cooking was bad or if she was too tired to eat. The whole family was relieved when the Nazis finally released her from the forced labor.

At the end of the job, she had lost weight and ruined her new pair of shoes. Several days passed before she recovered her usual energy and good disposition. We lived with the fear the Nazis might want more from her. I prayed they'd leave her alone.

Everything I feared about life under Hitler's yoke had come true.

Another spell of cold weather froze the mud and more snow fell. When it stopped, another thirty centimeters covered the ground. A frigid north wind moved it to form tall drifts that became almost impossible for me to plow through.

Mr. Schmidt came to see Papa one evening in early March as I washed our dinner dishes. He stamped the snow off his boots at the step before entering. "I got more good news from the BBC just now. The Russians have driven the Nazis out of Stalingrad. They credit the allied front in North Africa with taking some of the pressure off the Red Army."

Papa invited him to sit. "How about a glass of schnapps?"

"Sounds good. I haven't tasted of your fine brew for a while."

Papa poured a generous amount of the potent liquid in a water glass and handed it to his visitor. "I heard Field Marshal Montgomery finally got some help. American and Free French forces showed up to reinforce the British Army in Africa."

Mr. Schmidt took a generous sip and breathed a long sigh. "Some of your best." He leaned back in the chair and continued. "BBC says the Russians shattered the German lines, and the Wehrmacht is in full retreat."

Papa poured a like amount of schnapps into his glass and sipped it. "I'm thankful I failed my physical for military service or I'd be there now."

"BBC says casualties have been enormous."

"That just means they'll draft more young men from here. Hitler will never find enough soldiers to outlast the Russians."

I put our dishes in the cupboard and left the room. I couldn't bear to hear more talk about this awful war.

* * *

The weather turned windy and wet in March. Papa and Mama made plans for crops we would plant for the coming year. Thanks to another extra pig we'd hidden from the inspector, we had plenty of meat for our needs. Papa had put this one in a cage behind Mr. Schmidt's house. The Schmidts didn't keep pigs, so the inspector wouldn't look there.

Being a cautious person, Papa had taken to locking our door when we ate pork. We didn't tell people what sort of food we had and lived with fear that the wrong person might report us. We could never be sure who might bring tales to the Nazis.

Papa took me with him one evening to visit the Koeppels. It had been months since I'd seen Maria. While the men enjoyed their schnapps and talked about the war, Maria and I found a quiet corner and talked about more interesting things like hoping for the weather to warm so we could play outside with our dolls.

"I'm really glad you taught me to read and write when we were in Wolfskirchen," Maria said. "I'm ahead of everyone else in first grade."

"It's because you're smart," I told her. "A lot of kids only learn when someone makes them study."

Her expression turned sour. "Is Mrs. Diedendorph as mean to your class as she is to us?" Maria asked. "She gives us too much homework."

"That's a good thing," I said. "The bad part is when she tries to make us like the Nazis."

I looked up to pay attention to the grownups when I heard Papa's voice get louder. "We had the Gestapo at the station all day. They're still trying to find out who wrecked the train."

"Make sure you don't tell them anything."

"I'll make sure I don't wear my new boots while they're around. No telling what they're likely to find."

Mr. Koeppel took another sip of schnapps. "If they find anything, they're likely to make an example of the guilty one."

"We're lucky we don't live in Occupied France," Papa said. "The Vichy Government has organized a group they call the

Milice. They're modeled after the Gestapo, but people tell me they're even worse."

Mr. Koeppel threw back his head and laughed. "That's the first time I've heard we're lucky the Nazis made us German citizens."

How could the men laugh and joke about the Nazis? Fear of what they might do never seemed to leave me. I even woke at night after bad dreams of their cruelty.

Chapter 33

When mild weather arrived, Mama helped Papa plant our crops. After he came home from his job, they worked until dark every night and all day on Saturday and Sunday. She left me in charge of the house and Roger. By now I had plenty of experience taking care of the house. That wasn't much of a challenge. Keeping track of Roger was a bigger problem.

The little wild man had turned four, and Mama made him a cake using real sugar this time. He could run faster, and he wandered farther. He thought it was fun to chase the neighbor's chickens and interrupt Mr. Rolf by asking about a million questions while the man was trying to work. Only one thing helped me keep up with him. He was afraid of dogs, even small ones. If he encountered one on the street, he'd find his way home in a hurry.

Many of our neighbors owned dogs. They were mostly used for herding animals, especially sheep. They might challenge or bark at strangers or another dog who wandered by their property, but I didn't know of any that were really mean.

After an encounter with a cocker spaniel sent him running home, I tried to convince Roger that dogs wouldn't hurt him. "He just wants to get acquainted when he meets you. Talk to him and scratch his ears. He'll be your friend."

Roger's lower lip stuck out. "He's big and mean, and he barks at me when I walk by his house."

I didn't try too hard to calm his fears. He was easier to find when he stayed close to home. That didn't completely solve my problem because he could still find plenty of ways to get in trouble without going anywhere.

While I wasn't chasing after Roger, I kept the house clean and had dinner ready when my parents came home from the fields. Doing my own ironing became part of my routine. Then Mama washed my navy blue pleated skirt and left it for me. I laid it on the table but couldn't figure out how to handle the pleats.

Upset with my failure, I confessed to Mama that evening. "I don't know how to iron my Sunday skirt."

She gave me a quick hug. "Build up the fire in the kitchen stove and heat the iron. I'll show you how."

When the iron was hot, she laid my skirt flat on the dining table. "Do one pleat at a time. Run the iron down the pleat from top to bottom, then shift the skirt so the next one is straight. Do it exactly like you did the first."

I shifted the skirt to flatten the material. "I can do it."

She watched me until I'd finished the entire skirt. It looked like new, and I said, "I'll iron it by myself next time."

After Mama and I finished work on the skirt, Mr. Rolf showed up to visit with Papa. Mama cleaned off the table to make room for the men, and I found my place in the corner to sit and listen.

Mr. Rolf set his hat on an empty chair. "BBC reported the *Maquis* has conducted over a hundred attacks on rail lines. They've destroyed a few bridges and a lot of engines in those raids. It's hurting the Nazis' ability to move their war materials."

"They've been busy," Papa agreed. "The *Milice* have caught a few *Maquis* fighters. They're turning them over to the Gestapo for interrogation."

"After each act of sabotage, the Nazis have started executing villagers who live nearby." Mr. Rolf sounded angry as he pulled tobacco and a pipe from the bib pocket of his overalls. "It hasn't stopped the Resistance up to now."

"We haven't had much activity around here," Papa said. "It's harder to keep secrets this close to the heartland."

"Things aren't going well for the Nazis." Mr. Rolf paused to light his pipe. "They haven't invaded the British Isles yet, and they're retreating in Russia and North Africa as well."

I breathed in the smoke from Mr. Rolf's pipe. Mama said it was stinky, but I liked the strong smell of burning tobacco.

Papa leaned forward to scratch at a shoulder. "The Nazis are drafting more men from the village. They're taking them younger every month."

The toe of Mr. Rolf's boot banged against a table leg. "They're being sent to the slaughterhouse in Russia. Four more from Kaschel were reported killed in action last month. They are the *malgre nous*, the unwilling, and they're being forced to fight for the Nazis."

Papa heaved a long sigh. "Draftees are not all going to the Wehrmacht now. Two were inducted into the *Waffen SS* last month."

Mr. Rolf blew a puff of smoke toward the ceiling. "That's the wrong place for a true Alsatian. They'll have to fight against everything they believe in and threaten their own people. They took young Stephan Roebling in the *SS*. He hated the Nazis. He was reported killed in action yesterday."

I'd heard more than I wanted to hear, so I slipped away to lie in my bed and worry about the terrible mess we were in.

* * *

A few weeks later Papa took advantage of free grass for our two cows and let them graze on the small, unfenced tract of city-owned common ground south of the village. He sent me to drive them to the field on Saturday and Sunday afternoons. I'd watch them graze and chase them back when they wandered away from the common land. The railroad tracks ran nearby, and the town of Sarre Union was only four kilometers away. I couldn't leave the animals to fend for themselves, and they weren't good company. I could only daydream about having time to play with friends if I weren't babysitting the stupid cows.

We'd been awakened by several air raids recently. Factories in some of the nearby cities had been bombed by the Royal Air Force. Lately the Americans had joined in to increase the number of raids. I'd been scared and lost a lot of sleep when Papa made us seek shelter behind the couch each time we heard a siren.

"We'll never know where they might bomb," he'd insisted.

I knew Papa had probably been right, but it didn't keep me from being sleepy stuck out in this lonely field watching our cows munching grass. I stood, stretched, and walked up and down the side of the field to stay alert after losing sleep the previous night.

A passing train was always an event that broke the monotony. The plot of ground where the cattle grazed lay two hundred meters from the tracks. The afternoon was warm and cloudless, leaving me drowsy until I heard the train. The engine huffed, and I could hear the iron wheels click clacking on the rails. Smoke billowed from the stack of a coal-burner. It was pulling a string of boxcars, but I couldn't see what was in them.

The engineer blew his shrill whistle as he approached a crossroad, and I waved. He must not have seen me because he didn't wave back.

The engine passed by, and I had counted a dozen cars when two airplanes approached from the west. The first plane flipped sideways, and I saw the white star painted on the wing as it turned at the railroad track. Papa had told me the star meant it was an American fighter plane. It pointed its nose at the train and flew low over its entire length. The sharp pop, pop, pop of its guns drowned out the roar of the engine as it fired at the cars and the locomotive. The second plane followed the first to increase the damage.

Pieces of wood flew from the tops of the boxcars, and the loud screech of iron wheels sliding on the track hurt my ears as the engineer tried to stop the train. Terrified, I sank to my knees and covered my head in my hands.

I suddenly realized I was too close to the bullets hitting the train, and the cows made a mad dash toward the nearby woods. Attempting to rise and run at the same time, I tripped and fell headlong on the ground. After a second try, I ran back toward the road and a cement culvert I remembered. I dived through the opening and lay trembling on the mud-covered bottom. The dark inside smelled rotten and made my stomach threaten to bring up my lunch. Then I noticed the scratches on my hands and knees. I gulped a few times, and my thumping heart slowed. Curiosity made me turn back to watch from the end of the big cement pipe.

The airplanes circled back and made another run to shoot at the train. Then I heard booms in the distance, and tiny airplanes dove and soared over the town of Sarre Union, dropping bombs and shooting near the railroad station.

The train slowed to a stop. Workers on board screamed in terror as they ran away from the tracks, looking for a safe place to hide. They dived into ditches and hid behind trees. The line of railcars had passed me by when the shooting started, so the men didn't come close to my shelter in the culvert.

Two more airplanes came from the north, and I recognized the Iron Cross on their wings. German fighter planes. They started shooting at the Americans, and all the airplanes began to make wild turns as they shot at the others. I couldn't see if bullets hit any of them.

After a minute or two, the German planes flew away to the north, and the Americans chased them for a moment before heading west.

I stayed in the pipe, still scared and shaking, wondering if the airplanes would return. I thought they might have dropped bombs on the station in Sarre Union. *Would they drop bombs on the station in Kaschel where Papa worked?*

Minutes later, I heard my father call me. When I peeked out, he stood by the road, out of breath from running. When I crawled out of the culvert, his pale face was twisted by fear.

He gathered me in his arms. "Are you all right? Those planes had a dogfight. Bullets could have landed anywhere. You could have been killed."

The airplanes had disappeared. Papa was there, and my fear was gone. "I hid in the culvert to watch them fight. I think they hurt the train."

Papa held my hands and looked in my eyes. "The important thing is you're safe."

I'd forgotten about the cows. When I turned to look, they were back in the field, gobbling down the tall grass. They seemed to have forgotten the airplane battle.

* * *

A week later Mama got word the inspector counting pigs for the Nazis would be in the village. “We need to save another pig. He’ll leave us only one and that’s not enough.”

She grabbed a length of clothesline and tied one end around a little pig’s neck before handing the other end to me. “Take him down by the river and hide him where the inspector can’t find him. Here’s some feed and a pan for water. It should keep him occupied until we come for him after dark.”

I tried to lead the pig across the pasture adjoining our yard, but he didn’t want to follow. Frustrated, I finally picked him up and carried him into the narrow grove of trees by the river. When I located a patch of thick brush, I took him to the middle of the bushes and tied him to a small tree. Anyone walking by would be unlikely to see him there. After filling the pan with water from the Sarre, I set it and the feed within the pig’s reach.

Then I stepped back to survey my work. “That should keep you happy for the rest of the day. We’ll bring you home after dark.”

A sudden noise froze me in place. What if someone had seen me hide the pig? Then I saw the tree branch scraping through the overhanging limbs to crash on the ground. After recovering from my fright, I made my way home.

This time Mama’s plan worked perfectly. The inspector counted the pigs and announced he’d leave one for us. The rest would go to the Wehrmacht.

She went with me to bring the pig home after darkness fell. We’d have two pigs to slaughter after our first hard freeze. We’d managed to outwit the Nazis again.

As the middle of May approached, Papa brought home an underground newspaper printed in our local dialect. I had trouble reading French, but reading this one was easy. The top of the front page was covered with an account of a huge battle in Tunisia. I read over Papa's shoulder. The article said the German Army had been attacked by both the British and American Armies. Free French forces had joined in the fight as well. Casualties had been enormous, and the Nazis lost.

After the German Army surrendered, the Allies took a quarter million troops as prisoners of war. The article said Germany would no longer be a credible power in North Africa. Surviving units retreated to Italy to defend the European Continent.

Papa leaned back in his chair and exhaled a huge breath. "Hitler should negotiate a surrender now. He's hemmed in on all sides and will surely lose the war. The Russians are coming, and they'll kill everyone in their path. If Hitler would surrender, he could prevent a lot more bloodshed to come."

Mama folded her hands on top of the table. "Hitler will never surrender. He's crazy, and I don't think he knows how to give up. He doesn't care what happens to the German people."

My chin dropped to my chest as I left the room. Hitler would be sure to draft more young men from Kaschel to replace those he'd lost in North Africa.

A memory of young Stephan Roebling formed in my mind. I'd known him as a smart and friendly schoolboy who was always kind to smaller kids. The Nazis took him and sent him to die on the Russian front.

Chapter 34

Summer arrived warm and dry, and Papa cut our first hay crop of the year. The whole family helped bring in the harvest to fill the empty loft above the stalls. Since Roger had recently turned four, Papa said he was old enough to help and gave him a job. As the wagon was filled, Roger replaced me to walk on top of the stack and trample the hay down so we could haul more. Having grown taller lately, I had to scoop hay off the ground with a pitchfork and throw it onto the wagon. I could tell from looking at Roger he felt this important job made him a head taller than he'd been before. We'd have one more cutting in the fall, and the cows would have their winter feed.

Several days later, Papa returned from an evening visit with Mr. Schmidt, listening to his hidden radio. "The Allied Forces made an amphibious landing on Sicily today."

"What is amphibious?" I asked.

"It means they came in boats to land their soldiers on the beach." Mama pursed her lips as she laid her embroidery work on the table. "Sicily is just a big island. The Allies will have to invade the mainland to keep pushing the Nazis back. The German forces are sure to help the Italians resist."

Papa reached to close a kitchen window. "The Germans didn't do so well in Libya. I don't think the Allies will stop in Sicily. They'll attack the mainland."

"Anyway," Mama said, "Sicily is a long way from here. I don't think it will make our life any better. The Nazis might even make everything more difficult here."

I picked up my doll and retreated to the living room. Hearing more news of the war didn't appeal to me. I wanted to feel safe. I wanted the Nazis gone.

* * *

Our next-door neighbor, Mr. Rolf, kept goats. He milked two of them and always slaughtered a young one in the fall. Wanting to save money on their feed, he staked a half dozen of them out on small patches of untended grass in the neighborhood. After they'd grazed until one spot was bare, he'd move them to another.

The turmoil of war didn't prevent Roger and me from being kids. When Roger got bored, which was often, he'd look for ways to stir up a little excitement. The goats presented an opportunity. After Mr. Rolf tied his animals near our house along the farm road leading to the Sarre, Roger couldn't resist the temptation to visit the goats and spark some trouble.

I looked up from weeding the garden to see him slip down the path to the goats. Then he hustled back home to watch them from the road in front of our house. I couldn't see what he'd done, but I felt sure it was something he shouldn't do.

He didn't have to wait long for something to happen. The goats did what goats do. They scattered, looking for the best food they could find. Soon they ranged from the banks of the river to the middle of town. Some of them found Mayor Spengler's garden by his pasture along the river. They stayed to eat fresh beans and peas along with the tops of turnip and carrot plants. Later the mayor came to tend his crops and recognized the animals eating his vegetables. He stormed up the path to Mr. Rolf's house. I was outside, feeding the chickens, when he pounded on Mr. Rolf's front door.

"You turned your goats loose to eat my garden!"

Mr. Rolf's face turned red. "I tethered them along the road. It's about time for me to go move them."

"They moved because they weren't tied. You'll pay for the damage they did to my crops. You can't get away with stealing from the town's mayor. I represent the Third Reich."

Mr. Rolf spent the next hour searching the village for his goats. He shook his fist when he told Papa what happened. "Someone turned them loose and they ate the mayor's garden. Now, I'm in trouble with the fat old fool."

Papa pursed his lips and frowned. "Who would do something like that?"

Mr. Rolf growled under his breath and kicked at rocks in his path as he stomped back to his house.

I thought back over the morning and approached Papa. "Roger went to the goats this morning. He stood in the road and giggled as he watched them scatter."

Papa breathed a long sigh and wiped a hand through his hair. "Why didn't you stop him?"

My stomach tried to climb up to my throat. "I don't know."

Papa glared at me and shouted, "Roger, come here!"

My brother looked small when he got there. "Yes, Papa."

"Did you untie Mr. Rolf's goats?"

Roger's face paled. He looked around like he was seeking help. "It was Irene."

Papa cocked his head to glare at the boy. "I doubt it. This sounds more like something you'd do."

My trembling little brother hung his head and tried to sound innocent, but it didn't take long for Papa to force a confession.

Roger received a rare but energetic spanking for his behavior. Then I watched Papa drag him to Mr. Rolf's house to apologize. Roger pulled away and looked down like he was more afraid of confronting Mr. Rolf than being spanked.

He finally said he was sorry for turning the goats loose to roam, and Papa gave Mr. Rolf some money to pay the mayor for the damage the hungry animals did.

I didn't get off free. Papa made me stay home for a week, and I couldn't have friends over. Even worse, I had to write an apology to Mr. Rolf for my part in Roger's misadventure.

Roger sent a vengeful glance at me. I feared he'd find a way to get even.

* * *

July 14, Bastille Day, passed without notice, and I asked, "Why don't we celebrate?"

Papa's answer sounded gruff. "There is no reason to celebrate anything now that France is no longer independent."

Smothering summer heat covered the village. Sunlight penetrated scattered clouds to bake the rain-starved ground. Annette came to visit, so I fixed lunch for us. We ate slices of pork sausage with fresh green beans and potatoes. The temperature inside the house was a few degrees cooler, so we didn't venture outside.

Papa and Mama were away working in the fields, and Roger was taking his afternoon nap. He usually slept for more than an hour, so I was thankful my little brother wouldn't bother us for a while. Annette and I were busy talking about the upcoming school term when loud banging on the front door made me jump.

I ran to answer. Sergeant Schnabel and another German soldier stood on our step. The soldier carried a rifle slung across his shoulder. His insignia read *Waffen SS*. Startled, I struggled to control an involuntary shudder.

“We’re looking for deserters,” the burly sergeant announced. He loomed over me like a big storm cloud. The other soldier was short and heavy. He frowned as he stood back, looking left and right as if to guard against anyone approaching.

Frightened, it took me a few seconds to find my voice. “My parents are not home. We’re not hiding anyone.”

Sergeant Schnabel crossed his arms to glare at me. “We can search your property without them.”

My back stiffened as I answered. “Mama told me not to allow strangers inside our house.”

“We don’t need permission,” the SS soldier said. His hip batted me aside as he stormed through the doorway. “Don’t you know who we are? Stay out of my way.”

I bounced off the doorframe and held on to keep from falling. Everyone knew who the SS were. Enforcers for the Nazi party. His presence made my knees weak.

Annette and I backed against the wall. I tried to concentrate, but my churning stomach betrayed my fear as the Nazis searched our house.

There was no place to hide in the summer kitchen so the pair moved on to the larger kitchen and pantry. The sound of slamming doors and furniture crashing against a wall made me afraid they intended to break everything. Anger welled up from my stomach to replace the fear. In the living room, the noise made me think they might have broken our couch as they shoved it away from the wall. It rattled against an end table. Everything in the dining room was visible, so they didn’t disturb the furniture there.

Sergeant Schnabel motioned to the other. “Stay with the girls. I’ll check upstairs.”

My fear turned to panic as he mounted the steps. Roger was asleep in his room.

We heard the sergeant moving furniture and overturning beds while we cowered under the watchful eye of the overweight SS trooper. I bit my lip to keep from saying anything when he spit in a corner of the room. His lack of respect for our home disgusted me. I wanted to vomit.

A sudden cry from upstairs announced Schnabel had awakened Roger. He appeared at the top of the stairs crying, and I climbed the steps to help him down. He stood beside me, holding my hand, looking up at the slouching thug through tear-filled eyes.

When the scowling sergeant came back downstairs, the fat one motioned us outside. Annette's eyes were huge, her lips drawn. She tripped when he shoved us through the door. I managed to grab her arm to keep her from falling.

Outside, the SS soldier stopped to glance around our yard. "I'll look in the outhouse."

He returned with a shrug. The soldiers checked the woodpile first, then the animals' stalls in the back of the building, finding nothing.

Annette, Roger, and I stood shaking, and tears crept into my eyes when Sergeant Schnabel pointed to our hayloft above the stalls.

"A coward could hide up there."

He grabbed a pitchfork from the corner and climbed the ladder. In the loft, he drove the big six-tined fork into the stack of hay. The sharp tines would kill anyone who happened to be hiding there. After a dozen or more thrusts that found nothing, he threw a fork of hay outside before climbing down the ladder.

Annette and I held each other and sobbed as the loose hay covered the ground around us. Roger had stopped crying, but he kept a tight grip on my hand.

The SS soldier crossed his arms to stare at us. “If we find deserters, we’ll kill them. The Third Reich has no place for cowards. We might decide to kill anyone hiding them as well. Make sure you tell your parents what I said.”

Sergeant Schnabel waved a finger at my face. “I’ll be watching you.”

We stood by the stables, frightened, clinging to each other as the Nazi pair left.

Chapter 35

A few days after Sergeant Schnabel and the SS killer invaded our home, I spent the morning taking care of my little brother and gathering vegetables from our garden. I asked Roger to help me, but he preferred to play with his soccer ball. Mama would punish me if I swatted him, so I gave up and did the work myself. Lunch was ready when she came home from the fields at noon, and Roger smirked to show me he didn't have to obey.

That evening, Papa brought home another underground newspaper. He said, "Benito Mussolini has been deposed in Italy. The new government may be more inclined to seek peace."

He locked the doors and the three of us gathered around the table to read the news. Roger found something more interesting to do. The article explained that Italy wanted to sue for peace, but the Nazis refused to allow them to withdraw from their Pact of Steel.

"The Nazis will force them to fight," Papa said. "Just like they did in Vichy, France."

Mama looked up from the paper. "At least it will force the Germans to keep an army there. They won't be able to man all the fronts."

Papa cupped his chin in his hand. "The German Army is spread too thin, even with all the help they force France to give them."

Mama rose and turned to stare out the kitchen window. "It means they'll draft more of our unwilling young men and send them to die on the Russian plains. Germany is desperate to stop the Red Army from getting revenge for things Hitler did to them."

A pair of small articles near the bottom of the page caught my attention.

They first reported that French Communists had joined the Resistance in large numbers. Most of them had been motivated by Nazi attacks on Russia. Since the *Milice* was finding Jews in the south of France and handing them over to the Nazis for extermination, both groups were becoming a major force in the Resistance.

The other was even more shocking. The British Royal Air Force had retaliated for the deadly German attacks on London. A huge formation of RAF airplanes had firebombed Hamburg. Forty thousand people had been killed by the raid. The war was coming home to the Nazis.

A chilling thought struck me. *We are part of Germany now. Could the British airplanes bomb Kaschel?*

Papa stuffed the paper into the kitchen stove to burn. "Can't allow the Nazis to find out we have this."

As fall approached, life in the village didn't change much. We harvested our wheat, but the Nazis kept most of it. They took our second cutting of hay as well. The Third Reich took its toll from everyone, but city dwellers suffered most. Protests weren't allowed. Shortages during the winter months were certain to become a serious problem.

* * *

Papa came home from work one day with a large German police dog on a leash. "I found him wandering along the tracks after a troop train departed."

Mama pointed a finger at the animal. "We don't need a dog. We have enough trouble feeding ourselves."

When Roger saw the dog, his face turned pale. He climbed on top of the dining table.

Papa lifted his hands. "The tag on his collar says he belongs to an *Oberstleutnant* Braun in the Wehrmacht. The stationmaster says I found him and we'd be in serious trouble if we don't care for the officer's dog. He told me to keep it at home, and he'll try to locate the *Oberstleutnant*."

I wanted to make friends with the dog. When I held out my hand, he sniffed it. "He doesn't act like he's mean."

Papa nodded. "He's obviously well trained. We'll have to keep him. I have no choice."

Mama reached out to Roger. "Come down from the table. He won't hurt you."

Roger pulled away. "He doesn't like me."

Mama lifted him down and stood him on the floor, but he darted behind her, clutching her skirt. "He has big teeth. He wants to bite me."

After searching under the sink, I brought out a metal pan and filled it from the water bucket. "He must be thirsty."

I set the pan on the floor, and the dog promptly lapped up the water. "What's his name?" I asked.

"Wasn't on the tag," Papa said. "You can give him a name."

I'd never named an animal before. My mind raced through several possibilities before I had an inspiration. "He can be Otto. That's a German name."

I took him for a walk around the village while Papa cobbled together a rough doghouse for the animal and set it inside the woodshed.

Otto proved to be well mannered and accepted his place in the family. I went to see him often, bringing him food or rubbing his fur and talking to him. Afraid he might run away, we didn't remove his leash. I'd never owned a dog, and Otto made a good companion. Walking him around the village attracted a lot of attention. He'd wag his tail when people stopped to ask questions, and I'd explain how he came to stay with us.

Roger avoided Otto completely. I tried to persuade him to make friends with the dog, but he pulled away and refused to come near the animal.

Two weeks later, while Papa was away, *Oberstleutnant* Braun knocked on our kitchen door. "The stationmaster tells me you have my dog."

Mama's hands trembled, and she stammered before answering. "Yes, he was running loose near the station. My husband brought him home to keep him safe. Won't you come in?"

The perfectly creased uniform with symbols of his rank and the emblem of the German eagle clutching a swastika sewn on his tunic identified the man as a German officer.

He removed his cap and stepped inside. "Thank you."

Mama motioned to me. "Go bring Otto inside. His master is here to claim him."

Otto came out of his shelter to greet me when I ran to his doghouse. "Your master is here for you. You have to go."

Knowing he'd be leaving us, I wiped away a tear and gave him a goodbye hug before leading him inside.

The dog whined and wagged his tail when he saw his master. He pulled me across the floor to reach the man.

Roger retreated to the far corner of the room.

The *Oberstleutnant* bent to ruffle the dog's ears and took the leash I offered. "I see you've given him a new name, Otto. You'll use the proper one from now on. You should thank these fine people for their care, Prince. We need to catch the next train north."

The officer turned back after he'd stepped out the door. "Tell your husband the Third Reich appreciates his service. He is certainly a patriotic supporter of the Nazi cause."

When the officer disappeared down the street with his dog, Roger left his corner and stood in the center of the room, beaming. I tucked my chin against my chest and tried to hide my disappointment.

Mama stood with arms folded and a frown on her face. "Patriotic supporter my foot. We don't need his gratitude. He could have shown his appreciation with a small reward. At least, he could have paid the cost of feeding the animal."

* * *

Papa slammed the kitchen door and bounded into the room with a big grin. He'd been listening to Mr. Schmidt's hidden radio. "The Allies landed in force on mainland Italy. It appears they intend to stay."

I smiled as I watched Mama's reaction.

She raised her arms and looked toward the ceiling. "The Nazis will have to take charge and fight to keep the Italians from surrendering. If the Wehrmacht is tied up there, they won't be able to send those troops to the Russian front."

Papa slapped a fist into the other hand. "The British and Americans pushed them out of North Africa. I'm not sure the Nazis can prevent them from taking Italy."

My heart raced as I listened. Could it be possible they might come all the way to Alsace and chase the Germans away? Would the armies fight in Kaschel? Only shyness and fear kept me from joining Papa's celebration.

Mama reached out to touch my shoulder. "It's not likely to affect us here."

Three days later, we heard Italy had surrendered. One of our enemies had quit the war. That was the best news we'd heard in months. German troops would remain in place to occupy Italy and fight the Allies.

Our daily life continued despite the war news. School began, and Annette joined me as we started fourth grade in the rooms at City Hall. Our pudgy old teacher was Mr. Dietrich. He looked like a kindly grandfather, with his long gray hair and big belly. We soon learned his soft look was deceiving.

An ardent Nazi, he told us we would express absolute respect and loyalty to the party and the Third Reich at all times. After his rants about appreciating the opportunities to show our loyalty to Hitler, he sometimes found a little time to devote to our studies. More often he used the time to entertain us with stories of the bravery of our victorious Wehrmacht.

Loyalty to the Fuehrer took definite priority over learning.

Chapter 36

Roger's ability to get in trouble hit a new high shortly after the school term began. I wasn't home to help Mama keep track of him. Since it was only a short walk from our house to the school building, Roger came to meet me when classes ended. He liked to walk home with me and hear my stories about what happened during the day. When I turned to wave goodbye to Annette, he spotted an opportunity for a new adventure.

A team of two large draft horses pulled a pair of wagons hooked in trail down the street past my school. They were filled with wheat and headed for the mill. Roger ran alongside and jumped between the two big vehicles to grab the tailgate and climb aboard the lead wagon.

Realizing what he was doing, I screamed too late. "No!"

He was in the process of lifting himself to climb aboard when the wagon hit a big bump. His hands lost their grip, and he fell to the pavement between the wagons. He lay motionless for an instant, his head directly in line with the oncoming iron wheel of the second one.

The driver hadn't noticed the boy trying to climb onto the back of his wagon, and he allowed the horses to continue their slow movement down the street. Roger's head would certainly be crushed.

I watched in horror, unable to move, unable to make a sound.

At the last instant Roger's body jerked and he rolled toward the center of the wagon. The wheel brushed his hair as he escaped certain death. He didn't move as the rear wheels passed by him. The driver stopped the horses when bystanders got his attention. Roger lay still and silent behind the wagons when I reached him.

His eyes were open and his complexion was the color of chalk as I knelt beside him. He didn't acknowledge my presence for a moment. I reached to take his hand, and he finally exhaled a long breath. After I helped him sit up, he saw the bystanders surrounding us. He didn't appear to understand why they were all talking.

His voice cracked when he attempted to speak. "I fell."

I helped him up and led him home where Papa and Mama listened in shock to the story I told them and the way he looked.

Mama touched him with timid fingers. "Should we take him to the doctor?"

Papa shook his head. "What he needs is a good spanking. How could you be so foolish?"

Roger hung his head, but he didn't find an answer.

We were all completely subdued as we ate our evening meal in silence. Roger didn't protest when Mama put him to bed early.

At breakfast the next morning, he had recovered his normal spirit of adventure, and Papa's lecture about not taking foolish risks fell on deaf ears.

* * *

Papa and Mama sat at the dining table in deep conversation the next Saturday when I parked my bike after an afternoon visit to Annette. Her mother had served us slices of cake made with real sugar, and we amused ourselves by making fun of our teacher. We both giggled as we tried to outdo each other with funny stories about Mr. Dietrich. Knowing I would be late coming home, I tried to think of a good excuse. My parents' sad appearance caused me to stop as I entered the room.

"Is something wrong?"

Mama brushed back her hair and raised her eyes to mine. "We're just discussing all the men who've been drafted. They're taking them younger each month."

My happy mood disappeared. "Who got drafted?"

Papa answered, "The Berger boy that lives next to the station. He's barely seventeen, not old enough to be a soldier. He's in school, studying to be an accountant."

"We saw him in church last Sunday," I said. My stomach turned over. "He's not big and strong. He wears glasses."

"They're taking almost anyone now," Papa said. "The Nazis just want bodies to send to the Eastern Front. The Russians will kill them as fast as they show up."

"The Girauds were informed yesterday their son, Henri, is missing in action," Mama said. "He was in the army that attacked Stalingrad. He's either been shot or captured by the Russians. Either way, he's probably dead."

"His parents tried to get him to run away to avoid the draft, but he refused," Papa said. "They could have been sent to a concentration camp if he failed to report."

The cheerful afternoon I'd spent with Annette faded from my thoughts. Henri had always been my friend. He was the latest of several young men from the village who had been taken against their will. They had become the *malgre nous*, the unwilling, and they might never return.

* * *

It seemed like I'd just fallen asleep that night when Papa woke the family. The air raid siren screeched like an animal that had been hurt.

"Everybody up," Papa shouted. "Get behind the couch."

I climbed out of bed rubbing my eyes and stumbling to the top of the stairs. Gripping the rail to keep from falling, I made it down the steep steps and found my place behind the heavy piece of furniture. The whole family gathered there, and we waited for the sirens to stop. The drone of countless airplanes passing overhead kept me awake for a long time, and then the noise faded. I dozed for a few minutes until the sirens stopped.

Papa held the back of the couch and lifted himself up. "The airplanes are gone now. Everyone back to bed."

I'd just reached the top of the stairs when the sirens sounded again. Disappointed and sleepy, I stumbled down the steps once more to find my place in our shelter. My family crouched in our safe niche to await the passing of the English bombers.

The roar of hundreds of engines kept us still and frightened for what seemed like a long time. I huddled in the darkness, my back pressed against the wall and my feet tucked beneath the back of the couch. Cold air and the noise of the airplanes above kept me feeling miserable. I wanted to be in my bed, airplanes or no. The sirens finally stopped.

I'd just managed to crawl under the covers when they sounded once more.

As I forced myself out of bed again, I heard Mama complain. "This could last all night. Some poor German city is going through hell."

Papa's response sounded gruff. "Be thankful it's not Kaschel. Back to our shelter."

I crawled behind the couch and fell asleep this time.

Papa woke me later. "The sirens have finally stopped. We can go back to bed again. There were hundreds of bombers. They'll drop their bombs on some unfortunate German cities."

Daylight arrived all too soon. I brushed Mama's hand away when she shook me awake the next morning. Sirens had kept me from sleeping half the night, and I wasn't ready to get up.

After finishing my porridge, I ran to school to avoid being late. We spent a boring day learning why Europe would be a better place to live after all the undesirables were driven out or killed. Mr. Dietrich caught my head nodding and made me stand in the aisle so I'd stay awake to learn the lesson. Standing there like a fool made me feel like everyone was laughing at me.

Later I watched two of the boys join me. It didn't make me feel any better. Mr. Dietrich should have known we spent most of the night awake because of the air raid sirens.

That evening, Papa slammed the kitchen door and put his coat on its hook when he returned from listening to Mr. Schmidt's radio. "Thousands of British and American aircraft carpet-bombed German cities and military bases. Casualties have been horrific, and the bombers dropped leaflets telling the German people the bombing would stop when Hitler gave up his foolish plan to rule the world and surrendered."

Chapter 37

The winter sky promised more snow or wet weather when Papa shook raindrops from his coat after he came home from work. His boots gave way to a pair of house slippers. Then he pulled the underground newspaper I expected from an inside coat pocket and spread it on our table.

"Good news for a change." He picked up the front page and brought it closer to his eyes. "Free French forces from North Africa have liberated Corsica from the Germans. Along with the Resistance, most of the Italians changed sides and fought against the Nazis. The Wehrmacht was forced to evacuate their army from the island."

"Where is Corsica?" I asked.

Mama brought out a map and showed me where the island was. "It's close to Italy, but it is part of France."

Still puzzled, I asked another question. "I thought the Italians were friends with the Nazis. Why did they fight them?"

Papa laid the paper back on the table. "The Italians are trying to quit their alliance with Germany. They want the war to end."

The explanation didn't make a lot of sense. Figuring out what all these people were fighting about still puzzled me.

Later Opa came to visit with news of Uncle George. "The letter says he's still working on the farm near Marseilles. It was postmarked in Orleans. Something is wrong."

Mama looked aside. "Are you sure of the postmark?"

Opa nodded. "It's completely clear. I'm not mistaken."

She tugged at her apron. "That's not where he said the farm was located."

Papa hesitated, and his words came slow. "It sounds like he's hiding his location. I hope he didn't join the Resistance."

* * *

When the harsh weather arrived Mama's and my shoes were badly worn. They would never last through the season.

Papa bent to examine them and looked up at Mama. "The cobbler should be able to repair Irene's shoes to get her through the winter. Yours appear to be hopeless. I've looked everywhere, and I haven't found any to fit you."

Mama lifted her hands, palms up. "I have to find something."

Papa took a deep breath. "The Nazis have decreed that shoes with wooden soles will be sold so scarce materials can be diverted to the military. They're clumsy and not very comfortable, but they're all we can find now."

"Wooden shoes?" Mama gave a harsh frown and turned away.

"The cobbler has some," he said. "You can look at them when we take Irene's shoes for repair."

That afternoon we visited the man, and Papa explained what we needed. "I believe you can fix the child's shoes, but Mina's are gone. What do you propose?"

The man bent to examine mine and mumbled to himself as he ran his hands over them. "Take them off so I can see them better."

He pulled at the leather and poked a finger through a hole in one sole. "I can repair these to get you through the winter."

He looked at Mama's feet and reached for a pair on the shelf. "Try these on. They have leather uppers."

Mama put them on and made a face. She flung her hands in the air when she tried to walk. "They're completely stiff, and they make a terrible noise when they hit the floor."

The cobbler nodded. "That can't be helped. They seem to fit."

Mama's face wrinkled in a frown. "I suppose that's the best I can do."

Papa paid him, and we walked home. Mama's footsteps sounded like someone banging on the pavement with a stick. The cobbler kept my shoes to repair, so I walked down the cold street without them.

My stockings were soaked, and my toes felt like they had frozen when we arrived. Mama gave me her too large rubber boots to wear until my shoes were ready.

A week later, Mama had learned to walk without making so much noise with the wooden shoes, but she still didn't like them. "They feel too stiff."

My shoes had obviously been repaired, but I could wear them. Patches had become common in Kaschel.

* * *

Snow covered the ground, and Christmas was only three days away. We had a short vacation from school, and Mama used almost all of what was left of our sugar ration to make a small pound cake. The whole kitchen smelled good when I walked through.

She set the cake on the kitchen table to cool. "Don't anybody touch this. It's for Christmas Eve."

She put on her heavy coat and braved the snow to take care of our animals. I was in my room trying to sew up a rip in a sleeve of the dress I wanted to wear on Christmas day. Papa was due home from work soon, and Roger was somewhere being unusually quiet. He'd find a way to disrupt Mama's plan if one existed.

I opened my window to listen when I heard Papa talking about Christmas to Mama out by the chicken run. They came inside together stomping snow from their shoes on the front step.

I rushed to the top of the stairs to hear Papa tell her, "The stationmaster told me I could leave work at noon on Christmas Eve."

Mama's wooden soles clicked on the tile floor as she walked into the kitchen. Then she cried out in dismay, "Who took a bite out of my cake?"

"Irene, Roger, come here now." The tone of her voice told me she meant the *now*.

Roger stood in the doorway looking scared when I reached the bottom of the stairs. It appeared that someone was in serious trouble.

Mama pointed an accusing finger at Roger. "Did you take a bite out of the cake I baked for Christmas?"

His face lost color. "No, ma'am. It wasn't me."

The accusing finger pointed at me. "Did you take a bite of the cake?"

My legs felt weak, and I held onto the stair railing. "No, ma'am."

Papa stood with folded arms, a stern look on his face. "If we can't decide who is guilty, I'll have to spank you both."

He removed his belt and beckoned to Roger. "Come here."

Roger had already started to cry as he approached.

Papa took the little boy's hand and swung the belt. It made a loud smacking sound when it landed on my brother's backside.

Roger screamed like he was being eaten by the pigs. His voice screeched as he danced and dodged. The belt continued to smack his bottom.

I watched in horror as the spanking continued. "Stop! I bit the cake."

Papa released Roger and directed a firm gaze at me. "Why didn't you say so when your mother asked?"

I couldn't think of an answer.

Papa took my hand and swung the belt. Pain shot through my rear end, and it felt like I'd been burned.

I was already crying when Papa swung the belt again. Then I noticed Roger standing in a far corner of the room with his hand over his mouth, covering a giggle.

Another blow landed on the back of my legs.

"Stop," I screamed. "I didn't do it. Roger bit the cake."

Papa let the belt hang from his hand. "Are you sure? Why did you confess in the first place?"

I dried my tears on my sleeve and pointed at my little brother. "He giggled when you spanked me." My angry face delivered a message that my revenge would be worse than a spanking.

Papa released me and beckoned for Roger to come closer. "Why did you think it was so funny when I spanked your sister?"

Roger's chin fell to his chest. He squirmed and bit his lip. "I don't know."

"I think you lied to me, and your sister tried to save you," Papa said. "Is that true?"

Roger's eyes leaked more tears. "I'm sorry."

Papa took his hand and delivered another half dozen licks with his belt. "Now, what do you say to your sister?"

Roger turned toward me with downcast eyes and mumbled, "I'm sorry."

Then Papa gave me two more swats with the belt. "You should not tell lies, not even to save your brother from punishment he deserves."

Mama hid the cake on the top shelf of our cupboard, and we had to wait two more days for Christmas Eve.

After we'd eaten our holiday dinner, Mama cut the cake. Roger got the slice with the missing bite.

Chapter 38

I woke with a start when a passenger bumped my seat while walking down the narrow aisle of the airliner. I'd dozed off when boredom overcame me during the long day cooped up in the crowded airplane with nothing to do. A quick glance at my infant child assured me he was enjoying a peaceful nap in his safety hammock beside me.

Looking at my surroundings confirmed I wasn't the only one who had dozed off during our long journey. I leaned back against the headrest, and the steady drone of the plane's four big engines reminded me of sitting in our hideaway and listening to the American and British aircraft flying over Kaschel to drop bombs on Germany during the war.

My family had lost a lot of sleep rushing to our haven behind the couch whenever we heard air raid sirens. We'd huddle together for warmth to combat the near freezing temperature in the unheated room. Huge formations streamed overhead for what seemed like hours, and I quickly learned to bring a blanket with me as we waited for the all clear. The formations soon increased in the size and frequency of their raids. Clandestine radio broadcasts brought almost daily news of another German city demolished. Factories and transportation centers were reported to be utterly destroyed. Civilian casualties were high as well, especially during the nighttime attacks.

I'd lived in fear the airplanes might drop their bombs on Kaschel. We knew they attacked trains, and the railroad tracks passed close to the village. Papa worked at the station and switching yard, and we all feared he could be caught in an air raid.

Daylight raids became more frequent when the Americans brought their new aircraft with more accurate bomb sights. The *Luftwaffe* had suffered severe losses, and the Americans could attack during the daytime with less opposition. At school, we had frequent interruptions to take shelter as the fleets of Allied bombers passed overhead. My constant fear that they might drop a bomb on us remained as a vivid memory.

* * *

Planes flew over Kaschel, the sirens sounded, and we hid in our little space behind the sofa. It happened almost every day or night, and I was never able to stop being afraid. Everyone tried to live a normal life despite the frequent flyovers. Papa went to work, and Mama kept things neat and clean in the house. I went to school as usual.

Papa came home from work one day with drooping shoulders and wet, dull eyes. He took a seat at the kitchen table and held his head with both hands.

Mama lowered her voice to a hoarse whisper. “What’s wrong?”

Papa straightened in his chair and looked up. “The Wagner twins, Jacob and Hans, got their draft notices.”

Mama sank into an adjacent chair like a deflated balloon. “They’re only sixteen. How could the army use them?”

“The Fuehrer is desperate to stop the Russian advance. Stalin wants to make slaves of the Germans. The boys will wind up on the Eastern Front.”

I laid my hand on Papa’s arm. “When do they have to go?”

Papa’s fingers twitched as he reached out to hold me. “The Nazis didn’t give them any time. They leave next week.”

Tears wet my cheeks. "They're going to school in Sarregumines. They're too young to fight."

"They don't have a choice," Papa said. "If they fail to report, the Nazis will take their parents to a concentration camp and kill them."

My legs trembled when I sank down in my corner to hide my anger and fear. Jacob and Hans liked to tease me sometimes, but they were never mean. I remembered the time Hans gave me his apple when I forgot to bring my lunch. They were the nicest big boys I knew. They were too young to fight the Russians.

* * *

We braved the rain and cold weather until spring arrived. My school work was interrupted by our teacher's frequent discussions of our wonderful opportunities to support the Third Reich. More teenaged boys were drafted and we feared they would all be sent to the Russian front. Most went to the Wehrmacht, but some were required to serve in the dreaded *Waffen SS*.

Resistance newspapers told us the Red Army was relentless. The Nazis won a few battles, but the Russians continued their steady advance toward Germany. Hitler demanded more sacrifice from German citizens. Papa said the Fuehrer had gone crazy.

Mr. Schmidt walked across the street at suppertime. I listened as he brought more news of the war. "U.S. and British bombers attacked eight different German aircraft factories yesterday. BBC claims they destroyed one fourth of Nazi fighter plane output. Allied losses were minor."

Papa whistled under his breath. "If that's true, Hitler is in deep trouble."

"It could be worse," Mr. Schmidt said. "The swarm of bombers that pass over the village most days could destroy an entire city."

"I heard some encouraging news," Papa said. "The British have air dropped a huge load of weapons to the *Maquis* near Annency. That should equip them to stir up some real trouble for the Germans."

Mr. Schmidt drug a boot through the drifted snow. "The Underground is gaining strength fast. They could make a difference."

"I hope they hit the Vichy French forces as well," Papa said. "How about a glass of schnapps to celebrate before dinner?"

Mr. Schmidt grinned. "Sounds like an offer I can't refuse."

Days later, Papa came home with more good news after listening to the Schmidt's hidden radio. "BBC reports Allied Forces have achieved air superiority over the *Luftwaffe* in the skies over Germany and Western Europe. This will be a huge advantage when they invade the continent."

* * *

Warm weather and gentle rains had driven away the cold. After an early breakfast, Papa went to the barn, readying his farm equipment for spring planting. "I need to put in even bigger crops this year. The Nazis take almost half of what we produce."

Mama held her apron filled with eggs. "I don't know how you can do more. We work from sunup to sundown now."

Papa straightened and wiped his hands on his trousers. "The Nazis are holding Russian prisoners in a camp at Sarralbe. They'll let them out to work if we feed them."

Mama frowned. "Can we trust Russians?"

"They're not going anywhere. If they escaped and made their way back to the Red Army lines, they'd have to fight again. Worse, they might be shot as deserters. They're not treated well here, but it's better than their alternative. Only a few would go back if Germany offered to send them there."

"Are they in shape to work?"

Papa shook his head. "They're not in good health, but they're willing. Nazis usually give them half rations. What we feed them may be the only good meal they see all week."

Mama pursed her lips. "We can try it."

I listened to this discussion as I finished sweeping the steps. I'd heard everyone talking about Russian troops killing tens of thousands of German soldiers outside Moscow. The Red Army was brutal. The thought of having their prisoners on our farm scared me.

"I'll go to the camp and see what I can arrange. I should be home in an hour." Papa got on his bicycle and pedaled away.

It took more than an hour, but he pushed his bicycle as he returned with two pale, tall, and very thin, young men with hollow cheeks and vacant eyes. They were dressed in threadbare dark shirts and rumpled military trousers and what looked like their worn-out army boots.

Papa pointed to each of the prisoners when we came out to see them. "This is Alexei, and this is Viktor."

I nodded my greeting since I couldn't think of the proper words.

The men stood in silence while Papa harnessed the cows to the wagon. After a moment, he gestured to them and said, "Let's load the plow and these hand tools."

Alexei seemed to understand a little German and moved quickly while Viktor hesitated. He began to help after Alexei said something to him in Russian. They loaded a plow, a harrow, a pair of sturdy hoes, a rake, a brush hook, and an axe onto the wagon, and Papa gestured for them to climb aboard.

Looking at all those implements scared me. The tools could be used as weapons, and Papa would be alone with the prisoners.

After all three were seated in the wagon, they were ready to leave for the fields. Papa said, "We'll be home for lunch at noon. These men will be hungry."

When they returned, Mama had food ready. The men found a jug of milk, bread, boiled potatoes, sauerkraut, and a few slices of ham on the table.

Alexei dipped his face close to his plate and breathed in the aroma of the simple meal. A broad smile covered his face when he straightened. "Good."

I watched in awe as the prisoners ate as if they might never see food again. Not a crumb was left when they finished the meal.

The men spent the rest of the day preparing the land for planting crops, and Papa dismissed them to walk back to the prison camp. He'd arranged for the pair to work a full week, and they showed up at our house early the next morning. Mama fed them a bowl of oatmeal before they went to the fields.

During lunch, Alexei motioned for Roger to approach. "I have a thing for you," he said in broken German.

Always curious, Roger approached Alexei who held out a tiny wood carving of an airplane.

"For you," Alexei said.

Roger beamed, and I leaned toward him to examine the carving. It was delicate work and a good likeness of the Allied fighters that flew over Kaschel so frequently.

Roger handled it with care and awarded the Russian prisoner a big smile. "Thank you."

Papa looked closely at the little plane and reached into his wallet to bring out three or four small coins. He offered them to Alexei who waved them away.

"They're for you," Papa insisted.

After a brief hesitation, the man accepted the coins and dropped them in his pocket. "Can trade to guard for food. Much thank you."

Papa rose from his chair and waved the prisoners toward the door. "Daylight is wasting. Time to get to work."

When Friday arrived, the planting was done, and Papa took the men to my grandparents' house to help plant their garden.

That evening, we said goodbye to Alexei and Viktor. Their shoulders slumped when Papa sent them back to the camp. He shook hands with them and said, "Perhaps you can help us again when we harvest our crops."

Fearful for what awaited them, I choked at the thought of the hardship they suffered in the Nazi prison. I hoped they would survive to go home when the war ended. I could only wish them well during their time as prisoners.

A week later, we had just finished breakfast when Mr. Schmidt brought more news about the war. "American, British, and Polish troops have entered Rome. German resistance is crumbling. They're falling back to regroup."

Papa tipped his cap back. “If The Allies keep coming, they’ll be in France soon. The Nazis are in big trouble.”

Mama looked up from the sink where she washed our dishes. “I’ll believe it when I see them running away.”

“Our Vichy Government will probably fight against the Allies in the South of France,” Mr. Schmidt said. “We could have a big battle there.”

I shuddered and held my doll close as I listened from the corner. The armies might soon be fighting in Kaschel.

Chapter 39

On a Tuesday morning, the hot June day already felt like August as I swept our kitchen floor. Mama had heated water and filled two tubs for our laundry when Mr. Schmidt rushed across the street with news. He was out of breath when he reached our house. "The Allies have invaded at Normandy. I just heard it on the radio. Hundreds of ships stretch as far as the eye can see. Troops are arriving in landing craft and storming the beaches by the thousands."

Papa's eyebrows flew up at the news. "Where did they land?" He took off his hat to beat it against his leg.

"Somewhere around a town named Caen. It's about a hundred kilometers southeast of Cherbourg. Thousands of soldiers are pouring off the ships to flood the beaches."

"The newspaper says Nazis have pillboxes and machine guns sighted in on the shoreline from those cliffs," Papa said. "We had a training exercise there while I was stationed at Soissons. The cliffs overlook the beaches. There's nothing but flat sand. There's no cover. The Allies don't have a chance. It'll be mass murder, a slaughterhouse."

Mr. Rolf hurried over to join the group. "Is it the big invasion we've been expecting?"

"Appears to be," Mr. Schmidt said. "We can all listen to my radio in the basement."

"Better lock your doors and keep quiet. You don't want to lose your radio," Mama warned.

Mr. Schmidt chuckled. "They'd take it right after they shot me."

I tagged along as the men gathered to hear the BBC. They huddled close to the big console radio that crackled with static. I stood beside Papa's chair as we listened to the broadcast.

The daytime signal came in weak, so Mr. Schmidt played with the knobs and the antenna until we were able to understand the broadcast. "Our on-site announcer reports waves of American C-47 transports dropped hundreds, maybe thousands, of paratroopers behind the German lines. They could disrupt Nazi troop movements and protect bridges so Allied troops can move inland quickly when they gain a foothold. American and British fighter planes are attacking German batteries on the cliffs."

Stunned, I sank to the floor, picturing the Normandy Beach as Papa had described it. A vision of thousands of soldiers coming out of the water to a stretch of sand where Nazis could shoot down on them with big guns was too frightening to think about.

Mr. Rolf said, "They'll have to climb the cliffs to destroy those guns. It would be suicide to stay on the beach."

The announcer continued, "Hundreds of aircraft towing gliders are releasing them to land in shallow water close to shore. Others are landing behind German lines. Troops are wading through the surf to join their comrades on the beaches. Small groups of soldiers are attempting to scale the cliffs."

Papa held his head in his hands, "This is awful. If they get to the top, they'll be carrying rifles to attack concrete gun emplacements."

"The soldiers don't have a choice," Mr. Schmidt said. "They'll all die on the beach if they don't destroy those guns."

Papa breathed a long sigh. "Their best bet is to get close and use hand grenades. They'll need to land them inside the dug-in shelters to destroy the Nazi guns."

Mr. Schmidt closed the windows, and the room felt stuffy. I sank to my knees in a corner of the basement and tried not to think about the soldiers trying to climb the cliffs with Nazis shooting down at them. Fighting a queasy stomach and a strong urge to vomit, I sought comfort by rising to stand beside Papa.

He looked up and put an arm around me. "I know it's terrible, but the Allies will break through and come to help us."

Later the announcer repeated a message from the American commanding general. "Dwight Eisenhower asked all French citizens to remain calm and follow the instructions of your leaders. A premature uprising may prevent you from being of maximum help to your country during this critical hour. Be patient. Prepare."

The announcer couldn't give more details of the battle and repeated himself several times. The men finally left, and I followed Papa home. His assurances the Allies would come here didn't convince me. Visions of thousands of soldiers lying on an unprotected beach with machine gun bullets raining down on them filled my mind. I went to my room to lie in bed shaking. Then the flood of tears came.

* * *

A few days later, Papa brought home a Resistance newspaper. "The SS committed another atrocity too vile to comprehend."

He laid the paper on the dining table, and Mama sat down to read it. I read over her shoulder, and she explained the parts I couldn't understand. The article said "The *maquis* had been suspected of capturing a senior SS officer. An unconfirmed rumor said the Resistance had executed him in the village of Oradour-Sur-Glane.

The SS descended on the village and rounded up all the residents. The men were separated in groups and marched into barns. Women and children were herded into a church. The SS shot all the men. Then they ransacked and burned the houses in the village. Next, they locked the church doors and set it on fire. When the terrified women tried to escape with their children, the SS fired through the windows to kill them. They murdered every living person they found."

She stopped to wipe away tears. "Still not satisfied, the Nazis stopped the evening train and separated all the passengers bound for Oradour. The SS killed them and threw them into the fire."

My tears fell on the newspaper before I fled to my room. Why did the Nazis want to kill innocent people?

* * *

In the weeks that followed, the Allies broke out of their beachhead and advanced in several directions. I listened as Mama and Papa discussed the battles. Cherbourg fell, and the American General Bradley destroyed the Nazi forces around St. Lo. British and Canadian armies pushed eastward. The invasion proved to be a success, but casualties on both sides had been enormous.

Still horrified by the announcer's description of Allied troops on the Normandy beaches, I lost sleep every night from bad dreams. After begging off my chores the following Sunday, I spent the afternoon with Annette. The visit helped both of us feel better. We talked about our families and the war and wondered whether or not we'd have school in the fall.

My improved mood didn't last long. Papa brought home more terrible news. "The Wagner twins, Jacob and Hans, have been reported killed in action on the Eastern Front. They were only sixteen."

Mama collapsed into a chair wringing her hands. "That's the worst thing that could happen to a family. I must take their mother some food."

I slipped outside to be alone and suffer in silence. The twins had enjoyed teasing me, but they'd always been kind. I'd looked up to them. Taking the boys into military service had been cruel. They couldn't stop the Russians. Sending them to the Eastern Front had been murder. Their senseless death added one more tragedy we were forced to suffer.

Bad news kept coming. The next day Papa told us about another terrible event he'd heard about on Mr. Schmidt's radio. "The Germans launched a secret weapon today, the V-1 Rocket. This jet propelled flying bomb killed dozens of people in London. It's hard to intercept because it doesn't have a pilot, and it flies as fast as a fighter plane. It's not accurate, so they aim at the center of the city. The bomb flies until it runs out of fuel, and then it falls. It can't be aimed at the military, so it usually kills civilians when it crashes and explodes in the city."

Mama's voice sounded like she had something stuck in her throat. "That's not a weapon of war. It's a terror weapon."

Papa nodded agreement. "The British government is trying to evacuate the holdouts among women and children in London to rural areas."

Mama's eyes darted around the room, then stared at the ceiling. She sighed and mumbled. "This could turn the war around for Hitler if he has enough of these infernal machines. And just when we thought the Nazis were losing."

Chapter 40

I was helping Mama clean the kitchen when Roger's friend, Karl Scheuer, knocked on our door looking for Roger on a cloud-free Saturday. "My father is fishing at the Sarre, and I'm bringing his lunch. Could Roger come with me?"

Roger sprang from the corner where he'd been playing with a toy truck. "Can I go? Please."

Mama hesitated. Karl was about two years older than Roger and equally capable of getting into trouble.

Karl promised, "I'll just bring Papa his lunch, and we'll come home."

Roger pleaded, "We'll come straight home. I promise."

Mama cocked her head and shook a finger at my brother. "Don't play by the river. I'll have lunch ready in a half hour. You'd better be here to eat."

Roger flashed his best innocent look at Mama. "I'll be home."

As they left, the two boys skipped down the street. I didn't believe a word they said.

Lunch was soon ready, and Roger hadn't returned. A half hour later, he still wasn't home.

Finally, Mama looked at me. "Go see if the boys went to Mrs. Scheuer's house."

The Scheuers lived two blocks down the cross street, and I ran all the way. I was out of breath and sweating by the time I arrived. When Mrs. Scheuer answered the door, I asked, "Did Karl and Roger come back here?"

She shook her head. "No. I told Karl to hurry, and then I got busy and forgot. His lunch is already cold."

"Mama's worried they may be playing by the river."

"Neither of them can swim." Her eyes opened wide, and she wiped a hand across her forehead. "Come with me to look for them."

I had to run to keep up with her long steps. When we arrived at Mr. Scheuer's fishing hole, he was alone.

Mrs. Scheuer took a deep breath. "Karl promised to come straight home, and he hasn't shown up for lunch."

He lifted his bait from the water and leaned his pole against a tree. "Check the playground at the park and their friends' houses. I'll walk along the river and look for them."

We started back to the village, and Mrs. Scheuer said, "I'll check their friends'. Tell your mother to look in the park."

After I ran home, I tagged along with Mama. She asked everyone she saw if they'd seen the boys. Nobody had. We walked along some of the major streets and asked others. She got the same answers and finally went home to see if he'd returned.

By the middle of the afternoon, Mama and I were unable to sit or stand in one place. If a child fell in the river, he'd likely be swept away by the current. She stayed home to wait for Roger while I made the rounds to city hall, the churches, schoolrooms, and the soccer field without finding anyone who'd seen the boys.

An hour later, Mr. Scheuer came with Roger in tow. "The boys wandered through the woods along the river and upstream to the flour mill. They were fascinated by the big water wheel. When I found them, they were wading the shallows, throwing rocks at the wheel as it turned in the stream."

"Thank you." Mama clasped her hands together. "We were so frightened."

Mr. Scheuer turned to Roger with a stern look. "I hope you boys learned something."

My brother looked at his feet and mumbled, "Yes, sir."

"Good. My day of fishing was cut short, and I have a boy at home who needs a proper spanking."

When Mr. Scheuer was gone, Mama crossed her arms and faced Roger. "What caused you to break your promise and run away?"

Roger snuffled and wiped away a few tears. "I don't know."

She took his hand and led him inside. A moment later, I heard the sound of a leather strap smacking a soft target. Roger's yowls of pain told me he was paying the price for scaring us with his adventure.

When Papa came home from work, Mama told him what happened. His jaw tightened and his face darkened as he listened. Then he led Roger to our parlor, and I heard the popping sound of the strap on Roger's back side again. His howls were even louder this time.

The punishment must have done some good. For the next several days, Roger was quiet. He stayed home, and he did what Mama told him to do.

* * *

Later that week Papa returned from work sweating from the heat and sporting a big smile. "We have good news today."

Mama puffed out her cheeks and exhaled. "You'd best tell us. We haven't heard much good lately."

"Adolf Hitler had a rude surprise. He was holding a meeting in his secret lair when a bomb went off in the room. He lived through it, but he has a bad burn and a few bruises. It killed one and wounded a dozen of his military staff."

Mama's eyes lit up. "Too bad it wasn't him dead. Do they know who did it?"

"It was an officer named von Stauffenberg," he said. "The Resistance paper says a lot of the military officers want to end this war, but Hitler won't admit he's beaten. He expects his army to fight until they're dead."

"Maybe someone will try again."

"It will be difficult," Papa said. "He's likely to kill anyone he suspects. They reported that von Stauffenberg has already been executed."

I couldn't stay quiet. "Will the fighting end if someone kills Hitler?"

Papa patted my shoulder. "The Germans would probably try to negotiate an end to the war, but the Allies want to punish them. They'd need to agree on terms."

It took me a long time to fall asleep that night. I didn't always remember to say my prayers, but, this time, I prayed for the war to end.

A few days later Papa invited Mr. Rolf and Mr. Schmidt over to share a glass of schnapps. The men discussed the war. Papa opened the windows to capture the cooling breeze that removed some of the stale heat in the room, and I watched from the doorway to our winter kitchen.

Papa didn't use the tiny glasses for his liquor. He poured about four fingers of the sparkling clear liquid in water glasses and waited for the men to taste it.

Mr. Rolf took a small sip then smiled. "Just what I expected. Some of the best you've ever made."

Mr. Schmidt took a larger swallow and coughed. "Good as ever. I hear the German Army is retreating along the whole front in Normandy. The Americans are advancing everywhere."

Mr. Rolf scooted back in his chair. "If they keep it up, the Nazis will be defending their homeland before long."

"The French are beginning to make a difference," Papa said. "Free French troops are advancing with the Americans."

"The French Second Armored Division was part of the Normandy invasion," Mr. Rolf said. "They're using American tanks."

Mr. Schmidt's hand slapped the table. "About time the French did something."

Papa continued. "The *maquis* is coming alive, too. They are taking the fight to the Nazis and their collaborators. They have already shaved the heads of a few females who were too friendly with the Germans."

I hugged myself and listened in silence. Would the Nazis fight here if the Americans came to Kaschel? When armies fight, civilians could get hurt too. I'd heard that almost three thousand civilians had been killed in London by the flying bombs. It would have been more if the Royal Air Force hadn't managed to shoot down half of them before they reached their target. I wanted the Americans to come, but the thought of two armies fighting here scared me.

The men were smiling and slapping each other on the back when they finished the schnapps. I went to bed and pulled the sheet over my head, shaking and afraid, worried the war could really come to Kaschel.

Bad news was closer to home the next day. The sun sank behind the tops of trees bordering the Sarre as Mr. Rolf banged on our door. "Adolf, come quickly. A house is on fire."

I followed as Papa stormed outside. "Where?" he shouted.

Mama called after him. "I'll keep Roger at home."

Mr. Rolf was already running toward the column of smoke near the cemetery. “Looks like it might be the Blattner’s house.”

My shorter legs forced me to fall behind as the men raced to the fire. When they got to the street corner by the burning house, they stopped with several others before they arrived. When I finally caught up, I saw the SS troopers pointing their rifles at the villagers.

“Stay back,” a soldier shouted. “This is a military operation.”

Flames poured from the windows of the Blattner’s house. Smoke burned my eyes and made me cough. I felt heat from the flames from a half block away.

Looking past the soldiers, I saw Henri Blattner handcuffed and on his knees in the middle of the street. An SS man pointed a gun at his head. Another soldier used his rifle to block Henri’s parents from reaching their son.

Henri had been drafted at age sixteen and sent to the Eastern Front to fight the Russians.

Sergeant Schnabel stormed up to join the SS men keeping us away from the blaze. His legs were planted wide, and he bared his teeth as he shouted orders. “This man deserted his unit. His parents attempted to hide him. The Third Reich does not allow cowardice or disobedience. Henri Blattner will be taken to his base and shot for desertion.”

Henri’s mother tried to run to her son. “No!” she screamed! “He’s a child!”

The soldier shoved her back with the stock of his rifle, and she collapsed in tears.

Sergeant Schnabel lifted his pistol from its holster and waved it at onlookers. “This house is burned as punishment for housing a deserter. The same will happen to anyone who attempts to shirk their duty."

My shaking knees threatened to collapse. Nobody was safe from the Nazis.

Chapter 41

Another shoreline moved into view outside my window as the pilot came on the public address system. "Ladies and gentlemen, the land you see on the right side of the aircraft is Nova Scotia. We have reached the North American Continent. We'll land in New York in about two hours."

Our stewardess translated for me, and I tried out my limited English. "Thank you."

I reached to touch little Paul in his hammock and breathed a sigh of relief. Our trip neared its end. Dale had gone ahead to be released from the army. He'd be discharged, a civilian again, when he met us at the airport.

Living in Paris as a young woman had been an exciting time. Then I met and married an American soldier named Dale.

Friends had warned me to beware dating one of those rascals. "They are shallow, not interested in a long-term relationship, and they will soon return to the United States."

Dale's army salary was inadequate to support us, even with lower prices at the PX. He worked weekends at the army mess hall to earn a few dollars, and I added what I could save from my meager wages to pay for our trip to America.

My father didn't approve of my choice. He researched what he could learn about Kansas from the library, and his friends at the bar had described a few of the obstacles I'd face. "Kansas is like a furnace in summer, and arctic snowstorms paralyze it during winter. Fierce winds blow all the time. The weather changes from dust storms to snowdrifts in a single day."

I held out my hands, palms up. "I don't think it's quite that bad."

Papa shook his head. "Wait until you see a tornado. It will carry your house away with you in it. Outlaws and wild Indians live there, too."

Dale and I had lived in a sixth-floor walk-up apartment and shared a bathroom with the family next door. We bought a small Renault car on credit.

A momentary fear took my breath away. What if Dale wasn't at the airport to meet us? I'd spent the last of our money to pay for the airplane tickets.

After taking a few deep breaths to calm my fright, I reminded myself that we had mapped out our next moves. Our future was surely secure. We'd purchased a new Renault automobile, and Dale had shipped it to New York. It would take us to Kansas, and his family would welcome us while Dale started work. My fears were surely foolish.

We planned to live in Wichita where he would resume his old job. I looked forward to reaching a country my friends told me offered unlimited opportunity. Dale had already explained almost nobody spoke French or German there, so I would have to learn English to function. To date, I hadn't made much of an effort. Reassuring myself that my doubts about this new world were unfounded, I looked back to reflect on my fears when the end of World War II approached.

* * *

The weather stayed warm, and clouds filled the sky when Annette parked her bike by the garden where I rested on my knees pulling weeds. "Did you hear about Maria's uncle?"

"No. What happened?" I stood and brushed away the dirt. "Was it Nicolas? I saw him at church on Sunday."

"Yes. The SS came and took him away. They said he'll be taken to the big prison in Strasbourg."

I felt a sudden chill. "Why?"

Her hands lifted and fluttered. "They just took him and put him in their automobile without telling his wife anything."

"He has four children," I said. "He wasn't involved in the Resistance."

"It doesn't seem to matter to the Nazis. They send some people to forced labor camps, and some go to concentration camps. Some are kept in Strasbourg. I hear they work them all the time and don't give them enough food."

"Who's going to take care of the children?"

Annette shrugged. "His wife will have to do something. I suppose her parents will keep the children while she tries to find work."

We went inside to escape the heat, and I offered her a glass of tea. "It's weak. We are almost out of it, and Mama can't find any more to replace it."

"My father had good news when he came home for lunch today," Annette said. "The Allies have invaded the south of France. Free French forces landed with the Americans. They are moving inland. The Nazis are retreating."

I wanted to celebrate at the thought we might be liberated. "They might come to Alsace. I hope they run the Nazis all the way back to Berlin."

A week later we learned the French Army had liberated the cities of Toulon and Marseilles. The Wehrmacht offered little resistance before retreating, and the French arrival was met with huge celebrations in the freed cities.

Another week passed before Mr. Schmidt brought word that General De Gaulle led the Free French Army to take control of Paris. Everyone expected the Nazis to destroy the city, but they left it almost untouched when the Wehrmacht retreated without putting up a fight. The French flag flew over our capital city once more. Kaschel celebrated quietly, not giving the authorities an excuse to punish us.

* * *

The next day Mama went outside to repair a sagging gate to the chicken run. Roger played with his toys on the kitchen floor, and I had been told to keep him out of trouble. Mama's sudden scream got my attention.

"Irene, I need help. Come quickly!"

I arrived to find her hand caught in the gap between the gate and its post. She explained that a wind gust slammed the gate shut. The ring finger on her left hand suffered a deep cut, and the wound was badly soiled with dirt from the chicken run. After I held the gate open, she managed to pull her hand free.

She looked at the deep gash in her finger. "Bring me a fresh rag. I need to clean and bandage the cut."

After she'd washed her hand and doused the cut with schnapps, I helped her wrap the wound with a strip of cloth.

She looked at the bandaged finger and nodded approval. "It should heal now. I'll have to be careful and keep it clean."

But the wound didn't heal.

By morning the cut was red, swollen, and filled with pus. Her wedding ring threatened to cut off blood circulation to the finger.

"It hurts," she said.

Papa frowned when he came to look. "We have to get the ring off."

He soaped her finger and tugged on the ring. It was imbedded in the swollen flesh and didn't move. He managed to rotate it and tried again. It still wouldn't budge.

He finally gave up. "We need a doctor."

Mama shook her head. "The doctor in Sarre Union was drafted to care for German soldiers. He's not available for civilians."

"Ask the pastor at church," Papa said. "He may know someone who can help you. Go with her, Irene. I need to fix the gate. I'll look after Roger."

I walked with Mama to the parsonage, and the pastor looked at the wound.

He shook his head and didn't even attempt to remove the ring. "It has to be cut off. We'll have to find someone with the proper tools."

"What kind of tools?" Mama asked.

"I'm not sure." The pastor rubbed the side of his head. "We need something that will cut the ring and not your finger."

They discussed the problem for a time, and the pastor finally thought of a possible answer. "The Germans have a mechanic who maintains their vehicles. He might be able to find a tool that will work."

The thought of asking a Nazi for help scared me, but we had no choice. I followed them to the park where the German Army kept their heavy equipment. They had a utility vehicle, two trucks, a motorcycle, and, lately, a Panzer tank parked there. The mechanic stored his tools under a picnic pavilion. A Wehrmacht soldier sat at a table bonding a hot patch onto a big inner tube.

The pastor lifted a hand in greeting. "We're looking for your mechanic."

The soldier looked up. "That's me."

"Mrs. Reeb has a torn and swollen finger. We need someone who has a proper tool to remove her ring."

The mechanic stood. "Let me see the finger."

Mama stepped forward and showed him her wound.

He shook his head and whistled. "You do need help." He opened his tool box and rummaged through the top tray to retrieve a strange looking pair of pliers. "These are called nippers. They cut at the end of the tool."

Mama was soon seated at the table, and the soldier worked the nippers past the swollen flesh onto the ring. He looked up with a frown. "I'm not sure I can cut the ring without cutting your finger as well. At worst, it will be small, and you won't notice it against the big cut you already have."

Mama winced and nodded.

The soldier bent to the task, and we soon heard a distinct snip as the ring was severed. He used a different tool to widen the cut in the gold band and removed it from her finger. Smiling, he handed her the ring. "All done. Take it to a jeweler. He can make it look like new again."

Mama lifted the finger for a closer inspection, and a single drop of blood appeared where the tool had nicked the skin. With the ring removed, circulation returned to the wounded finger.

Mama smiled as she told him how much she appreciated his kindness, and our fears vanished as we made our way home.

Papa exhaled a deep breath when Mama showed him her finger. Then he rummaged in our closet and handed me a bottle of schnapps. "Take this to the soldier and thank him for me."

Relieved that Mama's finger would heal, I ran all the way.

A big grin appeared on the soldier's face when I delivered the bottle. "Thank you. It was nothing. I'll enjoy the schnapps."

As I made my way home, I realized I'd met a second Nazi who could be human.

* * *

Papa brought home a resistance newspaper later that week. He told us, "The *maquis* have become more active. They sabotaged several factories that support the Nazi war effort and concentrated on attacks to shut down railroad transportation."

Nazi retribution was swift. Dozens of underground prisoners were executed to send the message that opposition would not be tolerated. *Maquis* efforts to disrupt the occupiers only increased.

Another front page story caught Mama's eye. She pointed to the paper. "The Nazis have launched new rockets on London. They're called the V-2, and they fly at almost the speed of sound. British interceptors can't catch them."

Papa stared at the ceiling while pushing back his hair with both hands. "That leaves the city helpless against the rockets."

Mama ran her finger down the page. "It says artillery has shot down a few, but most of them have hit the city. The British are moving more women and children out in the countryside."

"How can they fight against a weapon like that?"

Mama looked up after she finished reading the article. "British and American forces try to bomb the launch sites, but Nazi camouflage makes them hard to find."

I sank into my corner. My chin touched my chest as I thought about the poor children who didn't know when the next bomb was coming. My hands shook as they covered my ears.

As fall approached, and the weather turned cooler, Papa returned from listening to Mr. Schmidt's radio. "The United States and Great Britain recognized the Provisional Government of the French Republic. It will be led by Charles De Gaulle. We'll have something to replace the Vichy Government when the Nazis are gone."

Several days later, Papa returned from work with drooping shoulders and dragging feet. When he entered the kitchen, he reached for the schnapps. After downing a drink directly from the bottle, he began to talk. "Two trains filled with German wounded passed through the station today. Blood seeped from the cars, and a ditch leading toward the Sarre ran red. Nazi officials boarded the train to conduct triage on the soldiers. Those hurt so badly they had little chance to survive were offloaded and taken to a camp where they will be left to die."

Mama stood close and wrapped an arm across his shoulders. "That's awful. Many of them are mere boys. They deserve a chance to live. Can't someone help them?"

Papa sighed. "They will save more lives if they concentrate on those with lesser injuries. Many of those rejected would probably die even if they received treatment, and the army doesn't have enough doctors to care for all of them."

Tears filled my eyes as I sat alone in my corner. We didn't even treat our animals like that. When one was sick or hurt, we tried to save it.

Papa continued. "They put up a big tent with a large red cross on top to treat others who might be saved with immediate care. The stationmaster says it's too little too late. They don't have doctors and nurses to staff this makeshift hospital."

Sobs wracked my body as I ran to my room to suffer in silence.

Chapter 42

One overcast evening, Papa finished his dinner and crossed the street to Mr. Schmidt's house for the latest war news. He returned with a huge smile on his face. "General Patton's army has captured the city of Nancy. The Americans are on their way to liberate us."

Excitement at the news made me want to dance. I'd been to Nancy. It wasn't far from Kaschel. The Americans would be here soon. The Nazis would finally be gone.

My fears took over when I had second thoughts. *What if they fight when the Americans get here? Would we be evacuated again?*

Papa motioned us to sit around the table. His voice was loud and gruff. "Hitler has lost his war. The crazy fool refuses to surrender."

Mama put a finger to her lips, then asked. "Is there no way to stop him?"

Papa's voice softened. "People have tried and failed. The army is taking sixteen-year-old boys to face American and Russian tanks. Most of them are sent to fight without training or proper weapons. They'll be killed within weeks."

Mama clutched Roger tighter. "We're losing a generation of young men fighting a war we didn't ask for."

Papa nodded. "The Wehrmacht has stopped sending death notices to families of soldiers on the Russian Front. There are too many."

My thoughts about being rescued didn't last long. Within minutes someone pounded on the door. When Papa answered, Sergeant Schnabel and an SS soldier shoved their way inside.

The burly SS man pointed his rifle. "Where are you hiding the draftee cowards?

Roger started to cry, and Mama took him in her arms.

Papa answered. "We are hiding nobody."

The overbearing sergeant glared at Papa. "If we find anyone, you will be shot for hiding a fugitive. Don't leave this room."

The four of us huddled together as the two Nazis rummaged through our house for a second time. The noise of doors slamming and furniture overturned filled my ears. Even though I knew no one was hiding, my body shook, and I clung to Mama. She promised Roger the soldiers would go away, but he didn't stop crying.

The Nazis stormed back into the room and left without speaking. When we looked at the rest of the house, we found overturned beds, scattered furniture, and clothing from our wardrobes strewn across the floor.

Mama crossed her arms and stared at the mess. "Swine."

We spent the next few hours cleaning up the damage.

* * *

A few days later Mr. Schmidt came to visit with more news. "The Americans are moving toward Kaschel, and the Free French are moving toward Strasbourg. I think the Nazis may be trapped."

As the Americans got closer, most villagers stayed near their homes. Soldiers in the Nazi garrison carried their weapons and posted lookouts for General Patton's approaching army. The Germans still patrolled the village. They were losing the war but still dangerous. I tried to stay away from them.

Papa commented. "Don't worry. This little Wehrmacht garrison won't fight the Americans. They wouldn't stand a chance."

The SS came to the village almost every day searching for deserters and draft dodgers. They dragged away another teenage boy who failed to report for the draft. We didn't know his fate. Nobody felt safe.

One evening, while I was supposed to be asleep, I heard Papa and Mama talking. Papa's voice was soft. "The Schmidt's son, Gerard, came home on leave after being wounded. They built a false wall at the end of a dormer in the attic. He is hiding in the narrow cubbyhole to avoid returning to his unit. The Wehrmacht is doomed. Going back would probably be suicide."

We learned that Patton's army liberated Metz. Two days later, they entered the Sarre basin. Papa and Mama spread a map on the dining table and followed the army's movements. The Americans were finally nearing Kaschel. We soon heard loud explosions in the distance. I clasped my hands together to keep them from shaking.

Mr. Schmidt invited us to share the unfinished basement under his house. Since we didn't have a safe place to stay, Papa was quick to accept.

We brought food, mattresses, and warm feather comforters to occupy a small corner of the big room. Mama brought a suitcase with a few changes of clothing for each of us. Papa helped Mr. Schmidt add heavy timbers to support the ceiling. I helped the women pile straw around the building and cover it with dirt and manure to protect the basement windows, blocking all the light. The inside of the big open room was pitch black. We brought a kerosene lamp and several candles to supplement our store of goods. Everyone hoped the room would keep us safe during the fighting. It was ready to shelter us.

Mr. Schmidt gave us the latest news. “General LeClerc led his army into Strasbourg. The Tricolor is flying from the cathedral.”

We cheered at this first visible sign the Nazis wouldn’t control our lives much longer.

Gerard climbed down from the attic to help the men stack furniture against the windows to make the dark shelter more secure. He walked with a limp and looked terribly thin. Hollow cheeks revealed the sharp bones of his face. After helping us, he returned to his cubbyhole.

Mr. Schmidt warned me again. “Don’t tell anyone Gerard is home.

The sound of artillery grew closer. Explosions made me cringe as I searched for a place to hide. We moved into the Schmidt’s basement. Four other families joined us as we all crowded in to share the large single room with the Schmidts. Each family chose a small area and settled in to wait. We brought a few things we would need, but the shelter was jammed with six families and all their kids. There wasn’t room to bring anything except necessities. The moisture and lack of fresh air made the dark and musty room smell terrible.

When Papa borrowed one of Mr. Roth’s goats to keep in the basement with us, I balked. “I’m not staying in this room with a goat.”

Papa insisted. “We may be here a long time. You children will need milk.”

“If the goat comes in, I’ll stay out. It stinks.”

Papa frowned at me. “It’s a nanny goat. We need the milk.”

I crossed my arms and stared up at him. “It’s me or the goat.”

He glared at me without speaking, and I was suddenly scared he might choose the goat. I'd be left outside by myself.

Mama laid a hand on his shoulder. "I think I'll be able to go outside long enough to milk the cows. The armies can't fight all the time."

Papa finally shrugged and returned the goat to Mr. Rolf.

Everyone brought lamps and candles, but the covered windows kept the basement dark and gloomy. Even with dim lights, too many people inside made the dank room smell worse. I didn't sleep well the first night.

Mr. Schmidt had the only indoor bathroom in our corner of the village. It was on the first floor, so we had to leave the safety of the basement to use it. The room was usually busy.

Artillery fire came closer during the next few days. Adults left to tend their livestock during periods of calm. Mama brought milk, so I was glad I refused to stay with the goat. After a trip outside, Papa said the Nazis stationed in Kaschel destroyed a few homes out of spite, and exploding shells caused scattered damage in the village. German troops began to slip away.

Snow and frequent rain added to our feeling of being prisoners in the crowded shelter. Even with cold weather, the basement became unbearable, hot and stuffy, with twenty-five bodies crammed into the small space. Roger and I sweated and quarreled. Mama returned from tending the cattle and pigs, still shivering as she scraped the thick mud from her shoes.

During the night, we heard a German tank leaving Kaschel, but not before a huge explosion shook the ground around us. The next morning Mr. Schmidt learned the owner of the house where the war machine was parked had refused to remain silent when the Wehrmacht left his basement filled with mines. The Nazis blew up his house before leaving.

* * *

Mr. Schmidt spent time outside and returned to talk to the group. “The big guns are getting closer. The Nazis are pulling out of Kaschel. Some are still here, but I don’t think they intend to fight. They’re moving all their equipment east.”

That evening, Gerard climbed down from the attic to join us. “I doubt if the SS will continue to check for deserters. They’re not strong enough to fight Patton’s army.”

He brought his violin with him, and my excitement made me forget the danger of being caught between two armies. Gerard played several folk songs everyone knew. People clapped and smiled. Mama and a neighbor lady even sang along with him. I grabbed Roger, and we danced in a tiny open space on the floor. Happy talk filled the room. I forgot my fear for an hour.

Two more days passed, and the smell of our overcrowded basement refuge became a noticeable stink. The goat wouldn’t have made any difference in the hot, stale air.

Papa and Mr. Schmidt went out to talk to neighbors. They returned with good news. “The Americans have taken Sarralbe, and they’re coming this way. We’ll soon be liberated.”

A few nearby explosions made us cower in our shelter. Artillery rounds landed in the village, and German eighty-eights answered. We huddled together in fear and waited.

Nobody slept that night. German trucks slipped and slid on the muddy streets as they left Kaschel. The sound of gunfire came closer. Other loud noises I couldn’t identify made me snuggle up to Mama and Roger.

Tears clouded my eyes. “I’m scared.”

Mama held me close. "It will soon be over. The Nazis are running."

A few minutes later, the stairway door slammed open. A young dark-skinned soldier holding a gun with a large knife on the end of the barrel stood on the steps. Fear caused me to sink to my knees and tremble. I'd heard the Americans had Negros in their army, but I'd never seen a black man before. His dull green clothing and round helmet looked different from the Wehrmacht uniform we were familiar with. His mud-spattered trousers looked too damp to protect him from the cold. I scurried to hide behind Mama and clutched her skirt as he shouted something in a language I didn't understand. The soldier's dark eyes moved to examine each corner of the room, and his gun pointed everywhere he looked.

Chapter 43

The man's uniform was soaked from his boots to the top of his head, making it hard to recognize who he was. He said something in a foreign language. My body froze in fear of the gun he held.

Gerard interpreted for us. "He wants to know if any Nazis are in the house."

Mr. Schmidt folded his arms and glared. "No Nazis in *my* house."

Gerard translated, and then he said, "This man is an American soldier. He's here to rescue us from the Nazis."

Mud made it hard to recognize who the soldier might be. His tightly drawn young face revealed anxiety as he examined the crowded basement room.

The soldier turned toward the top of the stairs and shouted to someone on the floor above.

After a deep voice responded, he nodded and spoke to Gerard again.

Gerard cleared his throat. "He says we must stay here. You can go home after the Americans confirm all the German troops are gone." He blinked, swallowed hard, and his voice softened. "The soldiers will search your houses. He says we are free of Nazi rule."

A stunned silence filled the room. It seemed unreal the Nazis could be gone. Looking around the room, I saw that everyone realized we had been liberated.

After another short talk with the soldier, Gerard told us more. "They will allow us to return upstairs after they finish searching for Nazis. You should be able to go home before dark."

The fresh air smelled good when we left the crowded chamber. After about an hour, the soldiers permitted us to go home. I only wanted to sit by myself and look at the sky. When I finally went to bed, I slept without fear a Nazi might burst into our house. We had been in that dark basement for more than a week.

* * *

The next morning, an American officer visited us. He spoke broken German and asked if we had space to house soldiers. Mama agreed to allow two of them to stay in our spare room. They would sleep there at night and report for duty during the day. The soldiers didn't look much older than some of the boys drafted by the Nazis. They were polite and quiet, and they didn't speak our language. Both of them were mud covered and weary, so Mama offered them hot water for a bath. They must not have understood because they refused.

Because of the language barrier, we didn't often attempt to talk with them. After a few days, Papa managed to connect with them. He offered a drink of his home-brewed schnapps.

The taller one cocked his head and frowned when he accepted the glass. Then he sniffed the contents and glanced at his companion. Finally, he took a small taste of the colorless brew. His eyes lit up, and he whistled. Then he took another sip.

The other soldier watched with interest and took the glass from his comrade. After he tasted the liquor, he let out a happy yelp and smacked the leg of his trousers. Then he held up the glass in a salute to Papa. They passed the drink back and forth until it was empty. Papa had made two new friends.

Opa and Oma housed four of the soldiers. I took her a basket of eggs the next morning and found the Americans eating breakfast. One of them offered me a chocolate bar and said something I couldn't understand. I hadn't seen chocolate in months. I found myself speechless.

Oma didn't let my silence stand. "Don't you remember how to say thank you?"

I finally found my voice to say the magic words. "*Vielen Dank.*"

The clean-shaven soldier nodded and smiled at me. Then I stayed to eat breakfast with them. The men devoured a large bowl of porridge and several thick slices of ham. The chocolate bar rested safely in my pocket. They said things to me in English, but I could only nod in response. I didn't understand their words.

Later, the soldiers walked outside to Oma's backyard while I helped her wash dishes. The sound of a gunshot behind the house had me searching for a place to hide. I peered out the window and saw the soldiers holding their rifles facing open fields. Then Oma's face turned red, and she rushed to the back door. I followed her outside to see what was going on. As we drew closer, another soldier fired his rifle, and a shower of glass exploded on top of the fence a hundred meters distant.

Oma charged the group, arms waving and shouting at them. I didn't understand. The men looked confused and lowered their rifles. One appeared to be trying to apologize as she rushed past them. She returned carrying a pair of her teacups the soldiers had been using for target practice.

She shook her fist at them. "Have you no respect?"

I couldn't understand their words, but the soldiers hung their heads and looked at the ground as she stopped to chastise them.

Oma faced them, hands on hips, with a frown and a clenched jaw. “These cups may mean nothing to you, but I use them. We can’t afford to buy more.” Then she stormed back inside.

The soldiers stood mute, looking at each other in embarrassment, then gathered their equipment and left.

The next morning an officer who spoke German arrived to apologize and explain the soldiers had admitted their disregard of her belongings. He promised it wouldn’t happen again.

* * *

American tanks continued to plow through the village daily, their engines roaring, heading east. Thc ground shook as they passed. The heavy vehicles tore up our roadways and left deep trenches in the soggy, unpaved streets as they moved to follow the retreating Germans.

We stayed inside most of the time, happy to have food, fresh air, and shelter. It was comforting to know the Americans were winning.

The Nazis were finally gone.

A small group of American soldiers remained in the village. They took over the Catholic Church and our schoolrooms to use as a field hospital. Several ambulances brought in loads of wounded Americans daily.

I cried at the sight of injured men who limped or were carried on stretchers from the trucks into the makeshift clinic.

“They don’t have enough doctors,” Papa explained, “or even beds, for them. They will be taken to a large hospital farther from the fighting when their condition is stable enough for them to travel.”

Tanks and trucks filled with American soldiers continued to pass through the village. I bundled up with Roger to watch them drive through Kaschel. They always smiled and waved at children. Bitter cold with rain and snow whipped by strong winds continued to torment us, so I didn't stay outside long.

In mid-December, Papa came home from work with frightening news. "The Wehrmacht attacked the American Army with a huge force near Bastogne. Hordes of Nazi tanks pierced the Allied lines and killed thousands of their troops. German radio reported they intend to drive the invaders back into the sea."

Mama had placed a French flag in our front window when the Americans came. After she and Papa had a quiet conversation I couldn't hear, she removed it and hid it away in a drawer.

"Why did you take our flag down?" I asked. "The Nazis are gone."

She pulled me close beside her. "The German counterattack may succeed. If the Nazis return, we could be imprisoned as disloyal to the Third Reich. We'll display it again if the Americans can hold the ground they've taken."

"I thought the Americans were winning."

Papa sat down in a kitchen chair. "They have been, but the Nazis counterattacked through the Ardennes Forest with a huge army. If they succeed, they'll split the American forces like they split the French from the Dutch and Belgian armies in 1940."

"Will the Nazis come back?" I asked.

"I hope not," Papa said. "But we can't be sure."

My heart pounded. Surely the Americans wouldn't let the Nazis return.

Papa listened to the news daily with neighbors for the next week and came home to tell us what happened. The American retreat had stopped, and they stood their ground and resumed their advance. Fierce fighting continued, and thousands of soldiers on both sides were slaughtered every day. Nothing changed in Kaschel.

The cold weather stayed with us, and we waded through mud and snow when we went outside. Christmas approached, and American trucks and tanks continued to pass through the village. Roger was fascinated and spent many hours bundled up in his winter coat and cap, watching American troops move through the village.

"Don't get close to the road because you could be run over by a truck," Mama warned.

Roger left the house to watch the procession of military vehicles two days before the holiday. After an hour, he returned with tears in his eyes and wailing about someone stealing from him.

"What happened?" Mama asked.

Roger pointed back to the street corner where he watched the vehicles pass through the village. "A soldier took my cap."

Mama's face wrinkled. "Why would he do that?"

"I was watching the trucks, and he shouted at me. I didn't understand, and he jumped down and took my cap."

Someone knocked at the kitchen door, and Mama went to meet a smiling American soldier.

He stood in the doorway holding Roger's cap and saying words we didn't understand. Then he approached Roger and held out the cap. It was filled with chocolate.

Roger hesitated before he took it. His tears had stopped and his eyes grew big and round as he looked at this treasure of sweets. He couldn't find his voice to respond as the soldier patted his head and turned to go.

Mama reached out to the soldier and spoke for my brother. "Thank you."

He appeared to understand that much of our language. "*Bitte,*" he answered in heavily accented German. "*Frohliche Weihnachten.*"

Then he turned away and ran back to his vehicle.

On Christmas Eve I had trouble going to sleep. I woke frequently during the night, excited and eager for the Christmas holiday, and morning finally arrived. A Christmas tree with candles lit the room, and evergreen branches hanging over doorways added a pleasant scent. Kris Kringle had found us and left presents for everyone. Oma and Opa came to share the big breakfast Mama prepared.

The soldiers in our spare room joined our gathering and brought more candy for Roger and me plus a bag of sugar for the women. They had packages of cigarettes for the men. Both of them celebrated with hugs for all when they learned Kris Kringle left them a bottle of Papa's schnapps.

Our fears the Germans might return faded. For the first time in five years, we celebrated Christmas free of Nazi rule.

Chapter 44

I tagged along with Papa to listen to the news on Mr. Schmidt's radio. Mrs. Schmidt joined me and offered a piece of chocolate American soldiers had given her. I was too busy enjoying the candy to pay attention when the broadcast started, but it quickly caught my interest.

The announcer described the situation on the Western Front: "The Americans have stopped the German offensive in the Ardennes and resumed their advance. Losses have been heavy on both sides. Failure to split the Allied lines has left the German Army disorganized and their reserves depleted. The destruction of the *Luftwaffe's* fighter planes gives Allied air power control of the skies over the battlefield."

Papa and Mr. Schmidt exchanged glances.

I finished eating my chocolate and licked the last sticky, sweet morsels from my fingers as the broadcast continued.

"The Nazis have been driven back, but their resistance continues. In Eastern France, the Wehrmacht is making a determined effort to hold on to Alsace. Hitler considers it to be a rightful part of Germany."

Mr. Schmidt kicked a table leg. "We've never been a rightful part of Germany. The Nazis invaded us."

"God willing, it won't ever happen again," Papa said.

The announcer told us more news closer to home." He said, "A major German offensive in the Vosges is tying up a large number of American and Free French divisions. American and German tanks are dueling as the Nazis attempt to avoid losing territory in the homeland. Americans control the sky, but the German Army is massed in the wooded mountains and refuse to retreat. Infantry units battle man to man in the mud and snow. Ice and glacial winds are taking a toll on both armies."

Tears filled my eyes when I thought of the young men I knew who'd been drafted in Kaschel being trapped in this awful battle. Annette told me that my friend, Klaus Berger, had been sent to the Vosges front with four weeks training and an obsolete rifle. The fighting couldn't continue forever. Nazis were losing the war.

The announcer's next words destroyed any hope I had for a quick end to the battles. "Hitler refuses to talk of surrender. He has ordered his army to fight to the death."

Papa pushed his chair back from the radio. "Hitler is insane. The advance of the Russian horde in the east frightens him. Most of the draftees from Kaschel are sent there. The Red Army won't show any mercy to survivors."

Mr. Schmidt pounded his knee with a clenched fist. "It appears they'll continue to kill each other until the German Army no longer exists."

When we got home, Papa told Mama to keep our French flag hidden away in a drawer. "Hitler is crazy. There's no way to know what he'll do next. It's still possible the Nazis could return."

* * *

The Americans took charge of providing security in Kaschel. A small number of their soldiers were stationed here. Army units continued to pass through the village, chasing after the retreating Wehrmacht.

The cold weather meant we had less outside work, and I was bored and felt cheated that I couldn't attend school. Mr. Diedendorf had disappeared, and the schoolroom was locked.

Disappointed, I asked Papa, “When can I go back to school?”

He shook his head. “I don’t know. Nobody seems to be in charge. I doubt if we’ll have school until the war ends.”

Not wanting to believe Papa’s answer, I complained to Mama. “It’s not fair. When we miss school, I don’t get to see Annette and all my friends.”

Mama tilted her head and lifted an eyebrow. “You could study at home while we wait for classes to resume.”

She spent time teaching me history and allowing me to read books written for older kids. She said she didn’t know enough to help me with the French language or arithmetic. Roger didn’t want to be left out, so Mama gave him lessons, too. He’d already learned numbers and writing simple words. She taught him to read and write more difficult material. He learned quickly, and I enjoyed hearing him read the stories aloud. It wasn’t the same as being in school, but we were learning, and reading was more fun than doing chores outside.

At work Papa got a new boss. He was definitely a French sympathizer, and he made a lot of changes at the station. Since the railroad no longer shipped goods for the Nazis, most trains were rerouted. He refused to allow trains to enter German-controlled areas. Workers spent a lot of time repairing track and bridges damaged in the fighting.

One afternoon while Mama, Roger, and I sat in our warm kitchen, Mama knitted a pair of stockings while she listened to me try to read a difficult book. When Papa came home from work, he pushed open the kitchen door and kicked snow off his boots on the outside step. He entered the cozy room with slumped shoulders. His face was drawn, and he brushed back his hair with shaking hands.

Mama went to him. “What’s wrong?”

He turned a dining chair and dropped into it with a heavy sigh. "The new stationmaster noticed my two stacks of lanterns and asked why I kept them separated. I couldn't lie to him."

Mama pinched her lips and shook her head slowly. "You told him you're colorblind?"

Papa nodded. "There was no way to hide it when he asked. He said I could work on track maintenance for now, but that job won't last forever. I won't be allowed to set signal lanterns anymore."

I listened in silence. Where would we get money to buy things if Papa lost his job? Maybe he could find another one.

Papa slapped the table top with an open hand. "I don't have any education. I'll never find another job in Kaschel."

Mama wrapped an arm around him. "We'll find a way to deal with it. Everyone knows you're a good worker."

Roger's bottom lip dropped. He gave Papa a hug.

Papa continued to go to the station each day and came home tired from the hard labor. On weekends, he found work helping neighbors make repairs to their homes. Though there hadn't been much heavy fighting in the village, a lot of houses suffered damage.

Village streets had been destroyed by heavy military vehicles. Windows and shutters were broken in many of the homes. Doors had been kicked in by Nazis and American troops searching for stragglers. They would have to be repaired. Artillery fire and exploding mines had destroyed several homes. The railroad station and business district suffered broken windows and serious theft.

Mama shrugged. "Everyone will have to repair the damage. Our house needs work, too."

Papa's hand rubbed at a temple. "Materials needed to repair the damage are hard to find. Most people don't have money and skills to repair their property. The elderly are especially vulnerable."

"You're working too hard," Mama said. "If you don't slow down, your health could suffer. We'd really be in bad shape then."

Papa's fists tightened. "We may have to make our living by farming. We'll save as much as we can now. I'll try to buy more fields when I have the opportunity."

Mama and I took on extra chores, allowing Papa to spend more time making money by helping neighbors with repairs in addition to taking care of our fields. We all did more to allow him time to make extra money. I did much of the cooking and housekeeping. Mama continued taking care of our cows and milked them. She also tried to keep up with cleaning and repairing the animal's pens and getting the garden ready for planting. Even Roger took care of the rabbits, pigs, and chickens after Mama threatened to spank him.

Chapter 45

Kaschel's mayor was nowhere to be seen. Neighbors said he was hiding at home with his wife and adult daughter. His office remained locked and vacant. I listened from my kitchen window to hear Mr. Schmidt and Mr. Rolf debate how we should punish Mayor Spengler for his treachery.

"We should hang him from the flagpole at city hall," Mr. Rolf suggested.

Mr. Schmidt argued, "A long prison term would be more reasonable."

Papa reminded the family the fat mayor should be made to pay for making our lives miserable under Nazi rule. "He's earned whatever happens to him. He's a Nazi at heart."

Mama's hands rested on her hips. "His daughter is as bad as he is. She entertained the Nazi soldiers occupying the village while we suffered their indignities."

My forehead knotted into a frown. "I don't understand. Why would she be nice to the Nazis?"

"She seems to like them better than us," Mama said. "They did special favors for her. She needs to be treated like a Nazi sympathizer." The corner of her mouth twisted upward like it did when she didn't want to answer.

Papa nodded. "I'll talk it over with Mr. Schmidt and his friends. We will find an appropriate way to let him know what the village thinks of him."

I added my thoughts. "He's a traitor. We ought to put him in prison."

Papa shook his head. "That's better treatment than he deserves. We'll find something more fitting for the fat old fool."

I still liked my idea. If he was in prison, I wouldn't have to look at him.

Our village trustees met a few days later and, after an argument that lasted all afternoon, selected a new mayor. Papa described the man they had chosen. "Mr. Hartmann is a retired railroad engineer who has always taken an interest in village affairs. Maybe he can help us get Kaschel back to something like normal. We lost an entire generation of young men."

Village work crews soon appeared to repair the nearby streets. Allied tanks and heavy trucks still drove along the roads leading east to chase the retreating Nazi army. No work was scheduled on this route until the military traffic had stopped. German language signs were torn down and replaced with the proper French street names. Signs at the entrances to Kaschel again read *Beinvenue a' Kaschel.* Our village had survived. It was becoming a happier place.

But the war continued.

Papa brought home news of the fighting in the Vosges Mountains around Colmar. "The Americans have begun to push the Nazis back, but the Wehrmacht counter-attacked in the mountains. Draftees from Kaschel have been sent there to fight in deep snow, and the Allies have difficulty moving their big vehicles to advance. Casualties on both sides are high."

We listened for the news and waited for Adolph Hitler and the Germans to surrender. Russian advances in the east and Allied pressure in the south and west gradually tightened the noose on the German armies.

* * *

A few nights later, Papa's face beamed when he came home from the corner bar. "Irene, I want you to fill a basket with all the rotted vegetables you can find. Go to the manure pile and find pieces of cow manure that are dry enough to hold together if you throw it. We need a lot of ammunition to celebrate an event."

I blinked, and my mouth fell open. "Why, Papa?"

His eyes twinkled. "We're going to have a party for our old Nazi mayor. We must all recognize everything he's done for the village."

I suspected Papa hadn't really answered my question. I'd never seen rotted potatoes and cow manure at a party. Confused, I grabbed a basket and went outside to do as he said. Adults could be hard to understand sometimes.

The next morning was Saturday. Mama served oatmeal porridge and pork sausage for breakfast. Roger and I ate second helpings. Papa usually left to work at odd jobs on Saturday, but he remained at the table and drank a second cup of coffee.

Puzzled, I asked, "Aren't you going to work?"

He shook his head. "Not this morning. We have a party to attend at ten o'clock."

I frowned. "Don't parties usually happen in the evening?"

"Yes," he said. "But this is a special recognition for our former mayor who was so thoughtful of our needs during the Nazi occupation. We'll use this occasion to express our gratitude for the way he treated us during his reign under the Third Reich. We're holding the celebration today so everyone will be able to attend."

Something didn't sound right. I thought Papa might be having fun with me.

When the clock struck ten, Papa took up the basket of manure and spoiled vegetables and led us to the street corner. Many of our neighbors were already gathered there, talking and laughing. Everyone appeared to be in a good mood. The sun shone brightly, but a cold wind bit through my winter coat. My fingers and nose were unprotected, and I still suspected Papa of fooling me about what kind of party this would be.

After we waited a few minutes, a farm wagon, pulled by a team of horses, stopped at the next intersection where another crowd of villagers gathered. It looked like our former mayor sitting on the driver's bench. I didn't recognize the smaller person who sat beside him. The noisy crowd surrounded the wagon and began to shout and throw things at the pair who covered their heads with their arms. After a few minutes, the jeering mob allowed the wagon to leave. A small group of men led by our new mayor marched behind the wagon.

The village postman walked ahead to lead the horses as the vehicle approached our corner. I recognized the shorter occupant as it arrived. "It's Mayor Spengler's daughter, Papa. She doesn't have any hair. What happened?"

He smiled and patted me on the back. "People who don't like Nazis cut it all off. It will help her remember we're French, and she should have been one of us." He pointed to our basket. "Grab a hand full of rotten potatoes to throw at them. They deserve to pay for the way they treated us under the Third Reich."

The unfortunate mayor and his daughter's clothing were soiled by dirty trash that had been thrown at them. They sat huddled together and wrapped their arms around their faces as the crowd pelted them with all sorts of disagreeable items. People laughed and jeered as they scored several direct hits on the unlucky pair. The lady standing beside me carried a bucket of cow manure, almost liquid, and a scoop. She flung the smelly mess onto the mayor and his daughter again and again. It splashed and covered the pair and the bench as well. They tried to duck and dodge, but both of them reeked of the manure.

Roger grabbed a few choice vegetables and threw them with more enthusiasm than accuracy. He didn't hit anyone, but he had fun trying.

I was tempted to feel sorry for them, but I remembered how miserable they'd made our lives while the Nazis ruled. They deserved what happened to them. I even jumped and cheered as I scored a hit on the fat mayor's head. When the wagon began to move toward the next street corner, our ammunition was gone.

Papa had a broad smile on his face when he picked up the empty basket and pointed our way home. "I hope the smelly old tyrant enjoyed the recognition we gave him."

I skipped with joy as we turned back toward our house, and I looked up at Mama. "Papa was right. This was better than jail."

Mama nodded. "This experience won't leave any doubt about how we remember what they did while the Nazis ruled."

* * *

Many of the houses in Kaschel needed repairs. Damaged roofs leaked when the spring rains arrived. Fences had been crushed by the passage of heavy military vehicles. Artillery shells tore through several homes, and a few were completely destroyed. Ditches and berms, dug by the Nazis, were scattered throughout the village. They would have to be filled and leveled to make the land useable again.

Papa found plenty of work on weekends. He used the money he'd earned to buy two small fields to make our farm bigger. Mama even found work repairing and cleaning homes for people who could afford to hire help, but she still found time to help Opa and Oma get their house in order. With our school closed, I was left at home to look after Roger. Fortunately, I was bigger than he. It took several threats from me to convince him to work, but the two of us were able to do most of Mama's and Papa's chores.

On an overcast morning, I waded the dingy snow to feed our sow. A big surprise greeted me. The huge animal lay on her side to nourish a new litter of baby pigs. The fat old hog greeted me with a satisfied grunt as I poured her ration into the trough. The little pigs were too busy scrambling to feed themselves to notice. The Nazis wouldn't take this litter from us. The happy sight made me want to dance.

My birthday arrived a few days later. I turned eleven years old, almost a grownup. The snowdrift beside our path had begun to melt, and a tiny stream of water started to shrink the gray mound and carry it away.

I stayed busy with chores and looked after Roger while Mama and Papa spent their days working for neighbors. That evening, Opa and Oma brought me a new sweater and joined us to celebrate my birthday. Papa slaughtered a rabbit and Mama prepared a big meal. She still had sugar from the Americans and made a big pound cake to mark the occasion. After she took it from the oven, she wagged a warning finger at Roger.

No bites were missing when she served it.

Not a single Nazi came around to ruin the celebration.

It was my best birthday ever.

Chapter 46

When classes resumed during the spring, the Lutheran and Catholic children were sent to separate schools. Lutherans were able to hire only one teacher for all grades. Students who graduated and passed tests to qualify could attend secondary school in Sarreguemines. Our new teacher promised us that school would be more organized in the fall. With the never-ending war as a distraction, it would be impossible for us to learn much. The first three grades attended morning classes, and the older grades were taught in the afternoon.

As he neared the end of second grade, Roger finally began to apply some effort to his studies. During the fall semester of his first grade, he'd been more interested in spreading mischief in the classroom. Staying out of trouble most of the time allowed him to do better with his schoolwork. He surprised the whole family when he brought home his first report card.

Mama looked up from the card with a smile. "This is a great report. We're proud of you."

Papa frowned. "Are you sure this card was meant for you?"

Roger became the top student in his class. My parents and I were shocked. It wasn't what he had led us to expect.

He didn't seem to notice he was doing anything different. "School is easy."

He'd learned a lot from French-speaking friends and didn't appear to see much difference when our school switched from German to French.

On the first day that classes resumed, the new teacher introduced herself. "My name is Marie Nicaise, and I must remind you that we are once again French citizens." She picked up an armload of books from her desk and stood before us. “Gather all your German textbooks and follow me.”

I scooped up all my books and trailed her outside, wondering why we were doing this.

Miss Nicaise dropped her armload of books on the ground behind the building. “Pile your texts on top of mine. They are written in a foreign language, and they teach Nazi propaganda.”

When all the books formed a mound, taller than my knees on the bare dirt, she brought out a can of kerosene and poured it over the pile. After allowing the books to soak for a moment, she lit a match and tossed it onto the mound. Flames shot up immediately, and everyone watched in silence as the books were consumed by the raging fire. Heat from the flames made me step away, and the black smoke followed to burn my eyes. It got in my lungs and choked me. I couldn’t stop coughing for several minutes.

I swallowed hard and fought back the urge to question what she’d done. I couldn’t think of the proper French words. Everything had changed again. We’d have to adapt.

The school didn’t have books to replace those she’d burned, so we copied our assignments and helpful information from the blackboard into our notebooks.

Miss Nicaise lectured us on being proud citizens of France again. “All students are forbidden to say anything in the German language. Our classes will be strictly conducted in French, and you must ignore the lies you learned under Nazi rule.”

Since I’d never studied French and we spoke the local patois at home, my knowledge of the language was sketchy, and I had trouble understanding her. For a while, I didn’t learn much.

I missed having Annette in class with me. We'd become best friends since we started school together. I raised my hand to ask a question when we started class the next day. "Why did they separate us from the Catholic students?"

Miss Nicaise shook her head. "I don't know. Both churches requested separate schools. When I asked the village council why, they didn't say, but they promised to consider all options for the fall term."

Her answer left me a ray of hope, but it didn't solve my problem. I still missed Annette. It wasn't fair to separate us for no good reason. Maybe they'd hire another teacher and put us all together in one school when September arrived.

* * *

German radio broadcasts reported the Wehrmacht's valiant stand brought the advance of Allied and Russian armies to a halt. They repeated a constant stream of promises from the German Government that the Fatherland would win this war and the Third Reich would endure.

BBC broadcasts told a different story. "German forces no longer have the ability to stop the Allied advance. The implacable Red Army is driving toward Berlin and slaughtering thousands of troops and civilians as they approach the German border. Countless civilians are being killed as the Soviet Army attempts to enter the Fatherland. Germany has pulled troops from the Western Front in an effort to stem the Russian tide. The Red Army continues to move closer to Berlin."

A few days after my eleventh birthday, I was helping Mama clean the kitchen when Papa returned from Mr. Schmidt's house after listening to his radio. His face was pale, and he muttered to himself as he sank into a kitchen chair.

Mama placed a hand on his shoulder. "What's wrong?"

He didn't respond immediately, and he looked like he'd seen a ghost. "The Americans and British destroyed Dresden. Hundreds of airplanes dropped incendiary bombs on the city. It was totally destroyed, and tens of thousands of civilians were burned alive."

"No." Mama frowned and shook her head. "Everyone goes to bomb shelters. The raid couldn't kill that many."

"They turned the city into a gigantic torch. Shelters couldn't protect people from the heat. Fires took all the oxygen and killed everyone in their path." Papa tilted his head back, his eyes fixed on the ceiling. "Oma worked in Dresden for two years after the First World War. She was a waitress in a big restaurant."

Mama took a deep breath. "Oma always said Dresden was a beautiful city. Until the war started and mail delivery stopped, she still wrote to a lady who lives there."

Papa continued. "Dresden doesn't have a lot of factories to build war materials. I don't understand why the Allies would destroy it."

Mama sat beside him. "Maybe Hitler will surrender now and end this awful war."

Papa spread his hands and sighed. "The Allies must be trying to force the German people to demand the Nazis surrender, but Hitler won't listen. He refuses to admit the war is lost."

I never thought I would be able to feel sorry for Nazis, but the vision of women, children, and old people caught in the fires haunted me for days. Why did the Allies destroy this beautiful city and kill everyone? Oma would be sad to hear this news. I wondered if her friend had survived.

Hitler didn't surrender, and Papa brought home more news of Dresden. "The city was filled with people fleeing the Russian advance. Most of them were living in the streets. I'm afraid casualties might be even worse than we thought."

Then we heard reports that Allied armies were holding back to allow the Russians to take Berlin. I was sure the Red Army would do terrible things to get even with the German people. Even General Patton's army failed to advance while the Soviets moved closer and slaughtered everyone in their path. It didn't seem to matter if they were military or civilian.

Crushed and scared, I tried to shut out the war news. It was too frightening, always about people getting killed. They never talked about good things happening. I couldn't escape from the stories. Even Roger was affected. He slept in the room next to mine. He didn't talk about the fighting, but I often heard him cry out during the night. Nobody seemed to talk about anything except the war. My parents couldn't understand why Hitler wouldn't accept reality. Germany was being destroyed.

Papa slammed the palm of his hand on the table top. "Hitler knows the Allies will hang him if he surrenders. He wants to bring the whole country down with him."

American and British Armies fought occasional skirmishes with the Germans, but they made little effort to reach Berlin. The news reported most of the Nazi forces were thrown into a desperate fight to stop the Red Army. The Wehrmacht was driven back repeatedly, and the Russian Army crossed the border into the homeland.

Still, Hitler refused to surrender.

Chapter 47

Snow and ice gradually melted as spring advanced. Dingy remnants on paths we'd trampled to feed our animals turned to mud. The temperature warmed, but cold spring winds still stung my skin through a heavy sweater. Each time I went out, Mama made me clean my shoes before I entered the house.

Roger forgot and left muddy tracks across the kitchen tile.

Mama shouted, "Look what you've done to my clean floor." She spanked him and sent him outside to scrape the mud off his shoes.

He wiped away tears on his shirt sleeve. "I won't do it again."

After seeing what happened to my brother, I made sure I didn't leave mud on the floor.

The war continued with the Russian Army forcing their way across Germany. The Allies fought occasional skirmishes, but they did not move to capture Berlin. The Wehrmacht was driven back repeatedly as the Russians stormed into the homeland.

Still, Hitler proclaimed that Germany would win the war.

Mama and Papa watched the forecasts, waiting for warmer weather before starting to prepare our fields for spring planting.

Papa planned to plant larger crops this year, and I would help him scatter seeds and manure to fertilize them. Since he no longer had a job, he hoped we could market what we didn't use at harvest time. I planned to sell produce at the Sarrealbe market again. We would need the money to replace the salary Papa lost.

The village continued to rebuild, and people tried to pick up the pieces of their old lives. Papa worked at odd jobs when he could find them. Many homes in Kaschel still needed repairs for damage suffered during the war. The last few American troops moved on, and our new government began to bring order to the chaos left by the Nazis.

Papa returned from the fields one mild spring evening to announce, "We'll wait for one more freezing night, then we can start planting our crops."

Mama had killed a chicken to add to the potatoes and sauerkraut she prepared. After wiping her hands on her apron, she said, "The food is ready."

We took our seats around the table, and Roger helped himself to a leg, a thigh, and both wings of the chicken. Mama wagged a finger at him, and he returned the leg and one wing to the platter.

She nailed him with a firm look. "You can't eat that much. We all need to eat."

A sudden crash startled me, and our front door flew open. Sergeant Schnabel stormed inside. His hair stuck out in all directions, and a scruffy beard covered his face. His rumpled civilian clothing made him look smaller, but he aimed a large pistol at Papa. "You will help me escape this despicable village tonight."

I froze.

Roger sobbed and ran to Mama.

She took him in her arms and murmured, "It's all right. The man won't hurt you."

Papa's voice was quiet. "Why me?"

The sergeant stood without moving. "You're the last house before the river. Nobody is likely to notice what goes on here."

Papa's face lost color, and he pursed his lip like he did when he was troubled. He turned his chair to face the Nazi sergeant. "You've done nothing to deserve help from this *despicable village*."

Schnabel waved the pistol. "You'll do it or I'll shoot your wife. Your daughter will be next. You can watch it happen."

Mama and Papa exchanged looks. I gripped the sides of my chair and bit my lip to remain silent.

I sat facing the sergeant's back and the open door. Something moved in the darkness outside. My heart pounded faster. Someone was out there.

Papa rose and ran his fingers through his hair. Then he gestured with open palms. "I don't own an automobile. How would I be able to help you escape?"

"Use your wagon." Schnabel waved his pistol at Papa.

"The Americans set up roadblocks. They won't let us pass. Where could you go?"

I couldn't take my eyes off the sergeant's pistol. My hands gripped each other to keep them from shaking. Roger's lips trembled as he leaned against Mama. She hugged him tighter.

Forcing my gaze away from the door, I looked at Mama. Her face had turned chalk white as she continued to hold onto Roger.

Schnabel pointed north with his pistol. "I have friends in Sitterswald. It's just across the Rhine. People there will hide me when I deliver the goods you'll haul. If we start early, we can make the trip in one day."

"The Allies will never allow me to travel to Germany. We're French now."

Schnabel smirked. "First you'll load the valuables and art I've collected here, and then you'll cover it with the food from your winter stores. You'll be taking it to your dear brother in

Sitterswald whose family is hungry. I'm your friend accompanying you on the trip."

Papa protested. "The cows are old. They might not make it that far."

The sergeant shook a fist at Papa. "Then you can help them pull."

"My family will be left without food."

The sergeant laughed. "They can beg from your neighbors."

Someone moved across the light from the open door. Who? Was he with Schnabel? I waited in silence, my heart racing and my hands trembling.

Papa's eyes rolled toward the ceiling, and he exhaled a big breath. "How do I know you won't shoot me after you deliver your loot?"

Mama released Roger and started to rise. Instead, she sagged forward, her elbows on the table, her hands holding her head. A shiver ran down my back even though the room was warm.

Leaning toward Papa, Schnabel grunted. "You'll have to take your chances. I'll shoot you here if you don't do as I say."

Fear cramped my stomach. Roger snuffled as he clung to Mama.

"Doesn't look like I have much choice." Papa shrugged.

Schnabel snickered and backed away from the family. He tucked the gun into his waistband and pointed a finger at Papa. "You have *no* choice."

The room became still and silent. I held my breath.

The shadow outside moved, and a man slipped through the open door, pointing a revolver at the Nazi sergeant. "Don't move a muscle."

I struggled to understand. The man looked familiar, and then I recognized him. "Uncle George!" I screamed.

He flashed a bitter smile at me but kept his gun pointed at Schnabel. "Looks like we have a change of plans, Nazi. Put your gun on the table. Carefully."

Fearing Schnabel might shoot Uncle George, I cringed.

Schnabel's hands shook. His eyes darted around the room. Then he lifted his pistol with two fingers and laid it on the table.

George's gaze stayed locked on the sergeant. "We need to turn you over to the authorities. They'll be more than happy to take care of you."

Schnabel's expression changed from arrogance to fright and back to arrogance. "If you try to stop me, my associates will make sure this family pays the price."

George laughed. "If you had any associates, they'd have helped you escape already."

"We can turn him over to the mayor," Papa said. "He works with the Americans."

Sweat appeared on Schnabel's brow. He stumbled as he tried to move away from George's pistol. He eyed his gun on the table. It was only a step away. "You can't turn me over to the French. They'll kill me."

Uncle George nodded. "Probably."

Schnabel's eyes darted around the room and fixed on his pistol.

"Don't even think about it." George's revolver didn't waver.

Schnabel's gaze measured George. Then his jaw firmed. He lunged for his weapon.

A blast from George's gun echoed across the room. Schnabel's body slammed against the table, driving it against the wall.

His fingers lost their grip, and the pistol clattered on the floor. His legs went limp, and he crumpled, his body brushing against me as he fell.

My ears rang. The acrid smell of gunpowder made my nose burn. Blood from the wound on the center of Schnabel's chest splashed onto the kitchen tile.

Uncle George kicked away the sergeant's gun and returned his to a coat pocket.

Roger and I gazed in horror at the dead man. Mama reached out and held us close, trying to shield us from viewing the body.

Uncle George knelt to wrap his arms around the three of us. "You're safe now.

My hands flew up to cover my eyes after the gunshot, and tears flowed when I opened them to see Schnabel's blood spreading across the floor. I wanted to shout with joy when I realized the Nazi was dead.

I couldn't take my eyes off the bloody corpse. I'd been frightened of him since he came to the village. Roger turned to look away. Mama's arms sheltered us, and her soft words eased my fear.

A sudden panic seized me. What would happen to Uncle George? Would he be in trouble for killing Schnabel?

Papa stared at George. "Where did you come from?"

George looked up from the dead sergeant. "I've been working my way home from the south of France. I came to you first to spare our parents from a sudden shock when I walked in. I heard this Nazi's threat from the open door. He's dead now. Don't worry."

Papa laid a hand on George's shoulder. "I'll tell the mayor what happened. He'll call the authorities."

George put out a hand to stop Papa. "We don't need to get involved in explaining. Losing this beast isn't worth it. Help me carry his carcass down to the Sarre and we'll throw him in the river. The current will take him away. He's a casualty of the war. That will be a decent burial by *Maquis* standards. You can tell the mayor you heard rumors this thief had a lot of stolen treasure hidden in the village. Someone should be able to locate it and return it to the owners."

Papa's mouth twisted in a grim line. "All right."

George stepped outside to see if a curious bystander might have heard the shot. He returned to say, "All clear."

The two men picked up the sergeant's body to carry it down the path to the river. I helped Mama clean to remove any traces that Schnabel had been here. I fought the urge to vomit as I mopped up the fresh blood.

When the men returned, we had removed all the evidence of what happened in the room. Neither Papa nor Uncle George said anything about the Nazi sergeant.

Later Mama went to bring my grandparents to join us. When she arrived with Opa and Oma, she smiled at them. "I told you he's safe."

George embraced his parents. Oma wept. The three of them held each other for a long time, and tears of happiness appeared in my eyes.

Oma spoke first. "We're so relieved you're home. We feared the *Milice* had found you. It's been a nightmare wondering if you were safe."

"I joined the *Maquis*," George said. "I couldn't spend the war hiding when my country suffered under the Nazi yoke. We fought for our freedom. I had to finish some business for the Resistance before I made my way home."

After bringing out a bottle of his schnapps, Papa poured a splash in glasses for each of us. Mine held about a spoonful and Mama put a pinch of sugar in it. Then Papa made a short toast to Uncle George's safe return. We all raised our glasses to his homecoming.

* * *

At the end of April, 1945, Papa brought word the Russian Army had entered Berlin. Hitler and Eva Braun committed suicide. We waited another anxious week before the Nazi government surrendered. The long war was over, and we were officially French citizens once more. The country could now start the process of recovery.

Our school reopened, and I was free to complete my elementary education by learning French. Catholic students were still separated from the Protestants, but Annette and I kept our close relationship alive with frequent visits on weekends. Continuing to surprise us, Roger maintained his status as the star student in his class. After he finished, he attended secondary school in Sarreguemines and graduated with honors.

Papa was able to buy more land and make our living by farming plus a few odd jobs to bring in extra money. He regretted losing his position with the railroad, but we didn't suffer. Kaschel began to recover from the war. The French Government allowed residents of Alsace to choose whether to be French or German. The province voted overwhelmingly to remain French, and our way of life returned to normal.

I graduated from the village school at age fourteen and spent a year training to be a secretary. Then I found work as a bookkeeper in a feed store and continued to help with the farm.

Mama made sure I never learned how to milk a cow.

After I turned seventeen, Papa decided I should become a married woman. He picked out a young man in the village. “Charles Dillmann would make you a good husband.”

The prospect of marrying a local farmer suggested by Papa didn’t appeal to me. The idea of spending my life in this small village made my decision to move to Paris a lot easier. I’d find work there and be close to my city relatives. Living the single life in Paris would be exciting. Papa didn’t approve, but he accepted my absence after I’d lived there a few years and not been murdered or suffered some other misfortune.

Everything changed the day I met an American soldier named Dale.

* * *

Sitting on the deck of our home in a quiet Midwestern neighborhood sixty years later, I enjoy the sight of well-kept lawns, nice houses obscured by plentiful trees, and the view of a pleasant valley descending to the small stream bordering a park. A forested hill on the other side gives me the impression of separation from the small city we call home. It also offers a great view of the fall foliage.

I smile when I recall my fears during that initial flight from Paris to New York. I had a lot to learn, and the support I received from family and friends in Kansas helped me adapt to life in America. I went to night school to learn English and became a proud United States citizen.

Dale and I didn’t get rich in this new world, but we’ve taken advantage of its freedoms and opportunities to face old age together in safety and comfort. I sometimes miss the simple life I enjoyed in Kaschel before and after the war, but I'm happy in America.

From the first, life was good in our new home. Dale's work led us to move a few times, and I assured my parents I was happy and secure here. Papa was skeptical. Several years after I arrived, Mama visited us to learn first-hand if I was telling the whole truth about my life in America. Papa was afraid to travel that far by airplane, so he didn't come with her. Mama stayed a month and met our family. She accompanied us on a tour of the western United States where we visited relatives, the Grand Canyon, and Yellowstone National Park.

On her return to Kaschel, Mama told stories of our beautiful and prosperous country. She assured Papa all was well with their daughter.

His concerns faded, and he finally made peace with my absence.

On numerous trips back to Kaschel over the years, I brought our children with me. We made the journey every three years and usually stayed several weeks. Dale managed to accompany us on a few of our visits. The children learned about their French relatives' lives and got to know their grandparents. These visits were joyful occasions. Their Opa and Oma were thrilled to show off the kids to the neighbors and spoiled them rotten. My father had purchased a diesel tractor to replace the cows for farm work. He delighted in driving it through the village to show our son the sights and show off his American grandson.

Later we took several trips to France with our grandkids. The vacation and learning about their ancestry proved to be a rewarding experience. They enjoyed getting in touch with their French heritage, and some even learned to speak the language. They all profited from their exposure to a different culture.

Roger brought his wife for a few visits, and we had the opportunity to show them the American way of life. He enjoyed the trips but was unwilling to consider leaving his beloved Kaschel. Other members of my extended family have visited on occasion. We welcomed them all and have maintained contact over the years.

Most of our children and grandchildren live nearby. Dale and I enjoy their proximity and the bonds of mutual love and support that strengthen family ties.

I still cherish memories of my early childhood in Kaschel, and I'm proud my family was able to overcome the hardships they faced during the war. The memories of my parents' strength and courage during those awful years still inspire me.

Life has been good, and I'm content.

About the Author

Doyle Suit grew up in the Ouachita Mountains during the depths of the great depression and World War II. He worked as a farm laborer, store clerk, carpenter's helper, butcher, construction laborer, tire salesman, lab technician, and soldier in the United States Army. A job as a draftsman for a major aircraft company led to a 44 year career as a design engineer who specialized in the design of cockpits for military aircraft. After he retired, he started writing historical fiction. His first novel, *Baker Mountain*, was published in 2013.

His short stories and articles have appeared in numerous publications including Cactus Country, My Dad is my Hero, Thin Threads, Storyteller Magazine, Bigfoot Confidential, and Good Old Days Magazine. He lives in Missouri, near his kids, grandkids, and a very young great granddaughter.

CPSIA information can be obtained
at www.ICGtesting.com
Printed in the USA
FFHW02n0718270818
48051754-51767FF